Sexy Living

Sexy Living

REGINA COLE

LYRICAL PRESS
Kensington Publishing Corp.
www.kensingtonbooks.com

LYRICAL PRESS BOOKS are published by

Kensington Publishing Corp.
119 West 40th Street
New York, NY 10018

All Kensington titles, imprints, and distributed lines are available at special quantity discounts for bulk purchases for sales promotion, premiums, fund-raising, educational, or institutional use. Special book excerpts or customized printings can also be created to fit specific needs. For details, write or phone the office of the Kensington Sales Manager: Kensington Publishing Corp., 119 West 40th Street, New York, NY 10018. Attn. Sales Department. Phone: 1-800-221-2647.

LYRICAL PRESS and the Lyrical logo are Reg. U.S. Pat. & TM Off.

First Electronic Edition: May 2017

ISBN-13: 978-1-5161-0373-7
ISBN-10: 1-5161-0373-4

First Print Edition: May 2017

ISBN-13: 978-1-5161-0393-5
ISBN-10: 1-5161-0393-9

Printed in the United States of America

Chapter 1

Before she'd left home, the thought of a November vacation in Hawaii had made Stacey Hough giddy. But now that it was actually happening, all she could think about were the drops of sweat wending their way down her spine as her sandals made flapping noises against the concrete walkway.

"Just a few more feet until air-conditioning," she said to herself, eyeing the resort's beautiful, air-conditioned tower of hotel rooms that would give her sanctuary. This was less than ideal. Her cousin would pick the hottest November on record to have her destination wedding.

Stacey upped her pace, trying to ignore the beads of moisture tickling her upper lip. That wasn't exactly fair. Sabrina couldn't have known how hot it would be. Besides, it wasn't the bride's fault that her maid of honor was sweating like a teenage boy who'd gotten caught watching Internet porn. That was all Stacey's doing.

"I'll go to the beach," she'd said to herself after lunch with the bride. It had been years since she'd been on a real vacation, and she had intended to enjoy it. Of course, she couldn't actually find the guts to put on the new swimsuit she'd bought for the trip. The imaginary confidence she'd been leaning on up until this point went *poof* in the harsh light of the tropical paradise. No way could she go out in any kind of swimwear. There were way too many witnesses. The trade-off was a nice walk. But what should have been a relaxing hour-long stroll along a beautiful coastline had turned into a hot, sandy trek across what might as well have been the Sahara, and had turned Stacey's joy at the vacation into a chore. It sucked, but the temporary discomfort would be over soon.

The artificially cooled air caressed Stacey's cheeks, and she gave a heavy sigh of relief as the glass hotel doors swung shut behind her. *Finally.* Punching the button for the elevator, she glanced upward.

Crap. Her strawberry-blond hair was frizzing around her forehead. Turning, she looked in the mirror that was mounted on the opposite wall and promptly blanched.

Good Lord, she looked like a nightmare. Red, sweaty, and frightening. If she ran into any small children on the way to her room, they'd probably need therapy for years to come.

This was why she stayed home. Work was safe. Work, she could throw herself into with abandon and not come out looking like a cartoon villain. Oh well. She had planned to shower before tonight's bachelorette party anyway. There were a couple of hours left for her to make herself look presentable.

The elevator doors glided open, and Stacey's stomach plummeted through the floor. Shit.

"Good Lord, Stacey, what happened to you? You look terrible!" Aunt Beatrice wasted no time in pointing out the obvious as she exited the elevator.

"I went for a run. I'm training for the Iron Man," Stacey joked drily as she passed her aunt.

Completely missing the sarcasm, Aunt Beatrice lit up with a smile. "Good! That is fabulous. You do need to exercise, but perhaps next time you should dress a bit differently? You aren't wearing the right attire, and there are sweat stains on—"

The doors shut then, and Stacey slumped against the back wall of the elevator.

Getting angry was exhausting and pointless. Aunt Beatrice had been dropping comments about her weight and other shortcomings since Stacey was in preschool. Her family had won the genetic lottery, and Stacey was the only exception. Not that she was ugly. She'd gotten the reddish-blond hair and blue eyes, sure, but the height and good metabolism had definitely skipped her. At least her own parents were vacationing in Europe, and unable to join in the fun of pointing out her faults. Fortunately, Bree was nothing like her mother in attitude. Bree was Stacey's favorite relative, and one of her closest friends. There wasn't much Stacey wouldn't endure for her, and that included record-high temperatures and snooty Aunt Beatrice.

When she finally arrived on her floor, Stacey dragged an arm across her cheeks and walked determinedly to her room. Tonight would be just what she needed. Bree always did wonders for Stacey's mood, and the other bridesmaid, Eliza, seemed really nice. They'd go out for pedicures, a fancy dinner, and then a night out dancing and cutting loose.

Stacey forced a smile. It would be a blast. Just the thing to help her shake off these blues.

The club beat drove through Stacey's body, urging her to move. A pleasant haze surrounded her brain, the light curtain of alcohol dulling her inhibitions.

"I didn't know you were such a good dancer, Stace!" Bree yelled to be heard over the thudding bass.

Stacey grinned and swiveled her hips, lifting her empty glass high. "Only when I'm thousands of miles away from home and slightly tipsy."

Nodding toward the empty glass, Bree smiled. "Another drink? I'm buying!"

"Seriously, stop it. Between you and Eliza getting me drinks, I'm going to be completely hammered." Stacey laughed. "I've already had enough. Just a water for me."

"Fine." Bree rolled her eyes. "Liza, another cosmo?"

Eliza, Bree's pretty, dark-haired friend from college, shook her head vehemently. Maybe a little too vehemently, because she stumbled backward a bit, knocking into a tall guy with gold chains decorating the space where his shirt was unbuttoned.

"Oh gosh, I'm sorry," Eliza stammered, regaining her balance. "I didn't mean to bump into you."

"No worries," he said, a wide, eager smile spreading across his face. "I was coming over here to talk to you, anyway. I talked to the bartender, she said you liked cosmos." He held out a pink cocktail to Eliza.

A brief flash of jealousy hit Stacey, but she tamped it down instantly. It wasn't like she wanted attention from a guy like Miami Vice here, but it would be nice to have a guy pay attention to her for once. The only men who looked her way were usually retirees or her gynecologist. And the gynecologist she had to pay.

She shook her head. Damn. This trip was really doing a number on her self-esteem. Every time she clawed her way back to her normal, cheerful mood, something else happened to piss all over it.

"No, that's okay. Thanks anyway." Eliza turned back to Stacey and Bree, but the guy grabbed Liza's shoulder.

Stacey's spine stiffened in anger.

"Hey, I'm talking to you. Don't be such a bitch." Miami Vice glared down at Eliza, but Bree grabbed her and pulled her away.

"What's the matter? Pussy got your tongue?" He laughed at his stupid joke, the sound carrying far in the break between songs.

That. Was. *Enough.*

Stacey shoved her way in front of Eliza and Sabrina, throwing her arms wide and blocking the guy from coming any closer. "She said she doesn't want a drink, you dickhead. Leave her alone."

For a moment, she was brave, she was strong, and the determination felt good. With her jaw clenched tight, she glared up at him, daring him to cross her.

Sadly, her moment of glory was short-lived.

"I was talking to your friend, you fat, ugly cunt. Fuck off." The guy walked straight into Stacey, muscling her out of his path. His foot hooked behind her heel, and his elbow went straight into her ribs. The ground rushed up at her, much too fast.

The sound of her head connecting with the hard dance floor echoed inside her skull, the pain and sound bouncing from side to side. Stacey blinked, but the club was still sideways. Her heart had stopped, but now it was launching itself into her throat.

It was hard to tell which hurt worse—the pain in her head or the shame of those ugly words.

"Stacey, say something! Oh God, you're really hurt, aren't you?" Bree was babbling above Stacey, her cold hand patting Stacey's cheek.

"I'm okay," Stacey ground out. God, even speaking hurt. "Just help me sit up."

Bree's arm snaked beneath Stacey's neck, and as she helped her rise into a sitting position, the nausea clogged Stacey's throat. Slamming her eyes shut, she concentrated on not throwing up.

"Oh shit," Bree said, and Stacey opened her eyes just in time to see Eliza's foot connect with the guy's crotch. She wanted to cheer, but just being upright was all she could manage at the moment.

It seemed like years later that Bree helped her to her feet, and the dance floor spun around Stacey. A ring of spectators surrounded them, and Stacey wanted to sink through the floor. Everyone had seen that, had heard the awful things the jackass had said. They'd seen her fall to the floor, the fat girl who shouldn't even be there.

There was a crack in her heart as wide as the one in her skull, and all Stacey wanted to do was run home to Atlanta and never show her face in public again.

Since she'd changed her flight so last-minute, she'd gotten stuck with one of the worst spots on the whole freaking plane. Back corner, in front of the lavatory, window seat. And her neighbor? Dude had to be pushing three hundred and fifty pounds himself.

She stared out the window, wishing the miles to fly by faster. The pressure of the elevation was causing her head to pound even harder than it had before she'd boarded.

"Ma'am, would you care for something to drink?"

Stacey jumped as she realized the flight attendant was talking to her. "Sorry, just ice water please."

"I like your eye makeup," the woman said as she dished ice into the plastic cup. "That shade of bronze really makes your blue eyes pop."

"Thanks," Stacey said lamely as she took her cup of water. Damn it, she should have taken the time to wash her face after the wedding. No, there hadn't been time, since she was trying to get out without too many guests noticing, but still. Her wedding makeup and hair probably looked really odd with her comfy pants and long-sleeved Mumford & Sons tee.

Sipping her water, Stacey scooched as close to the window as she possibly could get and opened her tablet. Blessing the free Wi-Fi on this flight, she started Googling.

This wedding had changed something inside her. Being there with her extended family, posing for pictures with the beautiful, perfect bridal party, and ruining Bree's bachelorette party had shown Stacey that she really didn't have a handle on life outside of work. In her job, she was confident, happy, complete. Outside of the city-planning department, in the "real life" zone? She really didn't like that Stacey at all.

It wasn't a surprise, of course. She'd rationalized it by reminding herself that most people didn't like themselves, right? It was a normal thing, at least in Stacey's experience. But when she'd been at the ER, hurting and alone, because she'd insisted she was fine and Eliza and Bree should go on and party, she'd realized that if she were someone else, anyone else, this wouldn't have happened.

Like it or not—and she didn't—a big part of her problem was her weight. Eighteen wasn't exactly the size models sported on the runway. And when she'd glimpsed the note the ER physician was scribbling in her chart, she'd caught the word *obese* only three words in.

Outside of her work accomplishments, what did she have? The most important thing about her, the most notable, was the size of her ass. And she was tired of it.

Page after page of results came back from her search.

"Good Lord," she muttered under her breath. How many freaking gyms were close to her apartment? A shit-ton, apparently.

Starting at the top, she clicked the first hit. Oh hell, no. Way too hard core for her. The home page touted the professional body-builders who used the gym, showing them in all their bronzed, oiled, and muscled perfection.

"Damn," her neighbor said, leaning closer to look over Stacey's shoulder. "She's freaking hot."

"Yeah," Stacey said, tilting her tablet the guy's way. "She's my girlfriend."

"Oh," he said, then turned back to his paperback.

Clicking back to the search results, Stacey scanned the names. All the common ones were there, the huge chains with instantly recognizable names, the typical eating-healthy groups advertising in banners across the top of each page.

A wave of tension crested over her shoulders. No, no, none of this was right. She didn't want to roll up into some huge mega-gym with thousands of people running on treadmills and be the fat chick everyone stared at. She needed help. Someone to show her how the heck to operate the stuff, how to do it right, without hurting or embarrassing herself.

A trainer. That's it. She needed to find a trainer.

As soon as the word popped into her brain, her headache eased off, and she smiled to herself. Yeah. This was right.

Clearing the search bar, she started again. Personal trainers within a five-mile radius of her apartment.

"Bingo," she said aloud. There it was. The name of the gym she'd be training at come Monday morning, if they had space for her. Healthy Living Training sounded perfect for her. Small, intimate, and encouraging. Training for people of all fitness levels.

It didn't hurt that the little picture under the *Meet Robert Liston, our founder and head trainer* tagline looked like it'd been peeled right out of a men's fashion magazine. The dude was *hot*.

And even though he'd never look at her twice, if she was going to be running her ass off, and sweating like a hooker in Hades, she'd like to do it while looking at a Greek god.

She might be a chubby girl, but damn it, her hormones worked just fine.

Chapter 2

The chill of the November morning threatened to seep down into Robert Liston's bones, but as he pushed through the doors, the warmth of the gym—his gym—chased it away. He smiled as he disabled the alarm system. The smell of new paint had finally faded, and the place was starting to take on a life of its own now.

"Hey, Rob. 'Morning."

Rob glanced over his shoulder as he threw the light switches to the ON position. "'Morning, Tony. You're here early."

The gym's first regular, a local attorney who'd signed up just after the doors had been unlocked in their old location for the first time, gave a million-watt grin. "Got a meeting this morning, and I can't miss my workout."

Rob nodded as Tony grabbed a towel and headed off to the cardio machines for a warm-up.

The warmth inside Rob's chest grew as he prepped the front counter for the day, and it didn't have anything to do with the space's new furnace. It was the vibe of the place. *His* place. More regulars were flowing in now, tossing cheerful greetings or early morning grunts his way.

The gym was finally looking like it was going to make it. *He'd* done that—nobody else. This was his dream, and if things kept up for the rest of the year the way they had been for the last couple of months, they'd be close to recouping the start-up costs and begin turning a profit. Maybe now his family would see—

"Ugh, why do we have to open so freaking early?" Brandi Matthews, his second-in-command and one of his closest friends, grumbled as she dumped her bag behind the counter. "Can't people work out in the afternoon?"

"Not if they want to keep their jobs," Rob said mildly as he punched the button on the Keurig. Brandi was a sweet person, but before her coffee she kind of hated life. He'd learned his lesson when she started working with him a year ago, and now, as soon as he set eyes on her, he got it brewing.

"Who needs a job? I could sell plasma."

"You'd get about fifty bucks a donation, and you can't do it more than once or twice a month, if I remember correctly."

"How much is rent on a park bench? I could eat Ramen."

"And that fluffy cat of yours would starve to death, because God forbid she eat anything but organic premium tuna."

Brandi, who'd been burying her face in her arms, raised her head long enough to arch a perfectly plucked brow at Rob. "You know she's got a sensitive digestive system."

"Bullshit. That cat is pickier than you are, and that's saying something." Rob deposited the mug beside Brandi's elbow with a smile. "Now, come on, princess. Suck it up. You've got a new client coming in soon."

Brandi snarled, but grabbed her mug and began sipping anyway.

The *thump* and *hum* of footsteps on the treadmill, the soft *click* of weight machines, the sound of voices and laughter swirled around him like a warm spring breeze. Rob closed his eyes, just for a minute. This was what peace felt like. Fulfillment. His family hadn't understood. After all, he was supposed to go to medical school, just like his dad had, his granddad too. But medicine hadn't called to him like this did. Like owning his own business, helping others achieve their potential, their goals. Dad didn't get it. Neither did Mom, or his two sisters. For the longest time, they'd all presumed he was pursuing a failing idea.

He cared about their opinions, but they hadn't stopped him. If anything, the negativity spurred him harder to make this a success.

His gym, Healthy Living, was situated right in the heart of Atlanta. In its first six months, membership numbers were growing, word was getting around, and their success seemed more likely now.

"You asleep? Come on, dude, I'm not running this place alone for the next two hours."

Rob opened his eyes to a now-smiling Brandi. Her mug was half-empty, so caffeine levels were approaching the safety zone.

"You really need to get a coffeemaker for your house, you know."

Brandi rolled her eyes. "Why would I do that when I can drink it here?"

"Because then maybe you'd be human before I inflicted you on people? You know Tony's terrified of you." Rob nodded his head at the weight bench closest to the counter, where Tony had set up shop.

Brandi's longing sigh was almost comedic. "That is the most beautiful man I've ever set eyes on. It should be illegal to be so sexy."

"Ask him out, already. I'm tired of you making puppy-dog eyes at him."

His simple, logical statement was answered with a murderous glare. "You're insane. I can't. He's gorgeous, successful . . . What if he says no? What if he already has a girlfriend? No, can't do it."

Rob shrugged. "You could do it if you wanted to. You aren't his trainer, so it's not against the rules. And he won't say no."

"How do you know that?"

"Because he's not an idiot, and he's not wearing a ring. You've been staring at him for months. You can't complain if you don't try."

"You're really one to talk about people's love lives, Rob. How long has it been since Rebecca left? Ten, eleven months? And you haven't so much as looked at another woman."

His temper stirred, but he clamped down on it. Brandi knew exactly what she was doing. Rebecca, his ex, was still a sore subject. He was the one who'd broken it off, but the whole sorry situation still chafed.

He could—and would—be the bigger man. "I'll let that slide. Come on, finish your go-juice. Isn't your new client supposed to be here in just a minute?" Rob clicked through the screens in their appointment calendar to get to today's. Yup, sure enough, there in the 5 a.m. slot was an unfamiliar name.

Brandi, who was still staring longingly at Tony's tensed lats, sighed. "Yeah, I guess so."

A cold breeze brushed by him then as the front door opened, and a body hustled through the doors into the warmth. Raindrops glistened on the hood of her jacket as she pushed it back, revealing long, strawberry-blonde curls. Bright blue eyes scanned the space, landing briefly on him, then glancing away just as quickly.

Her face was exquisite, her demeanor uncertain, as she shed her jacket and hung it on the rack near the doorway. She wore workout leggings and a baggy tee, which rode up just enough to let him see the generous curve of her ass as she hung up her jacket. Damn. She was no fitness model, but something about the way the woman was put together made his body sit up and take notice. And her smile as she approached Brandi at the front counter made him wonder if heaven was real and had really just walked into his gym.

"Hey, I'm here for the free pizza. Is it a buffet, or do I put my order in here?"

Her tone was light, but the nervousness behind her pleasant expression called to him. He stepped forward as Brandi laughed.

"Yeah, the pizza is imaginary, but I can promise you a kick-ass shake after your workout. You're Stacey, right?" Rob held out a hand, and she shook it.

The woman nodded. "Sadly, yes."

"Hey, no sadness here. You're going to love it. Maybe not today, but definitely soon. I promise. Let me get you our welcome packet, and then we'll get started."

Stacey unzipped her bag, and as Brandi turned toward the cabinet on the back wall, Rob grabbed her elbow.

"Bran, let me train her."

Brandi's huge brown eyes went wide. "Huh?"

Keeping his voice pitched low, Rob grabbed one of the green welcome packet envelopes as he answered. "I want to train her."

"But why? She's not exactly looking to take it to the next level. More like she's terrified to even get started."

Brandi was right. The guidelines they'd established for who took on which clients were there for a reason. Brandi was great at first-time gym-goers. Felicity was perfect for those who thrived on competition, and Silvio had the bodybuilding crowd down to a science. And Rob? He was the go-to guy for anyone who'd hit a wall. Those frustrated people who just wanted to push their bodies through to the next plane and reach a specific goal.

Where Stacey was concerned, he had to be honest, with himself at least. He had a specific goal of his own in mind.

"I know it, but I see something in her. I'm taking her on."

"Is that an order?"

He just cocked an eyebrow at her, wordless.

Brandi bit her full lower lip, and nodded. He'd probably played the boss card a little heavy just then, but it was perfectly justified in this case.

He wanted to help Stacey. He wanted to show her that this was inside her control, that she could do it, and he wanted to see her smile again. But this time without the fear behind it.

He was drawn to her. Honestly, he wasn't entirely sure if selfishness or altruism was motivating him at the moment, and he didn't really care.

Either way, the end result was the same.

Stacey hoped like hell that nobody could tell she was pants-pissing terrified. Gripping her hands into tight balls around the strap of her rain-dampened bag, she watched out of the corner of her eye as the two staff members held a whispered conversation on the other side of the counter from her.

They were probably fighting over who was going to be stuck training her. Her stomach flopped over in a lurching movement. Ugh. Her first day, and already they were sick of her?

"Stop it," she said under her breath as she unzipped her bag and dug through it for her water bottle. Beating herself up didn't help anything. She was here to get healthier, to like herself more. But that didn't stop her from sending up a silent prayer that the girl with the shiny brown ponytail would lose the coin toss and have to train her.

The guy? He was the one from the website, whose picture she'd drooled over for most of the flight home. She'd wanted to admire him from a distance. Having him be the one right beside the equipment on which she was sweating like a farm animal? Not cool. If she had to stay that close to him for an hour or two each day for the next few weeks, she'd definitely have a cardiac arrest. Beauty like that was meant to be admired from a safe distance. Did she want to get up close to him, see if his perfectly tousled sandy hair was as soft as it looked? Hell, yes. But no way. Maybe if she lost a hundred pounds she'd consider it later.

Her heart gave a nervous flutter as the pair turned toward her once again, a bright green folder in the guy's hand. He gave her a million-watt grin, teeth so straight and perfect they had to be the product of thousands of dollars' worth of dentistry.

"Well, Stacey, I'm looking forward to working with you. My name is Robert Liston, but you can call me Rob. Let's come over here and get acquainted before we get started."

There was no God. Well, if there was, he or she had a damn good sense of humor. This Greek statue was supposed to teach her how to get healthy? Without realizing it, she took a step backward toward the door.

He moved a little closer. Not so close that he invaded her personal space, but close enough for her to see a tiny curl of hair above his ear. It stuck out a bit. She seized onto the sight as if it were a badge of his humanity.

He's not perfect. Look, he has hairs out of place like a normal person.

"It's going to be okay. Come sit with me for a second."

She swallowed, which was hard to do, because her throat felt like it was full of sawdust. "Okay," she croaked, and followed him to a cluster of tables near the counter.

Rob pulled a chair out for her, and she pulled off her jacket before sinking into it.

"Tell me a little bit about why you're here today." His voice was kind, inviting. If she just closed her eyes, maybe she could pretend he was a priest or an elderly grandfather. But the sight of his handsome face had already burned into her retinas. All she could see when she blinked slowly was him.

With a deep breath for courage, Stacey spoke. "I'm the only person in my family who's overweight. I just got back from my cousin's wedding in Hawaii, and it was one of the most humiliating experiences of my life. I couldn't go swimming, or enjoy doing anything there because I'm so self-conscious. I'm tired of hating my body, and I want to do something to change it."

Oh God. Her throat was clogging with tears, and her vision had gone blurry. *Breathe, girl, come on, don't turn into a blubbering idiot in front of Chris Hemsworth's twin.*

"It's okay," Rob said, and then a warm weight was laid on top of her folded hands. He was touching her. He was comforting her.

"A lot of people come in here just like you. They're unhappy with how they look, how they feel. I can help you, Stacey, I promise you that. Together we can get your body healthy. But it's important for you to understand that a lot of this game is mental, too."

"What do you mean?" she sniffed.

"I mean that how you see yourself isn't dependent only on how you look. You've got to adjust your perspective. Right now, it's easy to see all the negatives."

She nodded, staring down at his large hand still covering hers.

"This process isn't easy. And it'll still be hard to focus on the positives. But it's something that you've got to start doing now."

"What positives? I like my hair and my eyes. That's about it."

"Come with me," Rob said, pulling Stacey to her feet. "Leave your stuff here on the table—Brandi will watch it."

"O—Okay."

Stacey let Rob lead her past the equipment down a long, narrow hallway. At the end, Rob turned the corner and pulled open a door.

"This is one of our classrooms. We do yoga, Pilates, and several other classes weekly. But for right now, focus on this mirror."

"Ugh." She couldn't hold back her groan. There was a wall of mirrors in front of her, ending just a couple of feet before the corners of the room. Full-length mirrors tended to ruin an otherwise good day for Stacey, which was why she didn't own one.

"Stand here." Rob positioned her in front of the mirror and stepped aside to remove himself from the reflection. He stood behind her left shoulder so she couldn't see him, not in the mirror nor from the corner of her eye.

"What do you see?"

She didn't want to look. God, why had she done this? She could have been completely happy in her apartment alone. Well, maybe not *completely* happy. But satisfied. Maybe not satisfied. Safe. *Safe* was the word.

"Come on, Stacey. Open your eyes for me."

That voice. Still kind, but now it held a note beneath it that wouldn't take any bullshit. Deep, masculine, demanding.

"Open them."

So she did. And then she winced.

"Tell me what you see when you look at yourself."

"I see a woman who's unattractive. A person I don't like much, if at all. Someone who will probably die alone."

She'd meant it as a joke, but for some reason, she couldn't laugh and neither did he. It was the truth, as she saw it anyway. Her chest felt heavy, and her eyes stung for a second.

"There. That's the dynamic that we want to change. Now I want you to look again, and find something positive to say about yourself."

Rolling her eyes, Stacey turned to Rob. "Seriously?"

There was zero hint of humor in his steely gray eyes. "Yes. Now." The demand would have been sexy if it wasn't so damn annoying.

Blowing an irritated breath up toward her forehead, Stacey faced the mirror again. She looked for a long moment, starting at her feet. They were laced into purple sneakers. Stretchy yoga pants didn't exactly hide the imperfections in her legs. The top she'd chosen, a green T-shirt that draped enough to hide her stomach, was tight in the upper arms. Her ponytail had gotten mussed in the hood of her coat.

"Something positive. Come on."

God, he was persistent.

She glanced over her shoulder as she spoke. "I came here today. I do want to see something positive in me. So I guess I'm proud of myself for taking the chance?"

"So you see determination."

A sudden smile broke out across her face. That wasn't so bad. Did she believe it? Hell, no. But this little woo-woo positivity exercise would probably be good for her in the long run. "Yeah. I guess I do."

"Good. When you look in the mirror, I want you to find something positive to focus on. Every time you look. Deal?"

She turned to Rob, who was holding out a hand for her to shake. "Yeah. Deal."

At the contact with his warm skin, her blood bubbled in her veins like champagne. A shiver went down her spine as the contact broke. Damn, it was going to be so hard to focus on anything with a man like that beside her the whole time.

"Great. Let's go get you warmed up, and we'll take you through your first session."

Stacey nodded. "Let's go."

Chapter 3

She'd been wrong. He wasn't a Greek statue at all. He was some kind of upper-level male demon with sculpted arms, an evil grin, and horns that protruded from his skull when he cracked the whip.

"Come on, Stacey, two more."

"I can't," she panted, gripping her trembling thigh muscles. This machine, some kind of leg press thing, was torture. She was laid out on her back, her knees shoved up toward her chest, and about a billion pounds of weight was holding her feet down and forcing her into a fetal position.

"You can do it. Now, push through it."

His eyes weren't soft gray like a dove. They were bleak and hard, like the side of an Antarctic submarine. Steel. Titanium. Harder and colder than ice.

"You're heartless."

"Yup. Come on, two more. Push through, you can do it."

Gritting her teeth so hard she thought they'd crack, Stacey sucked a breath in through her nose and pressed her heels down into the panel. Her calves screamed silently, trembling with the effort.

"Almost there, straighten your legs," Rob said as his hand went just below her knee. The soft touch seemed to urge her on, and with a massive grunt, she gave one last shove. Her legs were straight for one brilliant second, and she gave a grateful sigh.

"Slow back down. Control it, come on, don't drop it—ease it back."

"I can't," she gasped as her knees buckled. Rob grabbed her legs and steadied them, helping her bend them slowly back into the start position.

"It's okay. You can do this. Breathe a second, then we're going for the last one."

"You are a monster."

"I've been called worse."

Pressing her hand against her chest, Stacey closed her eyes and felt her heart *thump* hard against her palm. She might just have a heart attack lying here. Dropping dead didn't sound so bad at the moment. She was only forty-five minutes into her first hour-long session. Whatever was after this was sure to be even more hellish.

Her heart slowed just a touch. Somehow the handsome bastard must have heard it.

"Okay, knock this last one out. Come on, Stace."

She slitted her eyes open and glared at him.

"I'm not backing down. You saw determination in the mirror. Don't let that turn into stubbornness. One more press, I'm right here with you."

"I'm just doing this to shut you up," Stacey growled, and pressed down on the panel. God, it was so heavy, almost as if he'd added three or four more plates when she wasn't looking. Her body was screaming, threatening to burst from all the pressure.

"Don't give up, I've got you." Rob's strong hands rested on her knees, steadying them. He looked down, straight into her eyes. "Push, just a little further, you're almost there."

"Gaaaah!" The cry that came from Stacey was almost a grunt, or a guttural scream. She didn't care that she sounded like a cow giving birth. The plate stopped, her legs stretched as far as they could go.

"Good girl! Slow back down, control it, easy. Perfect."

The plates *click*ed back home. She was never moving again. The sweat had cemented her to this bench, and she'd die here. They could hold the funeral here, and bury her with this medieval torture device still attached. It could be her coffin.

"Give me your hand. I'll help you sit up."

Without thinking, she lifted her wrist limply. Rob's strong, warm hand circled it and gently pulled her upright.

The room spun around her for a second, and she swayed.

"Sit on the bench for a second. Here, take a swig." Rob guided her back to sit on the leg press bench and handed her the water bottle he'd clipped to a loop on his shorts.

The cool water soothed her raw throat, and she gulped it gratefully.

"You've done great. I know this is tough, but you're really muscling through it. Good work."

"You're just saying that because you're afraid I'll throw a brick through your window."

Rob arched a brow and smiled. "I don't think you're the criminal type."

"Don't tempt me," Stacey grumbled, a little irritated when he laughed. She hadn't been making a joke. Well, mostly not.

"Okay. Five-minute break, and then we'll hit the treadmill for the last ten."

That word. That evil, soul-sucking, terrifying word. It yanked the floor out from beneath Stacey, and she had to grip the bench to keep from toppling off of it. "What?"

"Treadmill. Breathe a second, and I'll meet you over there. We'll go for the one in the corner." Rob nodded toward a sleek gray model in the far corner of the gym. Nobody else was near it, fortunately. The front was nestled up against the corner, and the back of it faced her like a gauntlet of doom.

"Isn't there some other kind of thing we can do? The elliptical again, maybe?"

"I need to get your level on the treadmill. You can do it. I'll be right there with you every step. Don't wimp out on me now."

Rob winked at her, then walked away.

"He. Is. Evil." Stacey glared at his perfect glutes. His perfect shoulders. The defined muscles in his perfect calves. This wasn't what she'd expected. Whether or not it was good for her didn't matter. She wanted to kill him. Her body was in agony, her lungs were burning, and he had the audacity to smile and wink at her?

She'd tie his beautiful ass in knots.

Five minutes passed much more quickly than she thought was fair. Her water bottle empty, she glanced over at the treadmill again.

Shit. Rob had just arrived over there, draping a towel over his shoulder and waving back at her.

"Nooo," Stacey moaned, dropping her forehead into her hands. She stared at the industrial carpeting beneath her sneakered feet. Not one more minute. Her insides were confused when she looked at Rob, but her hands wanted nothing more than to wrap themselves around his neck and squeeze until those beautiful gray eyes popped out like marbles.

Despite herself, she laughed a little. Rob would probably think that was funny, and maybe even give her permission to do it if she actually got off her ass and did her last ten minutes on the treadmill.

Standing reluctantly, Stacey turned and wiped down the leg press bench like Rob had showed her. Once that was done, she crossed the floor to Rob's side.

"Let's get this over with, Marquis de Sade."

Rob gave a little bow and held his hand out to help her step onto the treadmill. It would have been charming, if she wasn't so determined that homicide was her only other option to deal with him.

"Okay. Let's start slow, at a three. We'll give you a second to get used to the motion, get your breath and heart rate steady, and then we're going to ease the speed up to see where you're comfortable."

"I'm comfortable at a three," Stacey said, her footsteps thumping rhythmically on the rubberized tread.

"We're pushing your comfort level today," Rob said, leaning against the front panel slightly. "Make sure you hold on to the handles to keep yourself steady, at least until you get used to it. Later on you can move your arms as you run."

"Run?" She arched a brow at him. "I don't run."

"You will." He grinned.

Hate. Him. All six feet of his handsome self. He was made up of ginseng, health food, and pure, unadulterated cruelty.

"Okay, let's push it up a bit." The panel beeped as Rob nudged the speed higher.

Three-point-five, four, four-point-five . . .

"Slow down!" Stacey panted, her feet flying on the moving belt beneath her. "I can't keep up!"

"Stay here for a second, you can do it. Don't give up."

"Don't tell me what to do!" Her knuckles had gone white on the bar in front of her.

"You're paying me to tell you what to do. Here, for thirty more seconds. Come on. Count them down."

"Twenty-nine," Stacey panted. Her breath was burning her from the inside out. "Twenty-eight."

Rob pushed off the panel and stepped toward the back of the treadmill. Wait a second, where the hell did he think he was going?

"Twenty-six." Stacey craned her neck to see where Rob had gone. Why had that bastard deserted her? "Where are—"

She didn't get a chance to finish answering the question. She'd twisted around so hard to look at him that her left hand lost its grip on the bar in front of her. Grabbing wildly, her balance suddenly thrown off, she stepped on the side rail instead of the tread. Her right foot dragged her backward and she fell.

Right on top of Rob.

Rob had only stepped aside because Brandi was waving at him frantically. But before he could reply to his assistant, he was knocked to the floor.

He stared at the ceiling for a moment before his head cleared and his instincts kicked in. Stacey. She'd fallen.

"Are you okay?" he asked as he sat up. She'd fallen across his legs, and was currently lying facedown across his lap.

"Oh God," she moaned, scrambling backward. "Oh God, oh God."

"Are you hurt? Here, let me help you up."

He was fine. He hadn't fallen that hard, and he was glad he'd been able to slow her descent somewhat. But her cheeks were fire-engine red, and she refused to meet his gaze as she scuttled away on her hands and knees like her panties were on fire.

"No, I'm good, I'm fine. I can't believe I fell on top of you. I'm so, so sorry."

"It was my fault," Rob said, standing and reaching a hand down to her to help her to her feet. She ignored it, planting her palms on the side rail of the treadmill and struggling to her feet. "I shouldn't have left your side."

Brandi. He looked over at her. She'd stepped forward to help them both up, but Rob waved her off. He needed to handle this on his own.

"Sit down here, and let me check you for injuries." He led Stacey to the nearest chair.

"I'm fine," she protested, but he ignored her.

Kneeling in front of her, he ran his hands over her knees. "Any pain here?"

"Just sore. "

Grasping her heel, he gently flexed and extended her leg. "Here?"

"No."

After repeating the motion with her other leg, and examining the skin of her hands and arms, Rob was satisfied.

"You were going to be sore anyway after this morning, but you may discover a couple of bruises after that fall. If you've got any severe pain or discomfort, I want you to call me immediately. No matter what time it is, day or night."

Stacey looked away. "I'm sure I'm fine. It was just stupid clumsiness."

"Look at me."

She didn't for a long moment, but Rob didn't budge. He just waited. He knew exactly what was running through her head at that moment, and he wasn't about to stand for it.

Eventually, she glanced his way, and he stared straight into her eyes.

"That happened because I left your side. I promised I wouldn't. I let you down. So, that was my fault, not yours. I should never have moved without telling you first. I'm sorry. Can you forgive me?"

She blinked, her cornflower-blue eyes looking a little wet. *God, please don't let her cry.* He was useless around crying women.

"It's not your fault."

"Don't avoid the question. I'm asking for your forgiveness."

Her voice was barely a whisper. "I forgive you."

"Thank you," he said, giving her a small smile. "There are five minutes left. When the horse throws you, you've got to get right back on."

"I am not getting on that treadmill again."

"This time we'll stay at a three. You can walk the whole time. And even if the building falls down around us, I promise I won't leave your side."

Stacey sniffed and rubbed her nose with the back of her hand. "Okay. Let's get this over with."

Not exactly the enthusiastic reply he'd been hoping for, but realistically it was a pretty good response. He'd really screwed up there.

Kicking himself mentally wouldn't help a damn thing, but he did it anyway.

Stacey was about as emotionally fragile as anyone he'd seen walking through his doors. The confidence she had was false bravado. Her self-esteem was in the crapper, and this was obviously a last-ditch attempt to feel better about herself.

This little incident had happened at the worst possible time.

"You ready?"

She was on the treadmill again, both feet on the side rails and both hands gripping the bar as if it was her last hope for survival. "Ready as I'm going to be."

He started it at a two. "There. Start a nice, slow walk."

She stumbled a little as she stepped onto the tread, but he was right there. Steadying her, talking her through, calming her fears. After a moment, she'd gotten the rhythm and was walking well.

"Head up, look straight ahead."

"I'd rather see my feet."

"I know, but you're more likely to fall that way." Rob leaned in closer. "If you do that, I'll just have to catch you again."

Her cheeks fired angrily, her eyes snapping electric-blue fire. But still she refused to look at him.

"We're going to bump it up to three, okay? Steady walk. Not too fast, just even. Concentrate on your breathing—keep it deep and even."

She nodded, and he bumped the speed up to a three.

For the next several minutes, he stood there, leaning against the front panel of the treadmill, counting Stacey's breaths. She was more comfortable now, her knuckles not looking so white as she gripped the bar in front of her. There was even a tiny swing to her hips that made him want to smile. She wasn't in shape, but that didn't seem to matter to his libido. Her shape now was pretty damn appealing, and when she had the confidence to match? She'd be breathtaking.

Maybe she'd surprise him. Maybe that little tumble hadn't wrecked the work they'd done this morning after all. But he'd have to watch very carefully, just to make sure.

Something like that could make a person regret they'd ever had the idea of working out in the first place. He didn't want to lose her because of a stupid mistake he'd made.

Lose her as a client, obviously. He shook his head inwardly. Weird things were popping into his head today.

"Thirty more seconds," Rob said. "You're doing great."

"Yeah. I'm pretty experienced at walking." The snarky tone was at least an indication that her spirit wasn't broken, so he was glad to hear it.

"Three. Two. One. There, all done."

The tread slowed to a stop, and Stacey folded her arms on the treadmill panel and slumped over them. "I want to die."

"No, you don't. You want to live, and this is the first step to doing that. Here." Rob handed her a bottle of water. "Drink that slowly. Catch your breath, and meet me over at the tables."

Stacey took the water and cracked the seal. Rob watched her for a moment, then he walked toward the front counter.

"I am so sorry," Brandi said when he got near. "I just wanted to tell you that I talked to Tony. I should have waited, I was just so excited. Is Stacey okay? Are you?"

"I'm fine, but I'm going to have to talk fast to keep her. She's embarrassed."

"Oh no," Brandi said, her full lips pulled downward. "I feel so awful. It's my fault."

"Stop. It was my fault for leaving the side of a brand-new client while she was testing her limits. It was a rookie mistake and she paid the price. I apologized profusely, and we'll both just hope that she doesn't let this stop her." Rob rapped his knuckles on the counter and turned toward the tables.

Stacey was already there, gathering up her things. If he didn't hurry, she might just run out the door and not come back.

"Sit down with me for just a second," Rob said as he neared.

Stacey glanced at her cell phone's screen. "I really need to get going. I've got to go home and shower before work."

"It will only take a second."

She bit her lip, but sank down in the chair he pulled out for her anyway.

Rob sat down across from her, folded his hands, and leaned forward.

"I am so glad you came in here today. I really enjoyed working with you."

Stacey shook her head and opened her mouth to speak, but Rob kept going.

"I want to tell you that you did amazing. You pushed your limits; you kept persevering. You can meet your goals if we keep working together. You're stronger than you know."

A wry smile crossed her face, and she looked down into her lap.

"So, I want you to practice positive thinking when you look in the mirror, and I'll see you tomorrow morning, same time."

Stacey pushed her chair back and gave him a polite wave. "See you." She turned and walked out the door.

Rob sank back into the chair, lacing his fingers over his belly. Hmm. Not exactly the most promising good-bye. But at this point he'd done all he could.

It was up to her now.

Chapter 4

Rob couldn't get her out of his mind for the rest of the day.

Fortunately—or unfortunately—he didn't have any other clients scheduled. Not like the free time benefited him. He couldn't focus on anything productive after the morning he'd had.

It wasn't just the way she'd left, although that definitely took up a good bit of his thought processes. It was *her*. Little snippets of memory had dogged him all damn day. The reddish hue to her blond ponytail as it swayed with her movements, catching the light. The way her Lycra pants clung to her rounded hips as she stretched upward to reach the pull-down bar. The way her otherwise-loose tee strained around her breasts.

He had it bad.

"Hey, boss," Silvio said, poking his head through the open door. "You staying? I was going to lock up."

"Nah," Rob said, closing the lid of his laptop with a sigh. "I'm heading out too."

Silvio paused, a frown looking out of place on his always-cheerful face. "It's not like you to be here so late. Everything okay?"

Rob debated for a minute before answering. Everything was fine, wasn't it? Other than the fact that he might have destroyed Stacey's already-shaky self-image that morning, and thus lost the chance to get to know her better. God. It'd been forever since he'd screwed something up so royally. If she showed up tomorrow, the relief might just make him collapse.

"Yeah, just got a lot on my mind." Rob stood and grabbed his jacket from the rack in the corner. "Nothing to worry about."

"Want to grab a beer?" Silvio scratched his chin as he waited for

Rob to punch in the alarm code. "I'm meeting a few buddies at Galley's down the street. You're welcome to hang with us if you want."

"Thanks, Silvio, but I'll take a rain check. I've got some research I need to do before tomorrow."

Silvio arched a dark brow at him, but smiled. "Okay, boss. Next time, then."

After the doors were locked, Rob and Silvio went their separate ways. The parking deck across the street was mostly empty at this time of night. After all, it was after nine on a Monday. Hardly the most bustling time for this area of downtown. As Rob flipped through his keys for the fob to his ancient BMW, he wondered what Stacey drove.

Her hair had been perfect, makeup neat, clothes obviously well made and new. She'd drive something nice. Not that it mattered. She'd probably be driving in the opposite direction of the gym to-morrow morning.

After cranking up the car, he waited a moment for the engine to warm up. Checking his cell phone's screen, he frowned. No missed calls or texts. He'd been halfway hoping that Stacey would call, just to tell him that she felt okay after that fall and she would be coming to the gym tomorrow.

Not likely.

Scowling down at the blue-green lights of his dash, Rob jerked the gearshift into REVERSE. He had to stop dwelling on her. He'd lost clients before, and he would lose them in the future. It wasn't a big deal. People relocated, decided they wanted different things, wanted fresh experiences. But he'd never lost a client because he'd done a bad job. And he was beginning to think that this morning he might have done just that for the first time.

As the tires rolled over the speed bump at the entrance to the park-ing deck, Rob cranked up his radio and nosed the BMW toward home in the suburbs. He'd be up late. Tonight he would research some new exercises for Stacey before bed, make sure he was extra-prepared for her to show up tomorrow.

And if she didn't? Well, her registration paperwork had her phone number and address. A phone call, an e-mail, somehow he'd reach out to her and try to convince her to give Healthy Living a second chance. Even if it wasn't with him as her trainer, he still wanted her to fulfill her potential.

Besides that? He wanted to see her again. He hadn't been this interested in a woman since Rebecca. And that was definitely something worth pursuing.

The next morning, five thirty came and went with no Stacey. Then six. Then six thirty. As he stared at the clock for what had to be the seventieth time since coming in that morning, a sharp poke in his ribs made him wince.

"What's eating you?" Brandi asked over her second cup of coffee. Usually at this point in her caffeine intake, she was almost downright pleasant. But today there was a serious tint to her expression.

"Client didn't show," Rob said shortly as he locked the computer screen. "No big deal."

"It was that Stacey Hough, wasn't it?" Brandi shook her head, causing her ponytail to swing back and forth with the motion. "God, I still feel terrible about that."

"I told you, it was my fault." A burst of laughter from the elliptical machines drew his attention. A couple of regulars were chatting, happy smiles on their faces.

That was good. So, why did the mirth make him want to jump out of his skin and break something?

He had to tone down the scowl that knitted his brows. It was bad for business.

"Hey, can you go to the Corner Café and get us some breakfast? I've been saving up my calories for one of those chocolate croissants."

Rob looked hard at her for a moment. "Why? You're acting suspicious."

Brandi snorted, curling her hand around her coffee mug. "Don't be stupid. You need a break; you're making people nervous with that pissy look on your face. Go and sit down to eat. Just bring me my bakery treat when you come back, okay? And you can buy it for me."

Damn it, she was right. He didn't bother to argue. "Yeah, okay."

Grabbing his coat from the office took just a moment, and then he was out the door and hustling down the windy sidewalk to the Corner Café. It was a cute little place, with vintage wooden floors, artsy décor, and a real community-hangout kind of vibe. Brandi was right. He needed to go chill for a while, forget that Stacey had basically stood him up, in a manner of speaking.

He shoved his hands into his pockets. It was a business problem, not a personal one. He needed to pull his head out of his ass.

Alternative rock music greeted him as soon as he pushed into the warmth of the Corner Café. They were just starting to get really busy with the morning crowd. As Rob joined the line that stood three people deep, a somewhat-familiar voice met his ear. He turned and looked at the line to his right.

"Yeah, seriously. I'm fine. It's crazy that you're even calling me on your honeymoon. And what the crap time is it there? Shouldn't you be snuggled up in bed with your new husband?"

Long strawberry-blond curls tumbled around the shoulder that was cradling the phone to her head. A purple scarf trailed one end down her back, the black wool of her coat grabbing onto the fringe and making it twist in odd ways.

A grin stretched across his lips. Well, damn. If it wasn't the phantom trainee herself. Stacey Hough was standing in line right next to him. If that wasn't fate screaming for them to continue their association, in whatever capacity, he didn't know what was.

"Sorry, Bree, but I'm about to order breakfast. I know, I know. Seriously, I'm fine. No lasting effects. Yes, I'd tell you. Okay. Have fun, and don't worry about me. Love you, talk to you soon. Bye-bye."

Stacey hung up the phone just as the customer in front of her took his muffin and left. She turned, looking down into her purse as she tucked her phone away.

Rob waited. Three, two . . . She looked his way.

"Good morning," he said simply.

Her jaw fell open for a second, and she blinked twice. "Uh, well, hi. 'Morning, I mean."

"Good to see you," he said.

"Ma'am, are you ready to order?" The cashier was waving at Stacey. Just then, the person in line ahead of Rob moved on.

With a look that could only be defined as pure unadulterated spite, Stacey stepped up to the counter.

"Yes. Can I get a large mocha, with double chocolate and extra whipped cream? Oh, and a cheese Danish. One of those big ones," she said, pointing at the bakery case beside her.

And then she looked at him again. The defiant tilt of her head was a definite challenge.

One he didn't intend to ignore.

Stacey wasn't sure where the demon on her shoulder had come from. It was childish. Petty, even. But for some reason, the fact that Rob had greeted her without a word about her nonappearance at the gym today rankled.

He was supposed to be irritated with her. Disappointed, even. But maybe he didn't care that she'd humiliated herself in front of his entire gym yesterday? Well, in that case, he could go suck a—

"Here you go, ma'am."

Stacey jumped as the cashier handed her change back. "Thank you."

"Yeah, can I get a large mocha, double chocolate, with whipped cream? And one of those big cheese Danishes, please."

Stacey whirled. What the crap?

"Sure. You want that Danish heated?"

Rob looked over to the other cashier, who was tucking Stacey's Danish into the toaster oven. "Sounds good."

"That'll be seven fifty-three."

As Rob handed his credit card to the cashier, he gave Stacey a broad smile.

Anger flared to life within her. What was he doing? There were probably more calories in this breakfast than he allotted himself for the whole freaking week! Why would he copy her order like that? Was he trying to embarrass her again? She hadn't taken him for an asshole, but maybe he was.

As the cashier returned with Stacey's coffee and her Danish, she turned away from him. It didn't matter. His little game had nothing to do with her. She'd just grab her usual table in the corner, have her breakfast, and read the morning paper before work, just like usual. Like yesterday had never happened. Like the guy at the counter was just some stranger, not the person she'd knocked off his feet and physically crushed yesterday.

Warmth climbed into her cheeks as she set her coffee down at the corner table. Ugh. Why'd she have to remember that again?

"Is this seat taken?"

Her gaze flew upward. Damn it. Damn it, damn it, triple damn. There he was, black hoodie framing his arm muscles, his V-necked shirt showing just a hint of chest hair.

Why couldn't he just leave her alone?

"Actually, yeah. My, uh, cousin Bree is meeting me here."

"Oh, isn't that the one who's on her honeymoon right now? You were kind of loud on the phone earlier."

"Shit."

Rob laughed at that and set his coffee down. "I won't bug you for long. Just wanted to have a little chat. If that's okay with you."

She wasn't okay with it. Not in the slightest bit. Not any more than she'd be okay with four root canals, or a monthly Pap smear.

"Okay, fine. Let's get this over with."

The chair scraped back, and Rob sat down across from her. His eyes were bright, his expression direct, and all she wanted to do was crawl under the table and die. Why wouldn't he just give up? She'd obviously given up on her resolution. One whole day. That was all she'd lasted. And now she was fine with embracing her workaholic lifestyle. She was cut out for that. Working out at a gym? That had been a momentary lapse of reason, and she'd regained her senses now.

"Wow," Rob said, setting his coffee down after a brief moment at his lips. He coughed and blinked hard. "That's incredibly sweet."

"Yup. I like it that way." Stacey took a long, deliberate sip. The hot, chocolaty coffee coated her throat as she swallowed.

"Why didn't you come to the gym this morning?"

There it was. The ten-ton elephant in the room. The billion-dollar question. The one topic she'd been dreading and the Band-Aid she wanted to rip off as quickly as possible.

She decided to do the only reasonable thing.

Lie.

"Sorry about that. Had some car trouble this morning."

She couldn't look at him. She'd never been a great liar.

"Oh. That's too bad. But you can come by this evening, and we'll make up the session."

Shit. She stabbed her pastry with her fork a little too hard. The *clink* of metal on ceramic was so loud that several people in line looked her way. "Can't. Have to work late."

"The gym's open 'til nine."

"I'm working 'til ten."

"Well, we can go over now if you want."

"I don't want. No gym clothes."

"We'll just talk over your training plan. No change of clothes needed."

It was getting hard to breathe. Her anger was clogging her throat, but the way he stared right into her eyes was disconcerting, almost arousing. He was leaning toward her, looking at her, only her. She wanted to get even closer to him, but the logical side of her brain was still active. Attack him right back; that was the only solution. "Why are you pushing me so hard?"

"Why are you pushing back?" he countered. When she fell silent, he took another sip of coffee, wincing slightly as he swallowed. Good. He should suffer for being such a pushy jerk.

He set his paper cup down and folded his arms on the table. She tried hard not to notice the obvious muscle definition under his form-fitting jacket.

"You paid for a trainer. A trainer's job is to help you push past what's stopping you and help you achieve your goals. So, that's what I'm doing. I'm trying to help you achieve your goals."

"Well, this morning my goal is to finish this conversation, then my breakfast, and get to work on time." Way more pointed than she'd have liked it to be, but maybe it would work. Why wouldn't he just roll over on this? Her shoulders were so tight they were sending a throbbing pain up her spine into her brain.

"But what about tomorrow morning? And the one after that?" His voice was low, insistent.

"I'll deal with them as they come."

"Stacey, look at me."

She stared down at her plate as hard as she could.

"Look at me."

Damn it. Her eyes met his, and her resolve faltered. Just for a second. How could it not? His chiseled features were beautiful, and those incredible gray eyes were trained directly on hers.

"The reason you came into my gym hasn't changed, has it? You told me that you wanted to like yourself. Can you truly say that you've achieved that goal after a single session?"

With him staring at her like that, she couldn't lie, so she settled for silence.

"Honestly, why didn't you come this morning?"

"Because I was embarrassed."

"Why?"

She glared at him. "Seriously? You've got the gall to ask me that? You were there. You saw what happened. I can't even run on the treadmill for five minutes without falling on my fat ass."

"Hey," he said sharply, his brows lowering slightly. "Don't talk about yourself that way."

She slapped the table so hard her palm stung. "But it's the truth! Do you want me to lie to myself? I'm not interested in that. I'd rather see things for how they are than pretend everything is hunky-dory." Her throat was thickening, but she fought the sensation.

"You've got some things you want to change about yourself. Do you think that calling yourself names and hating your body is going to do that?"

She didn't answer, just flicked a crumb off the edge of her Danish. She didn't want to look at him anymore. And not just because he was so handsome he made her teeth hurt. Because his words were too close to the truth, and she didn't want to hear them.

"Were you ever bullied when you were a kid?" His voice was soft.

"Everyone was bullied when they were a kid."

A warm hand covered hers suddenly, and she looked up at Rob.

"When that was happening, how did it make you feel?"

She shook her head. "You ask the dumbest questions. It was fan-freaking-tastic. How do you *think* I felt? It was awful."

"It's hard to be happy when someone's being mean to you all the time, isn't it?"

Staring at him for a long moment, she searched his face. There was only sincerity written there, his gray eyes more like a cloudy day than cold steel this morning.

"Yesterday you had a bad day. That was my fault. But what matters now is how you choose to react. Sure, you can quit and go back to what you were doing before."

He leaned forward and squeezed her hand. It was such a kind, friendly touch, not intimate at all, but for some reason a delicious shiver went straight up her arm and down her spine.

"But what you were doing before wasn't making you happy. Maybe you were right when you decided to try this. A change can make all the difference in the world in how you feel, how you see yourself. All I want is a chance to show you what you're capable of. Can you give me a month? Just one month to show you the beginnings of what you can do."

Her chest had tightened, and breathing was a chore. Her eyes were stinging, but she didn't dare rub them or close them for fear of the moisture spilling over. Why wouldn't he just give up on her? Why did it matter if she quit after one day?

"Why are you doing this?"

"Because I believe you can make this change."

She closed her eyes. She wanted so badly to believe that he honestly felt that way. It had been so long since someone had. At her job, yeah, people believed in her abilities. It was how she'd become so successful in the city-planning department in such a relatively short time. But she couldn't stay at work 24/7, and there was the problem. Her family. Her friends. They just saw her as the girl who could be counted on to water plants or to pet-sit. *Stacey's never busy; she can house-sit for us while we go on a fabulous spring break vacation. Oh, Stacey's single, we don't have to invite her to this couples' outing. Stacey doesn't have a date; she can babysit while we go out.*

Nobody really believed her life would ever be anything different from what it was now. And she was sick of it. She'd been convinced for so long that life was the way it was, and that there was nothing she could do to change it.

But this guy? She'd spent only an hour or so in his company. He couldn't really believe in her, not the way she craved. He was a businessman. All he was doing was looking out for his bottom line. It wouldn't look good to have a new client quit the same day she started, right?

Even though it was the truth, a little bit of the newborn hope inside her dimmed.

But she wanted so badly to believe. Maybe Rob was right, no

matter whether it was a sales pitch or a sincere concern. Maybe she was capable of more. And this just might be the first step she needed to take to discover her potential.

"Stacey?" He said her name softly—not quite a whisper, but not full-voiced, either. It was a sweet, inviting sound.

She opened her eyes, and squeezed his hand back.

"Okay. One month. I'll give it a shot."

A smile broke out across his face like a break in the winter clouds. She smiled back, unable to stop the expression.

"Great. Come by tonight. I've planned out a more detailed workout plan for you, and I want to get started as soon as we can."

Her hand felt cold when he withdrew his, and she put it in her lap. "You planned a workout schedule for me? After what happened yesterday?"

A boyish tilt to Rob's head made her heart flutter. "I wasn't about to give up on you. Not for one second."

She bit her lip and glanced away. Oh boy. He was way too good of a salesman. If he kept this up, she was going to have a crush on him the size of the giant peach downtown.

Of course, that wouldn't take much. She was already imagining what he'd look like naked.

Chapter 5

The sun was out when Stacey pulled her car into her assigned space. Finally. A December miracle. Atlanta wasn't exactly the snow capital of the world—it was her second winter here and she'd yet to see a flake—but the bleak and gray days had a bad habit of getting everyone down, especially her.

She hummed to herself as she shouldered her bag and bumped the driver's side door closed with her hip. Her heels *click*ed along the cracked walkway, keeping in time with her tune. The breeze was cold, but she didn't care. The blessed sunlight more than made up for the chill.

"'Morning," Hannah called as Stacey pushed through the revolving door into the lobby of the city planning building. The dark-haired receptionist grinned as Stacey leaned on the front counter.

"Good morning to you," Stacey said, perching her sunglasses on top of her head. "You're awful cheery."

"Walter isn't here today."

"That *is* something to celebrate." Stacey grinned back at Hannah. Walter was a typical city government bureaucrat—lots of bluster and guff, with zero skills or management ability to back it up. Most of their department did everything possible to avoid him. Unlucky for Hannah, she had to operate as Walter's personal assistant on most days. Lucky for Stacey, her own boss, Ed, was a jovial older guy who liked to laugh.

"Want to grab lunch at noon?"

Stacey unlocked her phone screen and checked her schedule. "That should be fine. I've got a meeting with Sky Power at eleven, but that's only supposed to last thirty minutes."

"Great." Just then, the phone rang, and Hannah rolled her eyes. "Duty calls. Catch you later."

Stacey waved and moved toward the elevators. Resuming her happy little hum, she punched the Up button and waited.

What an unexpectedly good morning. She hadn't thought she'd be able to feel this good after what had happened yesterday. Her job, which normally was her pride and joy, had been a chore the day before. All she'd wanted to do was go home, take a hot bath, and snuggle up on the couch with a bowl of ice cream and a Netflix marathon.

But the project she was heading up, the installation of solar panels for low-income housing units, was too important to her. It wasn't something she could just forget about because she'd made an ass of herself. So she'd knuckled down and gotten some work done.

The elevator chimed as it arrived on the third floor. The doors glided open, and Stacey stepped out, nearly bumping into Vance Farmer.

"Whoa, steady there, shortcake."

"Vance, how many times do I have to ask you not to call me that?" Stacey moved aside as quickly and politely as she could. Vance, who was at least twenty years older than she was, had a bad habit of not taking no for an answer. Of course, the only man who'd shown an interest in her in the last five years was a paunchy guy in his mid-forties with a receding hairline and the unfortunate habit of wearing Crocs. And shorts. Year-round.

It wasn't even that. She could forgive an unfortunate-looking guy, but the problem was that his personality was even less appealing than his appearance.

"Come on, don't be such a hard-ass. You're not getting any younger, you know."

Stacey didn't pause; she just walked down the hall, tossing her answer over her shoulder. "Vance, don't make me talk to HR again."

"Hey now . . ." His voice faded as she closed her office door behind her.

Dropping her bag onto its usual shelf behind her desk, Stacey turned and sighed. Her office, her palace. Here, she was tough and in charge, on top of the world. The frosted panels of glass that formed the front wall and door gave the place a light, airy feel, while the windows beside and behind her desk let the sunlight in.

Green plants were stationed in the corners of the room, a little feng shui for her mental calm. Sinking into her office chair, Stacey closed her eyes for a moment.

Rob. His words were still ringing in her ears. He believed in her. Of course, it might just be a line he fed to everyone who was ready to quit in order to get them to stick around and pay their monthly fees. Personal training wasn't cheap. But from the number of people she'd seen coming in and out of the new gym, he couldn't be that hard up for clients, could he?

She was reading too much into it.

Her fingers curled into the woven padding on the arms of her chair. Of course, it was delicious to dream about what it might be like to have someone like Rob interested in her.

Impossible? Sure. But wasn't that half the fun of a fantasy life? Imagining the impossible?

"You have got to be kidding me." Hannah's mouth had dropped open, revealing a little too much of her bite of burger.

"Whoa there, chew first, then react." Stacey laughed as she tossed Hannah a napkin.

"Sorry." Hannah's answer was muffled by both napkin and food. She swallowed and took a sip of water before speaking again. "You fell off the treadmill yesterday, right on top of him, and he cornered you in the coffee shop this morning to beg you to come back?"

"I don't know if *beg* is the right word." Stacey frowned at the French fry she was currently poking into a mound of ketchup. "He was just very encouraging."

"Oh puh-lease. I've never quit a gym or a trainer and had them run me down after the fact."

"That's because you change gyms like most people change pants."

Hannah grinned. "Okay, so I have commitment issues. But still, I've been around the block a few times. They'll sometimes send an e-mail, or leave you a voice mail. But if you run into them at the grocery store, or in line at the pharmacy, they'll just smile that awkward smile you see when you know someone but you don't know from where."

A drop of ketchup landed on Stacey's plate. "Well, you must not have made the same kind of impression on them that I did on Rob."

Hannah laughed. "Yeah, I never did sprawl across anyone's lap."

"Hey," Stacey growled in mock anger. "Watch it, girlie. I'd remind you that I'm planning the holiday party."

Hannah splayed a hand over her generous cleavage. "Don't sit me next to Walter. Or worse, Vance."

They both shuddered, then laughed. Stacey took another bite of her tuna salad sandwich, pretending not to notice as Hannah studied her.

"So, Rob. Is he hot?"

A piece of lettuce lodged in Stacey's windpipe and she coughed. Her eyes watered as she took a sip of her iced tea. "Why does that matter?"

"Because you get this really cute, bashful look on your face when you mention him."

Stacey's spine went cold. "I do not!"

"You totally do. It's cute. So, does he flirt with you?"

"God, no. Not at all. I mean, yeah, he's hot as hell, but he's totally out of my league. He's professional. No weirdness. It was just a really good sales pitch, that's all."

Hannah spun her straw and leaned forward, pinning Stacey with a mischievous look. It was almost impossible not to squirm in her chair, but Stacey thought she did an okay job. Mostly. Well, at least a fair job.

"That doesn't stop you from wondering, though, right?"

"I'm out of shape, not dead."

Hannah laughed again. "Yeah, I know the feeling. We serial dieters have to stick together. But you should have a little fun with him. Flirt."

Stacey blinked across the table. "You're insane."

Flapping a hand in the air, Hannah grabbed her fork. "I'm not saying you've got to try to drag him into bed. I'm just saying you should have a little practice. You know, be sassy. Get used to having some fun. If he's a ten like you say, get some practice on him. Then, flirting with a six down the line will be easy as pie." Hannah stopped, her fork in midair. "Mmm, pie."

A vehement head shake accompanied Stacey's stand. "Nope. No

pie. I've got to go to the gym tonight, and the last thing I need is another seven hundred calories today. I'm already regretting the fries."

Hannah whined, but followed Stacey to the register. As the cashier took Stacey's debit card, Hannah poked her in the side.

"So, you'll call me if anything happens tonight, right?"

"You are certifiably insane."

Hannah poked harder. "I'm stuck at home with Allen the emotionally constipated gamer and the kids. I have to get my romance somehow. Promise me."

"Okay!" Stacey jerked away. "You're evil. But I'll call you if the sky falls."

Satisfied, Hannah nodded and then proceeded to pay her own bill.

As Stacey shouldered her purse, she shook her head at her friend's insistence.

As if anything would happen between her and Rob. Ever. That was a scenario for the theater of her mind, and nowhere else.

The afternoon seemed to last forever. Rob tried to stay busy, but even training one of his favorite clients couldn't totally make him forget about the appointment he had with Stacey tonight.

For some reason, Stacey's agreement to give training with him another try had acted like a shot of pure adrenaline into his veins. There wasn't a reason that he could pinpoint, either. It was driving him crazy. It was like his mental video of her wouldn't stop playing, and it was all his favorite parts.

As the door swung shut behind Rob's last client of the day, Silvio waved at him from the smoothie bar.

"Your cell phone was buzzing over here a few minutes ago."

Rob's shoulders prickled. "Yeah?" Was she canceling? He sure as hell hoped not. He wasn't sure how long he could stalk that coffee shop in the hopes that she'd come back.

Unlocking the screen on his phone, Rob gave a sigh when he saw the number. Not Stacey. His father had called. A flash of worry gripped him.

"I'll be a few minutes. You okay out here?"

Silvio nodded as he rinsed out the blender's pitcher. "You got it."

Ducking into his office, Rob took a deep, calming breath. It might be nothing, but since his dad's last stint in the hospital, every phone call made him worry.

Some people were just larger than life, and Richard Liston was one of them. Rob had spent most of his life trying to live up to his dad's standards. More often than not, he failed. They'd clashed many times since Rob had announced his plans for his career, but lingering deep inside Rob was still the boyish urge to please his father. He doubted he'd ever outgrow that.

But his dad's recent health scares had been a devastating reminder of his father's mortality, and the heavy burden wasn't an easy one to bear.

Waiting wouldn't make it any easier, though. With a stab of his finger, he punched the CALL button. Only half a ring later, the call connected.

"Dr. Liston."

It didn't matter that he'd been retired for fifteen years. Rob's dad always introduced himself as a "doctor."

"Hey, Dad, it's Rob."

"Robert. Good to hear from you."

He sounded okay, that brusque tone within normal limits.

"How's that business coming? You ready to give up and go back to school yet?"

Rob folded his arms and leaned against his desk. Yeah, the good doctor was in fine form today. A little tension eased from his spine despite the probing questions. "No, things are actually going really well. Memberships are up, and we're getting more and more training clients too. We're shaping up just fine."

"Hmmph. Well, I suppose . . ." The dry tone of his dad's voice indicated that he was anything but pleased, but Rob had learned long ago that arguing got them nowhere.

"How are you? How's Mom?" It hadn't been long since he'd seen them. He'd left the gym to Brandi and Silvio back in September when his father had been hospitalized after a fall. They'd done a good job, but a new business needed to be encouraged to grow, and they'd had their hands full just maintaining. Rob had left too quickly, and he regretted it, but he still hadn't discovered how to be in two places at once. Charlotte was a four-hour drive from Atlanta. It wasn't like he could run back to see them every weekend. He wasn't even planning to make it back for Thanksgiving, a fact his mother didn't like at all.

"We're doing fine. Your mother's working on the Christmas play for the church. It's as terrible as usual."

"That's not fair. She does the best she can. But five-year-olds aren't exactly the best thespians."

His dad snorted, the noise coming loud into Rob's ear. "I've seen stray cats who could sing better."

Rob smiled despite himself. His dad might complain about his mom's involvement with the children's group at church, but he was always in the front pew cheering them on when they performed on stage.

"How are things going with you? Wasn't your cardiologist appointment earlier this week?"

"Fine. Everything's stable."

Rob ran his thumb across the desk beside him. "When do you go back?"

"Next month."

Well, that was different. Rob frowned. "I thought you went every six months."

"He just wants to check something again. Standard procedure for a male of my age. It's no big deal."

The urge to call his dad on the bullshit was strong, but if there was a person more stubborn than Rob himself it was Dr. Richard Liston. Rob set his jaw.

"Okay."

"I'll let you get back to your business. Just wanted to check in and see how things were going. Your mother misses you."

"I miss you guys too. I'll get up there soon, and we can do a makeup holiday meal."

"Sounds good. See you later."

"'Bye, Dad."

Rob ended the call and let the phone drop to his side.

Damn. It was hard to be so far away. But when his dad retired they'd moved up farther north to be closer to his mother's family.

Rob had already started college, so moving wasn't really in the cards for him then. It hadn't made that much of a difference before his business had started taking off. Now he was needed here, though, and couldn't just run back up to see his family every time he got worried about them.

Which was happening much more frequently than it used to.

A quick glance at the clock revealed that he only had a few more minutes before Stacey was scheduled to show up for their session. He had to shake off the worry about his family and get ready to focus. After what had happened yesterday, he had to be completely present and prepared during this session. She deserved no less than his best, and that was what she was going to get.

Laying his phone beside his closed laptop, Rob shoved off the desk and gave a good stretch before he opened the door.

As he exited the hallway and rounded the counter, an interesting sight met his gaze.

Silvio, dark bronze arms exposed by the fitted tank he wore, was leaning over the counter with his chiseled chin resting on his palm. Across from him stood a ponytailed and amused-looking Stacey. Silvio was making gooey eyes at her, and it looked like all Stacey wanted to do was burst out laughing.

Her expression eased his jealousy, and Rob grinned. He'd seen this act before. Silvio loved women. All shapes, sizes, ages, races—none of that mattered to him. He liked the way they responded to him, the way his compliments made them blush and giggle. The outrageous flirtations he engaged in gave him some kind of gratification.

But Stacey wasn't having any of it.

"You look so familiar. Didn't we have a class together? I could have sworn we had chemistry."

Rob snorted aloud as he came closer. Seriously? Silvio only employed the cheesy pickup lines when all his other tricks had failed.

"Nope, don't think so. Is Rob here?"

Rob was more than happy to act as her white knight. "Here I am. Sorry, Silvio's usually in heat."

Dark brows knitted together in irritation as Silvio straightened abruptly. "That's unfair, and not completely true."

"So the sky was gray today because all the blue was in my eyes?" Stacey deadpanned.

The laugh clogged Rob's throat so hard he had to cough to keep from choking. His eyes watered. Stacey helpfully *thwack*ed his back as he straightened.

"I can see that you're busy now," Silvio said. "But, beauty, if you ever find yourself feeling lonely, come speak to me. I don't believe in love at first sight, but I'd make an exception in your case."

Stacey bit her lip, squeezing her eyes tightly shut, but nodded.

As Silvio wandered off to lick his wounds, Stacey turned to Rob with the pained look of someone who had just been through the most exquisitely awkward experience but had no one to share it with.

"I'm—so, so sorry." Rob could barely get the words out from laughing.

"How—what was that? Was he for real? Is he practicing for some kind of soap opera?" Stacey's giggles were like a blast of fresh air, and they both laughed for a long moment before Rob answered.

"No, no, that's just how he is. A lot of women like that."

"That's insane. How can anyone take him seriously? He compared me to an angel. Seriously, who does that?" Wiping tears from her eyes, Stacey took a deep, steadying breath.

"He's a character. Anyway, laughing burns calories, but lifting weights burns more. Are you ready?"

"*Pffft.* I was born ready. The question is, are you ready?" Stacey shoved her sleeve up a bit and flexed her bicep. "For this gun show, that is?"

God, she was cute. Rob clutched his chest as if he'd been shot.

"Damn, girl, warn a man before you wield deadly weapons like that."

Stacey laughed again, and the sound warmed Rob all the way down to the toes of his sneakers. She had no clue how attractive she was to him, and that made her all the more irresistible.

"Okay, I'm ready. Hurt me."

And as Rob led her to the free weight section, he couldn't help but replay her laugh again in his mind. Such a light, musical sound. He'd like to hear it often.

Chapter 6

Stacey's face was flushed, her eyes focused straight upward. A bead of sweat rolled down her temple, but she ignored it. Rob stood by her side, coaching her through. Her muscles trembled as her arms locked, her body straining to meet his demands.

God, he loved his job.

"Great," he said, helping her put the bar on the cradle. "Breathe, then one more set of reps."

"Whew." Stacey took the towel he offered, and wiped her face. "That's tough."

"But you're killing it."

"That's because I've got a good coach," she said. And then she winked at him.

The expression wrapped around his midsection and yanked. Good God. Blood rushing, he busied himself wiping down the bar. Damn. This playful, confident attitude of hers was downright magnetic.

He'd have to watch himself. She was making it difficult to focus on the job at hand. He'd love to do some very different kinds of presses with her tonight.

"Come on, let's get to work. You can't just stare at me all night." Stacey lay back on the weight bench and reached for the bar.

"Why not?" He didn't regret the question, even though it was unplanned. She paused in her motion, her back arched, as she looked at him with one blond brow cocked.

"Hmm," she said, a slightly embarrassed smile lifting her reddened cheeks. "No reason, I guess."

He nodded toward the bar, and she lifted it with him spotting.

It was insane to hit on her, right? The gym's business wasn't solid yet. He was the one who'd insisted on the "no dating clients" rule, for crap's sake. She might be the first woman to tempt him since his ex-girlfriend had shown him that their relationship wasn't as strong as he'd imagined, but that didn't mean he should throw caution to the wind, did it?

Stacey groaned in exertion, the sensual sound doing all sorts of things to his too-eager body.

Jesus, he needed to get laid.

"Ten," he said, helping her rest the bar on its ledge. "Great work."

"Thanks," she said, sitting up on the bench and lacing her fingers together to stretch toward the sky. She arched her back, forcing her breasts tight against the material of her T-shirt. His cock twitched as he noticed her taut nipples.

Distraction—he needed a distraction. Ah, thank Christ. Silvio was waving to him from the front counter.

"Take a quick breather, I'll be right back."

Stacey nodded and sipped her water, and Rob trotted over to Silvio.

"Everyone else has gone, boss, and it's after nine. Want me to wait for you?"

Rob glanced at the clock. Wow, the time had really gotten away from them. Stacey had been late because of a problem at work, and then they'd talked for nearly an hour about Stacey's workout plan. The conversation had wandered into friendly chatting for quite a while, before Rob mentioned they still had a workout to do.

"No, you go ahead. I'll lock up."

Silvio nodded toward Stacey, who was bent over the bench she'd been using and wiping it down. The sight of her ass did beautiful, terrible things to Rob's already aching cock.

"She's really cute."

Rob shot a glare at Silvio. "Cute? No, she's not cute." *Cute* was for toddlers, puppies, and grandmas. Stacey Hough was hot, curvy, beautiful, fuckable, many different things. None of them "cute."

Silvio shrugged. "She does it for me. She's nice, too. I liked her laugh."

"Stay away from her."

"Whoa, man, no need to take my head off. She's not my client."

Rob forced his fists to relax and took a deep breath. "No, she isn't. Sorry. I just—" He couldn't explain. He fully intended to break his own fucking rule, so how could he? "Sorry."

"Don't worry about it—it's cool." Silvio pulled on his jacket. "I'll see you tomorrow, man."

"'Night," Rob said, watching as Silvio walked out the front door. Rob locked the thumbscrew behind him and flipped the neon OPEN sign to the *off* position.

"Are you keeping me in, or everyone else out?"

He turned. Stacey was there, a small smile on her face as she held her water bottle at waist height, fiddling with the lid, one hip jutted out slightly. Like she wanted to play the role of sex kitten, but wasn't sure how to go about it.

He could have told her that she was doing just fine.

"It's after closing time," he said in answer, smiling back. "You've got my undivided attention."

"What am I supposed to do with that?" She brought the bottle to her lips.

She was playing with fire, and he so badly wanted them both to burn. *Easy*, he cautioned himself, even though the wicked twinkle in her eye beckoned him onward.

"We should probably finish your workout. Just ten minutes on the treadmill or the elliptical, your choice."

She sighed. "If the choice is between bad and worse, I'll pick bad every time. Elliptical it is."

He followed her to the bank of machines across the right side of the gym's back wall. She mounted the one in the corner, and he stepped onto the one right beside her.

"You're doing it too?"

"I'm not always a heartless dictator," he said, turning the machine on.

"Pfft." She snorted, her arms swinging as she began the movements. "I've known you for just two days, and I can already see how pushy you are."

"You're the one who hired me. Don't whine because I'm doing my job well."

Her mouth formed an O, and her expression of outrage made him grin. "I am not whining! You're a bossy jerk."

"And you need to speed up," he said mildly, leaning over to punch up the resistance on her machine. "Come on, finish strong."

She glared dark thunder at him, but gripped the handles tighter and quickened her movements without further argument. The machines made the only noise in the large room, and they worked out together in silence for a while.

He watched every move she made, his own body handling the motion of the elliptical without any thought.

Her ponytail bobbed, and her cheeks were rosy and glistening with the effort. The shirt she wore had a V-neck, and a drop of perspiration wended its way down her cleavage. He wanted to pull that shirt off and see exactly what path it took. Her breasts shimmied slightly, the sports bra she wore not quite enough to stop her movements. And her nipples, God help him, were still prominent through the pale purple fabric.

"Eight minutes," she panted. "Just two more, right?"

"Yes," he said, leaning over to drop her speed back down. "Focus on your breathing. Deep, slow breaths, that's right. Ease your heart rate back down slowly."

She nodded, and he matched his speed to hers. The seconds wound down, and when they were done, Stacey stepped off her elliptical with a relieved sigh.

"So glad that's over," she said, lifting her hair from her neck and closing her eyes.

He had to recite the Gettysburg Address in his head to keep from cataloging all of her tantalizing physical attributes again. Staring at the free weights across the room, he went through as much of it as he could remember.

And dedicated to the proposition that all men are—

"—a shower," she was saying when he ran out of words.

"Say what?"

"I know the gym's closed, but is it okay if I grab a quick shower? It's so cold outside, I'd hate to go out with my clothes all sweaty."

"Sure," he said, hoping that his smile didn't look strained. "I've got some paperwork to do in the office, so it's no trouble."

She thanked him, grabbed her bag, and walked to the women's locker room.

He tried to forget that she was in there getting naked, in his locker room, alone.

He failed.

The cool water hitting her skin was absolute bliss, and Stacey tilted her chin upward to let it run through her hair.

She should've brought her conditioner, but she'd forgotten it in the haste of running home to pick up her workout gear. Oh well. Next time she'd be much more prepared.

As she quickly soaped up her skin, she took stock of her body. She felt good. Tired, that was for sure, but her muscles burned with a pleasant ache that reminded her that she had actually done some-thing with them. It was a good feeling, not one she was especially used to. Not since college had she really worked out, and the reality of using her muscles again was nice.

The soap ran down her body, little white rivers circling the drain. She smiled down at her feet, wiggling her toes in the bubbles atop her shower flip-flops.

Rob was really smoking hot. She had definitely made use of the idea Hannah had given her at lunch that day, flirting as hard as she could. And surprisingly, he seemed to respond really well to it. She had definitely noticed him checking her out once or twice.

It was insane. Rob was surrounded by hard bodies all day, every day. Yet he still acted like she was someone worth looking at. Crazy, but she wasn't about to question the fates about it. She would just revel in her newfound attractiveness, for however long it lasted.

She soaped up once more, then a quick rinse finished her shower. Upon opening the curtain, she shivered a little as the cool air hit her wet skin. The heat her workout had generated was gone now. She would be glad for a warm, dry towel and her fresh clothes.

Just as her fingers closed on her towel, a sudden popping sound was her only warning before darkness fell around her.

She froze. The drip of the showerhead was extra-loud in the dark. Okay, no biggie—she'd just wait for the lights to come back on.

But she waited. And waited. And they didn't.

"What the crap do I do?" Her voice echoed against the tiles. She shuffled forward, blindly feeling for her bag in the dark. Where was it? The benches were over here somewhere, weren't they?

"Ouch!" Her shin connected with the bench.

"Stacey?"

Oh God. Rob. She was naked; what the hell was she supposed to do?

"I'm okay." Her voice was more croak than anything else. She clutched her towel to her chest. "What happened?"

"The lights are on a timer, and I forgot to override it since we were here late. The utility room keys are in my car, so it'll take just a minute to fix the situation. Are you okay?"

Okay? No, she was not okay. She was naked, blind, shivering, and she didn't know where the hell her clothes were. But how could she tell him that?

"Umm, I'm okay enough, I guess, if you hurry. How long will it take?"

"I've got a flashlight on my phone. Let me help you get situated, and then I'll deal with the lights."

Shit. Why did he have to be so helpful?

She sighed. Wrapping her towel more tightly around her, she gave a slight nod in the dark. "Okay, I'll level with you. I've got my towel, but my clothes are across the room, I don't know where. Can you help me find them?"

She could tell he was smiling wickedly, even in the pitch-dark of the locker room. "So you're naked."

It wasn't a question, but she answered anyway. "Yes, I am, in fact, naked. That's typically how I shower. I find it's a lot easier to get clean without the clothes in the way."

Her snarky comment earned a laugh, and a sudden light from the doorway drew her gaze. She rounded her shoulders, embarrassed by the sight she must present.

The dim glow of the flashlight didn't offer much of a glimpse of Rob's face, but the expression she could discern was one of interest.

"Your bag is here."

Stacey reached for it, grateful. "Thank you. I'm sorry."

"Don't apologize to me. I'm the one who stranded you in the dark with no clothes. I should be apologizing to you." He turned the flashlight so she could see his face, and the wolf-like grin there made her heart *thump* hard against her ribs. "Although I couldn't have planned the timing any better if I had tried. You wear that towel well, Miss Hough."

Well, in for a penny . . .

"So, you like what you see?" She let one corner of the towel slip a little, giving him a better glimpse of the side of her breast. "You know, we are alone."

What was she hoping for here? That he'd rip the towel off of her and they would do incredibly nasty things to one another on the locker room bench? If she was being honest—yes. All of that. More. And a bag of chips.

"I had better leave, or what happens next will definitely fall outside the bonds of our client-trainer relationship."

"Who says we have to stay within those bonds?"

Rob closed his eyes, and Stacey held her breath to see what he would say next. It was all she could do to keep silent. But she had laid all her cards out on the table, and if he wanted to play, she would know soon.

Rob set his cell phone down, the flashlight beaming straight up in the blackness. He reached a hand forward and snagged the edge of her towel, not pulling, just holding. He stepped closer to her, not touching, but the heat from his body warmed her damp skin.

"Are you sure?"

Stacey slammed her eyes shut. Was she insane? Probably. But when was she ever going to have a chance like this again?

This was so far outside her comfort zone she was in another universe. She had never done this kind of thing before. Hell, she had only had sex with two other guys before. And those were months into their relationships. She had known this guy for two days, and here she was about to throw everything at him, when he was so far out of her league it was insane?

Yes. She was the one who wanted something different in life, and she was about to take the bull by the horns.

She dropped the towel.

Chapter 7

It worked. He hadn't expected it to, it was a stupid idea in the first place, but God help him, it had actually worked.

Rob had remembered the lights' auto-shutoff feature about three minutes before it happened. Plenty of time to go get the utility room keys and override the program. But then he had imagined Stacey in the shower and wondered exactly what she would do if confronted with a sudden blackout.

Was he a bastard? Probably. It had also been the single most brilliant idea he had ever had. And the worst. Because right now, in the dark, he held a damp towel—and a naked Stacey stood somewhere in front of him. But seeing her was nearly impossible.

He could only make out the barest outlines of her. The soft image of her pale skin in the flashlight's dim glow was more than enough to whet his imagination's appetite. Blood rushed to his cock, stiffening in response to her.

He dropped the towel on the bench beside them, stepping forward to bring her into his embrace. Bending down, he caught her lips in a kiss. Her skin was damp, cool from the moisture of the shower, and she smelled of flowers and soap. She leaned into him eagerly as his hands roamed her back, tangling in the wet ropes of her hair. She was delicious, sweet. Her mouth was open and inviting, her tongue questing into his mouth as if in search of hidden treasure.

With a groan, he gathered her closer to his body, not caring that her still-wet skin was dampening his clothes. She was soft, fitting so comfortably against him, as if she was made for him. His cock stiffened, eagerly pressing against the softness of her belly as he kissed her deeper, harder. His pulse rushed, his body straining with every nerve to take her—to make her his.

Pulling back, he looked down at her. God, why did that cell phone's flashlight have to be so weak? He could barely make out her features in the darkness. Her face was tilted up to look at him, but her expression was unreadable.

"If you're sure about this, then we'll do it. If you say no, this stops right here."

He waited, one heart-stopping second, for her answer.

"I'm sure." She reached up and caught the back of his neck, pulling him down to her once more.

This time, he didn't hold back. Crushing his mouth to hers, he pressed her backward toward the bench. Pausing only long enough to spread the damp towel on the bench, he then returned to her, kissing her deeply.

Her moans stirred him onward, giving license to his questing fingers. He wanted to touch her everywhere, to feel each part of her body as she eagerly responded to him. With every move he made, she met him. Each slide of his lips on hers, she echoed—each breath, each moan, each sigh. Touch for touch. He indulged them both, letting his fingers make their way down from her neck, to her shoulders, and then finally to rest against the softness of her breasts. She arched her back, pressing them firmly into his palms. They were full, so round they overflowed his hands.

He'd never imagined a woman could feel this way—so soft, so perfect. His ex was more classically beautiful, and physically smaller. But Stacey? His cock had never ached like this before. Ever.

Her nipples were pebbled against his palms, hard and begging for his attention. Gently, gently, he pinched, rolling them slightly between his thumbs and forefingers. Her gasp echoed in the darkness.

"Mmm," she moaned, the sound reaching beneath his pants and wrapping around his eager cock. "Ooooh."

"I want to see you," he said. He let go, reaching for the cell phone on the bench. His palm covered the light, plunging the locker room into complete darkness again. "You feel so amazing, Stacey. I want to see you."

"No." His wrist was suddenly enveloped in a small but strong grip. "This is perfect."

He wanted to argue, but then she reached forward and massaged his aching dick through the thin fabric of his pants. Her hand was hot, her fingers clever as they found and stroked his head in a slow, tantalizing circle. "Let's stay in the dark for now. Please?"

God, he couldn't deny her anything as long as her touch drove him this crazy. All he could think about was pressing her onto the bench and shoving his aching cock deep into her sweetness.

"In the dark. For now." He let the cell phone go, and the dim flashlight showed him the barest outline of her.

It was enough. It had to be.

She tugged at the hem of his shirt, and he helped her remove it. Her breaths were quick, her movements jerky. He stilled her, calmed her with hands and mouth and breath over skin. She trembled against him, kisses and touches becoming bolder with each passing moment.

The touch of her breasts against his bare chest was intoxicating, and he wanted so much more. Lust licked him up and down, and Stacey wielded it. He reached down and cupped her ass with both hands, bringing her high and hard against him. God, his pants were still in the way. He wanted his cock against her body in the worst way.

"These," she said as she ran her fingers beneath his waistband, "need to go."

Never one to disappoint a lady, he removed them as quickly as he could before pressing her back down on the locker room bench. Their breaths were loud and anxious in the silence.

As he knelt between her spread legs, a sudden, terrible thought struck him.

"I don't have a condom."

He knew what was the right thing to do, but damn, he hated it. He wasn't the kind of guy who would just take what was so freely offered without a thought. God, he wished he was, but he couldn't.

"It's okay."

"It's not. Not at all. Next time, I promise. For now? I just want to thank you for this."

With that, he knelt between her legs and buried his face between her thighs. Her shocked cries echoed off the ceiling as his tongue found her, surrounding her tender clit, flicking and stroking her softly.

Her fingers tangled in his hair, pulling in concert with his motions. She was so sweet, so wet, so ready for him. He had to make this good. God, she'd asked for this, together they'd decided, and the lack of a condom would not leave her wanting. He would make sure of that. Carefully, gently, he inserted a finger in time with the motions of his tongue.

Her hips twisted and bucked beneath him, clenching and twitching as her movements and his quickened. His balls ached like a toothache, his cock dripped precum, but still he could not stop. He would not stop. This might be all he could give her, but he'd be damned if he would let it go.

"Rob, I . . . I . . ."

He didn't lift his head to answer, just added a second finger and lightly nipped her clit. The extra pressure did it. Lifting her hips on a scream, Stacey shuddered and came.

He fell still, not moving as the remnants of her orgasm shuddered through her. Her gasps were ragged, the skin beneath his hands shivering.

"Oh my God," Stacey said, breathless, unevenly. "That was— I've never—"

"I'm about to split my skin here," Rob couldn't help but tell her. "You were delicious, you were incredible, and all I want to do is fuck you so hard right now."

Her fingers were there, searching for his hand. "It's okay, you can—"

He stopped her, not wanting to hear her affirmation. He couldn't take her up on it, but what he wouldn't give for a condom right then. "I won't, but God, I want to."

On his knees at the end of the long bench, Rob closed his hand over his aching hardness. His fingers still wet with her, the taste of her still on his lips, he closed his eyes as he tilted his chin skyward, reveling in the feeling. It wouldn't take long like this, too close already, but then a soft, questing hand felt its way up his thigh to cup his balls, and he moaned aloud.

"Let me." Her breath was on his cock, and he dripped even more. "I want to return the favor."

He let his hand fall away, and then her soft lips wrapped around his head. His hands balled into fists at his sides, and he gritted his teeth. The urge to thrust into her mouth was so strong, but he forced himself to remain still as she took him deep, her sweet tongue swirling around his cock head.

Her mouth was hot, wet, so sweet as she sucked him, her palm gently cupping his balls. The tight, swirling sensations gripped him, shooting fire through his blood as his nails dug into his palms. Too good, much too good. He wanted it to last, but there was no hope for it. The sensations were too incredible. He breathed hard, trying to hang on, but his lower back tightened in warning, and he spoke in a hoarse groan.

"I'm coming!"

But she didn't move away. Her lips worked around his cock as he lost himself into her waiting mouth.

It was the most intense orgasm he'd had in a very long time. In the darkness, there with her, he could almost believe that anything was possible. Hell, he would never have imagined this, and here they were.

For a long moment, it was quiet. Only her breath, and that was softer, more even now. She moved away and the sudden chill on the skin of his cock made him shake involuntarily.

Her voice was small in the dark. "Was that okay?"

He wanted to laugh. "You have to ask?"

"I can't see your face. But you sound pretty happy."

He stood on shaky legs. "I'm more than happy."

Reaching for his clothes, he wondered what he should say. *Thank you? Let's do that again?*

It wasn't like him to be so completely uncertain of himself. That wasn't Rob. Rob was the guy who made a decision and then put his head down while driving toward it. It was how he'd managed to build this business, shaky though it was, even though his entire family was against the idea.

But in this situation? With this woman?

"I should get the lights," he said. "I'll leave the phone here with you."

"Don't you need it to find the keys?"

"The streetlight will be enough."

He left the room, hoping a few minutes away would give him some much-needed clarity.

Stacey Hough had just befuddled the hell out of him.

Stacey dressed quickly, refusing to let the fact that her legs felt like Jell-O slow her down.

The weakness was from the workout, that was all. Her muscles were tired, unused to the way she'd pushed them. The fact that Robert Liston had just buried his face between her thighs had fuck-all to do with it.

She paused halfway through hooking her bra. Jesus. They'd really done that. She could still taste him, sweet and tangy, on her lips. What the hell had she been thinking? Obviously, she hadn't. But holy hell, she'd never had an orgasm like that before.

Her face got hot as she shoved her arms through her bra straps. Well, obviously she'd never had an orgasm like that before. How could she have when nobody had ever given her oral before? She wasn't exactly collecting notches on her headboard at home, after all. But to think that such a moment had just happened in the darkness of a locker room . . .

She'd stop thinking. That was it. Nonissue, right?

Fumbling for her shoes in the dark, she cursed when her knuckles brushed the bench. *Just keep your brain in the off position, Stacey. No need to think, no need to remember how Rob just kind of ran out of the room as if he'd forgotten that he left the stove on at home. No big deal, just like the time when—*

"Oh, thank Christ," she said as the lights popped back on. She jammed her feet into her shoes without bothering to unlace them first. The backs of the heels turned over, but she didn't stop to adjust them. Bundling her clothes and towel into a wad, she shoved them into her duffel bag and hightailed it out of the locker room.

"Sorry about that," Rob said as she met him near the front counter. "It's a really convenient feature, until it isn't."

"No big deal," she said, too brightly. God, what was wrong with her? Why couldn't she play this cool?

Rob looked down at the bundle of keys in his hand, turning them over with a soft jingle.

Wait a minute. Had something gone wrong? He'd said he enjoyed it, but why wasn't he looking her in the eye? Shit. Was all that stuff about men not respecting the girl in the morning actually true?

"I'm making a huge mess of this," Rob said as he pocketed the keys. "But I'll be honest with you. I wasn't planning that."

"Neither was I." She wanted to melt into the floor.

"I'm glad it happened, though."

Say what? Stacey blinked, but his expression didn't change. There was a warm, sated smile on his face.

"Can you repeat that?"

He laughed, and the sound made her heart fall over itself, then resume its beat in triple time. "I'm glad that happened. I do regret not having a condom, though."

Well, miracles did happen. "Next time?"

Her question was met with a nod as he slid closer, wrapping one arm around her waist. "Next time, for sure."

He bent his head down and kissed her again—long, slow, thorough. She let herself be swept away. How could she not? His arm was warm and hard against her back, his chest firm against her breasts, his tongue so demanding and careful as he tasted her.

She was falling, and she had no desire to slow her descent.

"We should get going," he murmured against her mouth. She sighed.

"Do we have to?"

His grin was almost hungry. "If you want to come back to my place . . ."

Never had an offer been more tempting, but at some point sanity had to return. Stacey moved backward, breaking the embrace. "I should get home." She had to create some distance in order to make some sense out of this. Any sense at all. There had to be some logic in this night, didn't there?

"I understand."

Rob walked Stacey to the door of the gym, and she shrugged into her coat as he made small talk about her workout routine. She nodded, said all the right things, but her brain was anywhere but on the amount of weights she should lift and number of reps she should do.

"So, tomorrow morning?"

That was the time she'd originally slated, but— Stacey looked around the deserted gym.

"Can we do another late session? This worked out really well."

His laugh echoed a bit in the empty space. "It did, didn't it? Tomorrow night works for me. I'll even take you out for a beer afterward. And now, if you don't mind . . ."

One last kiss seared her lips, and then Rob stepped back. "Good night, Stacey."

"'Night, Rob."

She smiled, then walked out of the gym's front door feeling like a meteor had struck her right between the eyeballs. Like a robot, she dug through her coat pocket and retrieved her keys. Fumbling for the correct button, she wondered if she'd ever manage to get into her freaking car and out of the cold. Her wet hair reminded her that she needed to hustle, but her fidgeting fingers weren't exactly cooperative.

Autopilot drove her to her building, and carried her up the three flights of stairs to her apartment. She'd just tossed her bag on the table in the foyer when her cell phone buzzed.

"Hannah?"

"You didn't call me." Her friend's voice was hushed, almost a whisper. Made sense, since it was way past her kiddos' bedtime.

"I just got home."

"Really? That's a hell of a long workout."

Stacey collapsed onto her couch with a huge sigh. "You have no. Freaking. Clue."

Hannah couldn't manage to control her squeal of delight when Stacey broke the news, but the conversation got cut short when Hannah had to get her toddler back to sleep. But Stacey grinned anyway as she began getting ready for bed herself.

She'd done it. Practice? Hell, she'd skipped straight from practice to the big game, and she'd sunk the winning shot. As to what she did with the trophy?

She could figure that out tomorrow. Now she had a whole night to replay the most delicious experience through the theater of her mind, and she intended to enjoy every second of it.

Chapter 8

"You're joking."

"Nope," Stacey smiled around the straw she'd just put in her mouth. The strawberry-banana protein smoothie she'd picked up at the gym before work tasted amazing. And the quick glimpse she'd gotten of Rob? Totally made the extra trip worth it.

"You flirted, everyone left, the lights went out, and you sixty-nined in the locker room?!" Hannah's squeal was much too loud, and Stacey shushed her.

"Do you mind? I don't want everyone and their uncle to know!" Stacey hissed, then sat back in her office chair with a contented smile. "And it wasn't sixty-nine. We took turns."

"I've never done anything that sexy in my life," Hannah moaned, leaning against Stacey's desk and grabbing her stapler to toy with it. "Hottest thing I've ever done was make out in the back of Allen's mom's station wagon when we were fourteen."

Stacey put her empty cup aside and wiggled her mouse to wake her computer. "I'll give you all the gory details you want, but you've got to let me get back to work. I've got cost projections to finish, a report to type up, e-mails to send—"

"I get it," Hannah said, closing the stapler with a *snap*. Her short brown hair bounced around her ears as she whirled to face Stacey. "But you've got to tell me one thing first. Are you guys seeing one another? Was this a onetime thing?"

Stacey frowned, a little of her morning glow fading at the question. "I wish I could say, but I don't know. It wasn't planned at all. We're still seeing one another at the gym, because he's my trainer, but as far as anything else?" Stacey shrugged, and one strawberry-blond curl fell in front of her shoulder with the motion. She tossed it back with a quick flick of her wrist.

"How was he this morning?"

The memory popped into her mind's eye, and she smiled. He'd looked amazing, dressed in a form-fitting white HEALTHY LIVING TRAINING tee and black track pants. His arms were definitely shown to advantage in the form-fitting shirt, his sandy hair perfectly tousled. He'd winked at her, those steely gray eyes looking bright and interested.

"Good. He didn't say anything out of the ordinary."

"And you're meeting him tonight. What if it happens again?"

"Then I'll have another incredible orgasm?" Stacey laughed at Hannah's delighted shock. "Seriously, it probably won't. It had to be a fluke, a onetime deal. I mean, it's not like we planned it."

"Planned what?" Vance stuck his head through Stacey's office door, causing both her and Hannah to jump.

"Nothing, why do you ask?" Her cheeks were burning, damn it. Why hadn't she asked Hannah to lock the door behind them?

"You were being loud in here." Vance's beady eyes scanned them both.

"We'll quiet down, sorry to disturb you," Hannah said before turning her back on him. "Anyway, Stacey, at the holiday party, I'll be happy to help with the decorations. Now, you were saying gold and black for the colors, yes?"

Stacey nodded, keeping up the conversation until a disappointed-looking Vance disappeared. Hannah shut and locked the door, and they breathed a collective sigh of relief.

"That was much too close," Stacey groaned, placing a hand on her midsection to steady her breath. "The last thing I need is Vance sticking his nose into my love life."

"It's not your love life he's after," Hannah said, her freckles bunching up as she wrinkled her nose in obvious distaste. "He's been trying to find out the details on your solar panel project."

"What?" The floor beneath Stacey seemed to wobble, and she clutched the arms of her chair as she leaned forward.

"I caught him reading some pages on the fax machine yesterday."

"The fax machine? But hardly anyone he deals with faxes anything anymore. I thought the utility services had all gone digital."

"They have," Hannah said. "When I asked him what was up, he blustered and stuttered, but he dropped the pages and left. Know what they were?"

Stacey's stomach sank. "They were the budget reports from the housing project, weren't they?"

Hannah's solemn nod was enough confirmation.

Shit. This was the last thing she needed. Her last project had been scuttled by competition from her own department, and it looked like this one would face the same fate if she wasn't careful. The constant battle of an underfunded department was competition for the dollars. But Stacey wouldn't lose, not this time. This project would save the city money, and it would also provide some much-needed updates to the government housing projects. But only if she could make her presentation shine and win the city council's approval.

"I'm sorry," Hannah said. "If I'd known they were coming, I would have waited for them."

"It's not your fault. I'll just have to be more careful. I've only got a day left to polish up this presentation, so until then, I'll just have to keep everything under lock and key." Stacey forced a smile and took another sip of her smoothie. There was nothing left but warm foam and no flavor. Just like her morning. Brilliant at the start, and then full of disappointment.

Hannah frowned as she smoothed her knee-length black pencil skirt. "Sorry, I didn't mean to bring you down. I just thought you should know."

Stacey smiled at her friend as she tossed her cup into the trash. "No, I'm glad you did. And thanks for covering for me. You're the best."

Hannah grinned. "I still want to know every little detail. Want to grab lunch later?"

"It's got to be healthy."

"Oooh, trying to impress our trainer?" Hannah's wink was just this side of ridiculous, and Stacey laughed.

"Think it'll get me a gold star?"

"It might get you that sixty-nine," Hannah cracked as she left the office.

A bit of her good mood restored, Stacey hummed to herself as she opened her project file. Vance wasn't a big enough threat to her project on his own. Yes, it would take a bit of the department's budget to pull off, but it was a good thing. She'd show the council exactly what they needed to do, and then everything would work out.

And as for her and Rob? Well, a little more flirting practice sure wouldn't hurt. And she'd just have a salad for lunch. Maybe Hannah was right. Stacey smiled down at her keyboard. It was certainly worth a shot.

Rob had to hand it to her. She was more focused and driven than he'd ever seen her tonight. She'd come in with bright eyes and a will to work, and he'd really put her through her paces. Heck, he'd just given her a break, and she was already champing at the bit to get back to it.

"Sure you've got your breath?"

Stacey nodded as she settled back down on the weight bench. "If you're going to take me out for a drink, I've got to get this done."

A delicious hunger curled in his belly. "What makes you think I'll be satisfied with just a drink?"

She ignored that. "Or dinner, your choice." She grunted as Rob helped her lift the bar into position. "Nothing too fancy, since you're making me sweat like a racehorse and I won't have the chance to get pretty."

Rob's laugh echoed in the otherwise empty gym. "Bar food all right?"

"As long as you're not counting my—*oomph*—calories. I'm in desperate need of a greasy cheeseburger. I had a small salad for lunch, so I'm starving now."

"We'll talk nutrition tomorrow." Rob stood by as Stacey continued her set of reps.

That little line between her eyebrows only appeared when she was focused and centered. He'd started watching out for it early on in her workout tonight.

She seemed different. The flirting, for one thing. She'd had an air of affected confidence before, but it seemed that tonight she was much more comfortable around him.

Of course, that probably had everything to do with the fact that they'd been together last night. She was as into him as he was her, and it felt damn good. It was fun, actually. He hadn't done any flirting at all since Rebecca. With his business and his dad's health, finding a new relationship had taken a back burner. Just that day, he'd gotten another worrying text from his mom. Dr. Liston never rested during the daytime, and he'd had his second nap of the day after lunch.

Rob shook his head. Focus. Stacey. Maybe he should consider taking things further with her. Of course, there was the inherent problem of their trainer/trainee relationship, but a barrier like that could be overcome somehow. For the moment, the delicious distraction was good enough for him, and, he hoped, for her.

"Eight, up, good. Nine, breathe through it." Rob stood by her side, ready to jump in if her arms buckled. Even though her muscles trembled and her cheeks were on fire, that little line between her brows was furrowed and her eyes were calm and focused.

"Last one, ready, ten!" Rob helped her rack the bar, and she instantly bounced off the bench as if she'd just heard her name called on *The Price Is Right*.

"I did it," she said, eyes sparkling and voice breathy. "I really, really did it!"

She threw her arms around him, and without thinking, Rob hugged her back. She laughed and squeezed him hard.

And when she pulled back, grinning widely, he leaned forward and pressed a kiss on her smiling mouth.

Her eyes slid closed and she leaned into him, twining her arms around his neck. His tongue darted out to taste her, tracing her full lower lip for the barest of seconds before reality doused him like a bucket of ice water.

He pulled away.

What the hell was he doing? The gym was still open. There were only a couple of clients left, and they were getting ready to leave, but still, completely unprofessional. He wasn't even really sure why he'd done it. Was it because he was proud of her? Was it to share in the incredible joy she was showing in her accomplishment? Or was it because he hadn't gotten near enough of her last night?

He looked into her eyes. They were wide, a bit dazed-looking, but hot, hungry. She leaned in again.

Shit. Not again. He really shouldn't have done that. He stepped back, breaking their contact, and shoved his fingers through his hair.

"Yeah, great job. We'll stop there tonight."

She stared at him for a long moment, as if unsure what had just happened. Awkwardness flooded the space between them as Stacey wiped her face with the small gym towel. Rob kicked himself mentally. Shit. Why had he done that? Mixed signals. He would have to stop the flirting during training times with her. Obviously neither of them could keep it simple.

"I'll let you get ready to go while I shut down the front counter. Meet me at the front door when you're done."

She blinked. "You still want to go out to eat?"

"I told you I would. Why would I have changed my mind? If you still want to, we'll go."

"Sure," Stacey said with a hesitant smile. "No problem."

As Rob walked away, he squared his shoulders. She had done incredibly well today. She could really accomplish great things here if she stuck with it. He just had to keep their association out of the gym during opening hours.

A few moments of meditation in his office helped him clear his head. It had only been excitement. He was proud of her, that was all. And the touch had just sparked memories of the previous night. No more, no less. He sat down in front of his laptop to shut it down, then stilled for a moment.

She was in the locker room now, grabbing a shower. The smell of her soap was still fresh in his memory, the taste of her, the sound of her cries as the darkness surrounded them both.

He winced and adjusted his pants, which had grown uncomfortably tight in the crotch.

He had to stay away. Keeping this—whatever it was—away from the gym was crucial. Last night had worked out fine, but what if someone came back next time?

Shaking off the thoughts, he finished packing up his things and shrugged into his coat. The office door *click*ed shut behind him, and as he began shutting down the computer at the front desk, the sound of footsteps drew his gaze upward.

She'd taken her hair down and brushed it out. Her cheeks were still a bit pink from the heat of her shower, but that just made her blue eyes seem brighter. The corners of his lips curled upward despite himself.

"I hope I didn't keep you waiting." Stacey wrapped her scarf around her neck. "Sorry I didn't bring any nicer clothes. I didn't really know what to plan for."

"Want to take a rain check?"

"You're not getting out of this that easily. Come on. I could use a beer." Stacey's grin was a touch too broad to be totally honest, but he let it go. He was just glad he hadn't scared her off.

"Beer it is, then. Where would you like to go?"

"Know where Mitch's Tavern is?"

"That's a couple streets over on Peachtree, right?"

Stacey nodded as Rob shouldered the strap of his laptop bag and rounded the corner. "Yeah. It's a tiny, dark little hole-in-the-wall. But they have great sandwiches and cold beer. I love that place."

"Mitch's it is, then. You can ride with me, if you'd like to."

Stacey shook her head and passed him as he held open the door for her. "No, it's actually closer to my apartment, so I'll take my car home and just walk over. See you there," she said with a wave as Rob tested the locked door.

Rob waited for a minute on the cold sidewalk, watching as she hurried away. Damn. She was cute.

He'd really have to watch himself around her.

Chapter 9

The cold night air seemed to slam through her as Stacey hurried to the parking deck. She wasn't sure whether the cold was numbing her brain or if it was the weirdness with Rob just then. Why hadn't she packed some nicer clothes? It had seemed like a good idea to grab some leggings and a comfy tunic top, but it was hardly date-night appropriate.

Date. Was that what they were doing? She'd thought so, but then that kiss—which was amazing, and his reaction—which was awful.

Her breath fogged out in front of her as she fumbled with her keys. She didn't know what to think. He'd come on to her, but then he had pulled back so quickly she almost had whiplash.

She paused before closing the driver's side door. That kiss, though. He'd really laid one on her. Intense, sexy, it carried with it all the memories of the night before, and the promise of more to come.

"Get going, weirdo. Don't make him think you ditched him."

Her own voice broke her reverie, and she shut the car door. She cranked the engine, and a cheery Christmas tune came through the speakers as the cabin came to life. Sighing beneath her breath, she put the car in REVERSE.

Her cell phone's *buzz* in her pocket made her put on the brakes before she even started rolling.

"Hello?"

"Hey! Am I interrupting anything? Some post-workout nookie, maybe?"

Hannah. No patience at all. Stacey shook her head as she put the call on speaker and tucked it into her hands-free cradle. The car wound its way through the dark, serpentine corridors of the parking deck.

"No, no nookie. I flirted my ass off, he kissed me, then it got weird. But we're going out for a drink right now."

"'Weird'?"

"Yeah. He pulled away really fast, and then he was acting all blustery and bossy and just—" Stacey rolled her eyes. "Weird."

Hannah's whistle filled the car cabin. "Girl, please. Don't read too much into that. He's totally into you. It's going to be awesome. Have fun, and tell me all about it in the morning."

"You know I will." Stacey's car rolled to a stop at the parking deck exit booth. "Let me go before I get on the road."

"Nighty night! Don't do anything I wouldn't do." The wink was obvious in Hannah's tone.

Stacey swiped her monthly pass card at the terminal and waited for the barrier to rise. It had been a good night after all, hadn't it? Maybe the weirdness was just Rob's way of reacting to whatever they had going on. After all, it wasn't like Stacey had expected this, either. And the night was only partially over. When was the last time she'd been on an actual, honest-to-God date? It was hard to remember. Maybe a year ago? Eighteen months?

Trent was—when? Halloween? *Last* Halloween?

The stoplight was red. Stacey used the rearview to check her reflection briefly. She did look like she'd just spent ninety minutes in the gym, but at least she smelled nice and he'd already seen her. She'd tried to look as cute as possible before getting to the gym, and the decline in her appearance was pretty much his fault anyway.

"It's going to be fine," she said to the nervous-looking girl in the mirror. "Just a casual drink. You can do this, flirting isn't that hard. Just suck it up, smile, and do your best."

Feeling a little bit better, she readjusted the mirror and waited for the light to turn green. Once it did, her toe pressed lightly on the accelerator, and she began to cross through the intersection.

The glance both ways was habit, but the pickup roaring directly at her was a complete surprise.

The impact, when it came, was sudden, sharp, and incredibly

loud. Without thinking, Stacey slammed her eyes shut and braced herself, but it was too late.

Tires screeched. Glass showered over her right side as her body connected with the driver's side door. The air bags deployed. She wanted to cry out, to scream, but her heart was in her throat blocking the way. Clinging to the steering wheel, she rode out the impact until the car came to a drunken stop, halfway up on the sidewalk with a pickup truck's grille much closer to her than it should have been, stuck against the crumpled passenger side of her car.

I'm alive, she thought for a brief, euphoric moment before everything went dark.

Rob dragged a finger through the condensation on the dark wood of the table just inside Mitch's Tavern. The music was low, conversation and laughter buzzing around him. It was the perfect place for a casual dinner with a friend. But his particular friend wasn't there yet, and he was starting to get a little worried.

It was her idea to go out, so where was she? He frowned down at his cell phone's screen. Nine thirty-eight. It had been over half an hour since they'd left the gym together. He'd been sitting here alone for nearly twenty minutes.

Had she run scared again? The only thing that had happened since last night was that kiss. His stomach tightened. She'd enjoyed it just as much as he had, but then he'd pulled back. The bewildered expression in her blue eyes still stung.

She'd agreed to come out with him, though, so that was something. She didn't seem like the kind of woman who'd stand him up like that, even though he had sent mixed signals.

"Would you like to order something?" The server, a young guy with thick dreads and a ready smile, stopped by the table.

"No, thanks, I'm going to wait for her. She'll be here in a minute."

"Okay, man."

As the server walked away, Rob picked up his phone. She had seemed a bit edgy on the way out the door. That too-bright smile stuck out in his mind's eye. Something was off. He just needed to call her.

Two rings, three. He looked over at the booth across the aisle, where a couple was chatting over a basket of nachos. Six. Seven.

He was about to hang up when her voice mail kicked on.

"Hi, you've reached Stacey Hough, deputy director of city planning. Please leave your name, number, and a detailed message—"

Before the recording finished, his phone *beep*ed and he looked at the screen. Stacey was calling him.

He clicked over with a relieved sigh.

"Stacey, hi. I was starting to wonder where you are. Everything okay?"

The sound of sirens registered for a brief half second before the reply came.

"This is EMS. Are you local? Do you know Stacey?"

Rob's shoulders tensed, and his guts twisted. "Yes, and yes. What happened?"

He tossed a couple of bucks on the table in thanks for the water and was heading down the narrow stairs to the sidewalk before the EMS tech had finished her reply.

"We're on the way to Charter Memorial. Your friend was in a car accident. Can you meet us there and give us some information on her? We couldn't find any ID at the scene, and she's unconscious."

"I'm heading there now."

"Go to the emergency department."

The call disconnected, and Rob shoved the phone into his jacket pocket. It was a damn good thing his gym's records were web-based. He'd be able to give a half-decent medical history on Stacey. And since part of the gym's signed agreement included giving health information to medical professionals in the event of emergency, he didn't have to worry about the legalities of it.

Damn. Guilt swallowed him as he slammed the car door behind him and cranked the engine. If she hadn't been heading out with him, then maybe—

He shut the thought down as he pulled out into the street. The blame game wouldn't help her now. God, they hadn't said how badly she was hurt. But unconscious? It didn't always take a hard hit to be knocked out, though, he knew that.

He stopped at the red light on Ivy before turning right. Blue lights flickered on the buildings lining the street. His guts twisted in on themselves, becoming origami as he slowly advanced toward the chaos.

A car accident. A gray pickup truck had T-boned a white Jetta, and the pair of vehicles were completely blocking his lane. A cop with a flashlight was directing traffic onto the side street.

"Shit," Rob breathed as he moved through the intersection and onto Madder Avenue. "That's got to be it."

The traffic was unusually thick because of the forced detour, and Rob's frustration tightened his grip on the wheel. That was no tiny fender bender Stacey had been involved in. She could have some pretty severe injuries.

"Please let her be okay," he muttered as he pressed harder on the gas pedal, blissfully free of the worst road congestion.

He shouldn't have kissed her. If he hadn't, then maybe she'd have ridden with him over to the bar. But he'd put the awkward distance between them, and now she was on her way to the hospital. The guilt ground and chewed at his insides, and the sickening feeling tightened his guts into knots.

Charter Hospital was only about three miles away, but the drive seemed to take forever. By the time he'd thrown his gearshift into PARK, he had enough nervous energy stored up to run a marathon.

The automatic doors didn't open fast enough. He turned sideways to fit through the opening doors, and three long strides took him to the counter.

"Stacey Hough just arrived by ambulance. They told me to come."

The man behind the counter didn't seem fazed, or even interested. He barely glanced at Rob before asking, "Patient name?"

"Stacey. Hough," Rob repeated through gritted teeth.

The keys clicked as the man typed. Rob fought to keep still. It was a losing battle. He needed to go find her, to help in what little way he could, to make up for this somehow. No matter how much of a freak accident this had been, he couldn't absolve his feelings of guilt until he had seen her and had done what he could.

"I don't see a patient by that name."

"I know they beat me here, but she was unconscious. I gave them her first name, but the call was so brief that they might not know her full name."

"What was the nature of her emergency?" The man arched a brow in Rob's direction.

"Car accident." The words felt awful as they fell from his lips. God, why her?

The man nodded. "Entered the system as Jane Doe. You can go through to the nurses' station." His hand moved beneath the counter, and a low buzzer sounded. The door to the right of the counter swung open. Rob nodded his thanks and walked through.

The rabbit warren of a hospital always made him vaguely uneasy. It was too closed off, too artificially bright and sterile. He'd gotten more exposure to them during recent months, with his dad's testing and hospital stays, but now the discomfort seemed to loom larger than ever.

He followed the signs past the triage stations and stopped when he reached a huge counter, surrounded on all sides by frosted glass–enclosed treatment rooms, any of which could be holding an unconscious Stacey.

"Excuse me." He waved down a scrubs-clad woman who had been riffling through a pile of paperwork. "I'm here for Stacey Hough, she just came in via ambulance as a Jane Doe. They needed some information about her."

The woman nodded. "Yes, thanks for coming so quickly. Come over here with me, and I'll get you set up with someone who can grab that info from you." She started toward the bay of desks on the opposite side of the ward, but Rob couldn't stop himself from asking.

"Is she okay?"

The woman looked at him for a brief moment.

"I don't have any information on her right now. Let's just get the demographics in, and then we'll go from there."

Rob nodded, and as much as he wanted to argue, to force them to let him see her, he followed after the nurse.

He had to do what he could to help. And right now, that meant following her instructions. As much as he hated it.

Chapter 10

When Stacey opened her eyes, all she could see was white—a harsh, too-bright wash of light. Her breath caught in her throat as she wondered if she was dead. But then *beeps* crashed through her consciousness, and the low hum of voices surrounded her. She blinked hard, but the shapes around her only darkened a little, never coalescing into real objects.

"She's back. Stacey, can you hear me?"

"Yes." Was that her voice? It was more like a croak. Totally unrecognizable.

"Do you know what day it is?"

"Tuesday. Was I in an accident? It feels like a dream."

"Yeah, you're right. On both counts. But don't worry, you're going to be okay. The doctor's coming in and he's going to check you out."

Injuries? Oh yeah. Her brain had been swimming so fast that the vague, uncomfortable feeling had seemed like background noise, but when she focused on it, it roared to life. Pain. It blossomed along her right leg, curling up insidiously to the right side of her ribs and spreading until her entire body flamed with it. She gasped, and the friendly man who had been speaking to her patted her hand.

"It's okay, we've got you. This will make you more comfortable, but it will also let you sleep."

There was a little twinge in the back of her hand, a cool sensation as if someone was pouring chilled water into her vein, and then a blanket of comfort settled softly over her. Her eyes closed.

When she woke this time, it really felt like waking. The *beeps* were fewer now, not as many voices, either. Her head was foggy, probably from medication, but at least she was conscious. Body one giant ache, head full of cotton. Wow, she was in great shape.

She looked around. Hospital room, but not of the comfortable variety, if there was such a thing. This one was austere. There was the usual medical bric-a-brac along the bedside, an IV pole with those little machines that controlled medications, that kind of thing. A bedside table with a phone was there, too, but there was no recliner, no couch, nothing more for visitors to sit on than one hard plastic chair.

"I must be in the ER."

Her voice broke the quiet, bringing her back to herself a bit. That was right. The pickup truck had sideswiped her. She didn't even know how she'd gotten here, though she guessed an ambulance had been involved. She was alive, but she was alone.

Damn. She picked at the threading edge of the white hospital sheet. Well, at least her fingers still worked. Her knuckles were rough and reddened, probably from the air bag.

She had lived and worked in Atlanta for almost two years. Her family lived miles away, up in North Carolina, but never before had she felt this isolated in the city. She had friends, of course, but nobody whom she could call on in this situation. They all had their own lives, their own problems. Who would come rushing to the emergency room just to sit by her side in the middle of the night?

Bree would have, but she was in Hawaii with her new husband. Hannah would want to, but she couldn't leave the kids in the middle of the night. Justine, Kelly, Tasha? No, they weren't close enough for Stacey to bother them at this time of night.

The bland white room went wavy as she looked at it through unshed tears. Even though she and her parents weren't on the best of terms, for a moment she really just wanted her mom.

A knock on the door came.

"Yes?"

A nurse, who seemed to belong to the friendly voice from before, poked his head through the crack in the door. "Oh good, you're awake. The doctor's tied up with another patient, so in the meantime, do you feel like a visitor? He's been sitting out here for two hours now."

Stacey's eyes widened in surprise. "A visitor? Yes, but who is it?"

"It's me." Rob stepped through the door.

Stacey's heart thumped a little harder. Even through the haze of pain and drugs, she still couldn't pretend to be unaffected by him. It was maddening. "Rob? Why are you here? I mean, it's good to see you, but . . ."

"I was calling you to see where you were. The EMS tech answered, and asked if I knew who you were. They couldn't find any identification before they loaded you up, so they asked me to meet them at the hospital. I hope you don't mind." Rob shoved his hands in his pockets, and he stood close to the door, as if unsure of his welcome.

"That's really nice of you. Of course I don't mind. Do you want to sit down?" She indicated the hard-backed chair at her bedside. The dull throb down her right side was becoming less dull every minute, but politeness—and the fact that Rob would come to the hospital for her so late at night—won over.

"Thanks," he said, and eased onto the chair beside her.

For a moment, there were no words between them. Stacey didn't know where to look, so she settled for a spot just above his left shoulder. There was a scuff mark on the wall there.

"Sorry," she said, when the silence got to her.

"You've got nothing to apologize for. I saw your car; clearly the other guy was at fault."

She shook her head. "I'm not talking about the wreck. I promised you that I'd give this a shot. And here I am, only a few days in and laid up already." Her gaze fell to the speckled industrial flooring. "I guess my training might be over, at this point. I've got no idea what is going on with me physically, but recovery is bound to take a while."

A furrow appeared between Rob's brows. "Don't say that. You can't make assumptions until you've got the whole story."

She wanted to respond, but a knock on the frosted glass door interrupted. It slid open.

"Ms. Hough? I'm Dr. Calhoun. I'd like to discuss your condition." A slender, dark-skinned man entered with a polite, terse wave.

"I should go, give you some privacy." Rob stood.

The words were out of her mouth before she even realized she was saying them. "No, please stay."

He stopped. "Are you sure?"

Stacey gave a quick glance to the doctor, who was shuffling through a large file in his hands. "I'm kind of fuzzy-headed from the meds, and I don't really want to be alone. Do you mind?"

Rob sank back into the chair. "No. I'll stay with you."

"Thanks." She wanted to reach out, grab his hand, but she tucked her fingers beneath the sheets instead.

Afraid to meet the doctor's—or Rob's—gaze, she trained her sights on the wall just past the doctor's left ear.

"I know you don't feel like it now, but you were pretty lucky." Dr. Calhoun gave a somber nod her way. "You do have some bone bruises on your right leg, and some soft tissue injury. With the swelling, it's difficult to determine whether there's a small fracture or not. But you won't need any surgery, as long as everything heals properly."

"That's . . . good." She wasn't so sure that it was, but it felt less bad, somehow. She didn't know what to think. Her brain was a swirling morass of confusion and unease.

"You'll have to see orthopedics. We'll set you up with an appointment with them tomorrow morning. If there is a break, you may need a cast for the leg."

A cast? Stacey's mouth went bone-dry. "I guess that means I can't put weight on it?"

Dr. Calhoun shook his head. "No. You won't want to, anyway. It'll be pretty painful for a while."

"Now I regret that third-floor walk-up. So they'll see me tomorrow. Do I have to stay here overnight?"

"You suffered a concussion, but we can release you if you've got someone who can stay with you and monitor you for signs of further brain injury. Since you lost consciousness, it's something we need to keep a tight check on."

"What if I don't have anyone?" She hated saying it in front of Rob, but what choice did she have? "Does that mean I have to stay here?"

Dr. Calhoun's handsome face—much too serious to start with— sobered further. "It's our extreme recommendation that you be monitored for the next forty-eight hours."

Her fingers curled into the white fabric of the sheets as her eyes burned. So stupid. She should be grateful to be alive, thankful that she hadn't died in that wreck, happy that she'd scraped by with only minor injuries. Instead, she was sweating about a couple of days stuck in the hospital. The thought of being cooped up here, alone the whole time, made her want to scream.

No help for it. She opened her mouth to admit it, but—

"She'll stay with me."

Chapter 11

The words escaped him before he realized it, but he wouldn't have taken them back anyway.

Dr. Calhoun raised an eyebrow. "Your relation?"

"Friend. No stairs at my place and I can arrange the next few days off to stay with her." Rob looked over at Stacey, whose face had gone as pale as the sheet she was clutching for dear life. "I can't let you be stuck here alone."

"But—"

"The discharge paperwork will have the symptoms you need to watch for. We'll issue a loaner wheelchair for you to get around with. Do not under any circumstances put weight on that foot until after you've seen Orthopedics. Here are the medications you'll be taking."

As Dr. Calhoun rattled off Stacey's instructions, Rob pulled his cell from his pocket, already mentally writing up a to-do list. He'd have Brandi and Felicity split his clients. Was Stacey allergic to dogs? He hoped not. That was the one wrinkle that might drop this plan straight in the crapper.

". . . reactions that could occur. All right, I'll call the nurse in here to take out your IV and then you'll be all set."

"Thank you," Stacey said, her voice as thin as hospital soup. The door rasped shut behind Dr. Calhoun, and Rob felt a sudden pang of doubt. He'd charged in, as usual, but maybe that wasn't the right thing to have done.

"Stacey, if you would rather stay here, I'll—"

"No, that's not it." Stacey's voice quavered slightly. "You've just— I—" Her hands covered her face and her shoulders shook.

Rob's guts tightened into a knot and he moved to her side instantly.

Sitting on the edge of the bed beside her, he gently wrapped his arms around her. "Hey. It's okay. You've had a rough night."

Her sobs came from somewhere deep inside, and he held her as they rocked through her body. Closing his eyes, he willed himself to stay calm and quiet, to let the emotions she needed to purge move through her.

He'd wanted to hold her again, but not like this.

Gone was her usual snap, her snark, the easy wit she relied on to shield her true feelings, and that, more than anything, made him twist into knots inside. Not because he was attracted to her—he was—or because he felt guilty—he did—but because she did not deserve this.

"Thank you," she said, when she could speak. She rubbed at her cheeks, and he leaned back to give her some space, keeping one hand in contact with her shoulder. "You've just met me, but you've done so much for me. I can't thank you enough."

"It's not a big deal. Unless you're not a dog person."

A tremulous smile stretched her lips. "I love dogs."

"Then get ready, because Custard's a whole lot of hound. She'll happily curl up next to you while you convalesce."

Her voice was still quavering, and her cheeks were red and shiny with the dampness of her tears, but her brows had lifted in what he thought was genuine interest.

"She's a mastiff. Huge paws, slobber, wrinkles, the whole nine yards."

"Sounds awesome." Stacey sniffed, then her head fell back against the pillows and she blew out a long breath through her nose. A furrow appeared on her forehead.

"Are you hurting?"

She didn't open her eyes to answer. "Yeah, I am. The leg's starting to get some feeling back in it, and when I breathe things are getting more and more sore. I think the meds are wearing off."

He was up and moving toward the door already. "I'll get the nurse."

"You don't have to . . ."

He didn't hear if she said anything else because he was on the other side of the door.

Dr. Calhoun stood at the nurses' station, conversing with the woman who'd taken Stacey's demographics from him hours before. Rob stood a respectful distance away, so as not to crowd or overhear whatever—or whomever—they were discussing. While he waited, he glanced at the wall behind the U-shaped counter. A large clock proclaimed it to be nearly one in the morning. Damn. Custard was going to be pissed at him.

Dr. Calhoun handed a folder to the nurse and turned Rob's way. Rob nodded politely, figuring the doctor was on his way to his next patient, but the man stopped beside Rob.

"We'll be releasing her into your care. Are you sure you're willing to be responsible for her? It's important that she come straight back here if she has any worsening symptoms."

Rob looked straight into Dr. Calhoun's serious brown eyes. "I'm sure. I'm not about to let her suffer through this alone."

A long moment passed, but Dr. Calhoun nodded. "All right, then. Marie has her discharge paperwork."

"Before you go, she's beginning to get more uncomfortable. Will she be getting any more pain meds before being discharged?"

The doctor frowned. "I don't want to medicate her too heavily because of the brain trauma. But I'll leave orders for another half dose of pain relief before she goes."

"Thank you, sir." Rob shook Dr. Calhoun's hand and then watched as he walked away.

When Rob stepped back into Stacey's room, she was talking on the room's corded telephone.

"No, honestly, I'm okay. I'm so sorry to be bothering you so late. I wouldn't even have called you except that I have no idea where my cell phone is and I remembered the presentation to the city council is tomorrow morning. I'm not going to be able to make it, obviously."

Rob moved to step back into the hallway, intending to give her privacy, but Stacey shook her head and beckoned him in.

"Yeah. Some bumps and bruises, nothing too major." She paused, listening, and shoved her hair back from her forehead, which was reddened from contact with the air bag. The movement began absentmindedly but cut off halfway with a wince and a pained gasp. "Sorry, just moved a way I shouldn't have."

Rob sank into the chair by her bedside and pretended to be interested in his phone. He wasn't. He was watching her move too slowly, too gingerly to adjust the hair that had been bothering her.

Damn. Just hours ago she'd been doing a hell of a job at the gym. He'd been planning to get her back into bed and explore the attraction between them. It had been a brilliant connection. And now . . . Now . . .

"They'll just have to delay it. There's no one else who can present the project to them like it needs to be presented. A couple of weeks should do it. Please, do you mind passing on the message for me?"

She was right. Not just about her work problem, but about everything. Nothing was over. Not the gym, not the chemistry between them. If, that is, she was still interested.

"Thank you. You're the best, Hannah. Get back to sleep. I promise I'll call you after I see the orthopedist tomorrow. Love you too. 'Bye."

Stacey pressed the red button on the phone and placed it back on the table beside her. "Sorry. I was supposed to do this big presentation tomorrow."

Rob nodded. "Things might be put off for a little while, but I think you'll be able to get everything back on track really soon."

Her smile was thin, strained.

"The nurse will be coming in with some more meds soon. Close your eyes. You've got to be tired."

"You don't mind?"

How could he? "No. Just rest. I'll be here."

Her eyelids fluttered closed. He allowed himself to brush a knuckle over the back of her hand as he looked down at her.

So determined. She'd flirted with him shamelessly. Regret flooded him that he'd missed the opportunity of a dinner with her tonight.

They would make up the lost time over the next forty-eight hours. He didn't intend to let her out of his sight.

Things definitely got worse before they got better. She couldn't sleep, though she tried.

Stacey's pain level kept rising, like floodwaters in a basement.

Steady, unrelenting, almost so gradual that she didn't realize she was being overtaken until it had almost happened.

Rob definitely kept her as distracted as possible. He told her about Custard, and Custard's sometimes-boyfriend Max, a mutt who belonged to Silvio from the gym. Stacey laughed at the stories, but she couldn't keep up her interest long.

"Sorry," she said when Rob's concern showed on his face. He was too handsome for that furrow between his brows. "My leg is starting to scream at me."

"Your breathing is shallow." He stood by the bedside, gently brushing a stray hair from her forehead. "Too shallow, too fast."

"I'm remembering what it's like to run on the treadmill." Her voice quavered. Damn it. She did not want to cry in front of him again.

He smiled at her lame joke. "I know." He looked toward the exit. "I'll go check on your meds."

"No need," said the nurse as she moved through the door. "Here they are."

With quick, deft motions, the nurse scrubbed the IV port with an alcohol pad and popped a syringe on it. The meds hit her vein, cooling her arm from the inside. Within a moment, a fuzzy dulling sensation coated her brain and she relaxed against the bed.

"We'll let this IV run while I give your discharge instructions. Now, are you the husband?"

Stacey shot a quick glance at the nurse, then back at Rob. Hopefully he wouldn't be insulted.

"Friend," Rob corrected gently. "But I'll be taking care of her for the next few days."

"All right, then. These are the symptoms you need to watch for. If any of these happen, you need to come back right away."

As she rattled off the list of symptoms, Stacey listened with half an ear. Mostly, though, she watched Rob. He nodded throughout the speech, asking specific questions, getting clarification on points, and being much more thorough than Stacey herself could have been. Of course, concentrating wasn't exactly super-easy with her system loaded with pain meds. God, he was handsome. Why was he so eager to help her? He was so out of her league he might as well be a New York Yankee, and she was stuck in T-ball. She wondered if he gave his one-night stands gift baskets like Derek Jeter. Could she expect one after their encounter in the locker room? A giggle escaped her.

"You okay?" the nurse asked, with one eyebrow hiked.

"Fine," Stacey said, composing herself. "Sorry, was a little distracted."

The nurse continued. "The paperwork I'm giving you will have all this information on it for reference, as well as the phone number in case you've got any questions. Now, here are your prescriptions." She handed two paper slips to Stacey. "The pain medicine I just gave you should last about four hours, so you should pick this up on your way home. For the next day, take your dose every four hours. After tomorrow you can stretch them as much as you're comfortable with."

Rob took the prescriptions that Stacey handed him as the nurse began removing the IV line. Another nurse poked her head in the door.

"Ms. Hough?"

"Yes?"

"A policeman is here about your accident. Do you feel up to talking to him?"

Oh great. More fun on this night that refused to end. Stacey gave a reluctant nod. "I can, if he needs me to."

"Briefly," Rob added.

Whoa. Stacey gave him a quick look. Was it her imagination, or did he sound a little protective there? It was probably the drugs. She shouldn't read into things like that. But, God, did she want to. Having a handsome, strong man stick up for her in this situation would make anyone melt, and she just wasn't that strong at the moment.

A little, silent prayer escaped her.

Please don't let me fall in love with him. It would be too easy to imagine that his physical interest meant something more. That his care and friendship signaled the start of something between them. It was a mistake she'd made in the past, but a repeat this time would hurt her so much more. The stakes were higher, because despite the fact that she didn't know him well, she genuinely liked Rob. Sure, she'd been using him as a practice flirt, but she'd dared to hope that maybe they could really become friends.

The policeman entered and introduced himself as the nurse finished up by bandaging Stacey's arm where the IV catheter had been.

"I'm Officer Foreman, Atlanta PD. Sorry about your accident, ma'am. I just need to get your side of the events as they happened."

"No problem," Stacey said. "It happened pretty fast, but there wasn't much to it. I had just left the parking deck, and I stopped at the light. When it turned green, I stepped on the gas, and then I saw the truck out of the corner of my eye. I didn't have time to do anything. And then"—she shrugged one shoulder—"that was that."

"Were you on your cell phone at the time?" The cop stared straight at her, even though the point of his pen was tapping on a small notebook held in his hand.

The question was so unexpected it took her a moment to process it. "What? No."

"No texting at all? Maybe fiddling with your GPS?"

"What exactly are you implying?" Rob said, stepping forward. Stacey was glad for the interference. Officer Foreman had a stern, almost mean look in his eye, and she couldn't stop herself from shrinking into the bed under his glare.

"Please answer the question, Ms. Hough."

She paused a moment for a cleansing breath.

"No. I was not on my phone, I was not fiddling with a GPS, and if you've got any more questions, you can direct them to my lawyer." Her voice was cool, but the tears welling in the corners of her eyes belied her calm demeanor. She hoped the jackass cop didn't notice them.

"We're done here," Rob said, stepping between them. "If you'll excuse us, she's being discharged."

The cop shot a look at Rob, not quite a glare but definitely a warning. But he gave Stacey a curt nod and left the room.

The silence fell then, Stacey's machines having been silenced by the nurse before she'd exited. It was like a blanket of ice. Rob didn't look at her. His gaze was trained on the door where Officer Dickhead had just left. But his hands were balled into fists at his sides.

"I guess the other driver is trying to blame me for the wreck," she said. It was obvious, but she had to break the silence somehow. If only to assure herself that the encounter had actually happened and was not a product of her pain medication. "It looks like I'll need a lawyer."

"We'll worry about that tomorrow. Come on, your chariot's

arrived." Rob indicated the wheelchair that an orderly had wheeled over next to the bed. Stacey's belongings were packed in a white plastic bag marked PROPERTY OF PATIENT on the side, and hung on a hook at the back of the wheelchair.

"If you want to get your vehicle, we can meet you at the side entrance," the orderly said.

Rob nodded, and gathered up Stacey's discharge paperwork. "I'll see you out there."

Stacey watched as he left the room.

The orderly helped her swing her legs off the side of the bed and transfer her to the wheelchair without putting any weight on her leg.

"Your boyfriend is cute," the orderly said as he took the brakes off.

"Thanks, but he's not my boyfriend," Stacey said.

She closed her eyes as the wheelchair rolled through the maze of hallways toward the exit. Exhaustion saturated her. All she wanted was to crawl into her own bed and sleep for about a week, but she couldn't. There were prescriptions to pick up, doctors to see, a lawyer to contact. The tasks stacked one on top of another, and the discomfort nipping at the edges of her consciousness made them seem insurmountable.

At least she had Rob to help, for now. She'd just have to make sure she understood that his kindness was just that.

Reading too much into it would ruin whatever thing they'd just started.

Chapter 12

The twenty-four-hour pharmacy was surprisingly crowded for four thirty in the morning. Rob waited at the counter, hoping they'd hurry up. Stacey was sleeping in the car. She hadn't made it out of the hospital parking lot before passing out. Fortunately, the light snore coming from her was reassuring that it was, indeed, normal sleep. But he wanted to get her tucked into bed now. The delay was chafing.

The clerk waved him over.

"We'll need to see some identification."

Rob pulled his wallet from his pocket and flipped open to his license.

The clerk cocked a brow at him. "This isn't your prescription."

Rob's already thin patience snapped. "No, it isn't. It's my girl-friend's. She's spent the entire night in the ER after being T-boned by some asshole who ran a red light. Right now she's so exhausted that she's sleeping in my car, with bruised ribs and a broken leg. In six hours we have to be at the orthopedist's office so he can schedule surgery. Now, do you want me to yank the rental wheelchair out of the trunk, wake her up, and wheel her in here so you can see her face yourself, or can you let me sign for her meds since they aren't even fucking narcotics?"

Totally true? No. Completely believable? Judging from the clerk's pale expression and deft motions at the cash register, most definitely.

"Have a nice morning, sir."

Rob nodded curtly and took the bag of meds. It wasn't like him to be a dick, but goddamn it, tonight was more than enough. Stacey had had enough. He wouldn't put her through one more minute of irritation.

Back at the car, he got behind the wheel. Stacey moved in her sleep, wincing and mumbling something.

"It's okay. We'll be at my place in just a few minutes."

He hit the highway and counted the exits. The road was lonely, only one or two other vehicles running the blacktop with them. The radio buzzed low, giving just enough sound to distract Rob from Stacey's soft breaths. His exit, finally. Second road on the right. He let out a sigh of relief as he cruised into his driveway.

His condo was nice. Not luxury, by any means, but there was some space to breathe, a small yard for Custard to play in, and lucky for him, a spare bedroom. He wasn't so much of a bastard that he'd force her to share the bed when she felt like shit.

Glancing at the drizzly night sky, Rob hurried to the trunk of the car. The wheelchair was easy enough to expand and set up by the passenger side. It quickly became dotted with rain.

"Stacey," he said as he opened the door. "We've got to hurry so you don't get too wet. It's starting to rain."

"Hmmm?" She blinked at him, blue eyes confused. "Wet?"

Not waiting to explain further, he helped her swing her legs out of the car. Then, with gentle, easy movements, he transferred her to the wheelchair. Fortunately the home health tech who had attended his dad last time had given Rob some tips, and he was grateful for them now.

"Sorry," Stacey said as he unlocked the brakes, rain falling in fat drops all around them. "I didn't mean to fall asleep on you there."

"It's okay. Come on. We're going to get you to bed." He wheeled her quickly up the brick walk.

His place wasn't exactly wheelchair-friendly, but it beat a third-floor walk-up all to hell. He maneuvered the chair up the two steps of his front stoop, and by the time he'd unlocked the door and wheeled Stacey into the foyer they were both drenched.

A huge brown ball of wrinkles, slobber, and love greeted him with a thumping tail as she sat watching Rob remove his coat.

"Stacey, this is Custard."

"Hi, Custard," Stacey said, the smile on her pale face making Rob's tension ease just a bit. She held out a hand and Custard covered it with kisses.

"Come on, girl, time for a potty break." Rob patted his knee and moved toward the back door. There was an awning that extended past his patio, so Custard at least could enjoy the night without being soaked. Once the dog was outside, Rob went back to his patient.

"It's really nice of you to do this. Are you sure you're up for it, though?" Stacey had obviously spent the last few minutes fighting a sense of guilty obligation. It was written all over the down-turned corners of her pink lips. "Maybe tomorrow I can go—"

"Save it," Rob said, wheeling her into his bedroom. "I promised Dr. Calhoun. Forty-eight hours in my company can't be so bad, can it? Am I that much of a bastard?"

"No, no, that's not it at all," she said, twisting her head to look at him. The movement was too much, and she gasped, stilling instantly. A pang of guilt gripped him. He shouldn't tease her right now.

"Sit right here," he said, locking the wheelchair brakes.

"What choice do I have? What am I going to do, power-roll down the highway?" She sounded grumpy, and he was kind of glad. At least some of her spirit had come back. He liked the vinegar-filled Stacey. He went into his closet and rifled through his things. Grabbing an old T-shirt, soft from repeated washings, and a pair of baggy basketball shorts, he came back into the room.

"Here," he said. "It's not exactly fancy, but it'll be more comfortable than sleeping in your wet stuff."

Stacey took the shirt and shorts from him. Her cheeks reddened as she looked at the labels.

"What's wrong?" he asked.

"I don't know how to say this out loud. God, this is embarrassing."

"What is it?" Had he done something to hurt her feelings? "Just tell me."

She didn't look at his face, choosing instead to focus on his feet as if they were the most exciting things in the room. "Your clothes won't fit me. They're too small."

Oh. *Oh.* Jesus Christ, he was an asshole.

Her cheeks were red with embarrassment. "I can probably squeeze into the shirt, but I'd be afraid of stretching it out."

"It's okay," Rob said. "Don't worry about it at all. I just wanted you to be comfortable, and I wasn't thinking. Here"—he ducked into the bathroom and came back a second later—"you can wear this if you want."

His robe, a comfy, beaten terry-cloth affair, seemed to ease some of her disquiet. "Thanks."

He moved the chair to the edge of the bed. At his direction, Stacey wound her arms around his neck. There was a faint hint of her perfume, along with the slightly antiseptic smell of the hospital clinging to her. Damn it. He hated that this was happening to her. She didn't look in his eyes as he lifted her from chair to bed. Probably for the best. This proximity had him wondering about kissing her again. Joining her in the bed. Soothing her sore and broken body with sweet caresses.

Had to be the exhaustion talking.

"Want me to help you get changed?"

Her head shake had to give her whiplash if the wreck hadn't already. "Nope, I can do it, thanks."

For a moment he wondered if he should be hurt or offended, but he let it go.

"I'll let you get changed, but I'll be just on the other side of the door. If it starts hurting too much, call me and I can help."

"I can do it." Stacey waved him off. "Seriously, I'll be fine."

He didn't argue, even though he was pretty sure she should have help. As he moved down the hall, Custard was already standing at the back door, her tail wagging lazily.

"Come on in, slobberchops." Rob locked the door behind Custard and gave her the Milkbone she'd been eyeing since paw hit hardwood. With his mutt crunching on her treat behind him, he moved down the hallway to wait outside the bedroom door.

A muffled curse made him lay a hand on the door. "Stacey? Are you okay?"

"God*damn it*." She yelled it, so he pushed the door open.

"Stacey, don't—"

He stopped dead. She stared at him, blue eyes wide. She'd removed her top and bra, and was sitting shirtless on the edge of his bed, trying to reach the T-shirt that had slipped onto the floor. And she had the most beautiful, full, round breasts he'd ever seen.

"Goddamn," he echoed.

She had died. The car accident was finally over, and the archangel had decided that she belonged in hell. Her punishment was for Robert Liston to see her naked.

A sound—almost a squawk—escaped her, but she couldn't move. Her muscles had seized up in protest against the movements she'd made, and she was frozen in that position. One arm reaching toward the floor, the other hand braced against the bed, and her breasts hanging free.

For an impossibly long moment, he stared, and she stared back. Why wouldn't he say something? Why couldn't she move? The pain in her body warred with her mind's frantic need to jerk backward, cover herself, and the stalemate wouldn't break.

"I'm sorry," Rob said, finally turning his head to the side. "It sounded like you were hurting."

"I was. I am. But—shit," she wheezed as the discomfort flared again. "I need help. I dropped the shirt and I could use a hand sitting upright again, but I'm half-naked and I'm so, so fucking sorry you had to see that."

He moved toward her, keeping his head turned. "Stacey, I invaded your privacy. You don't need to apologize for anything."

"A sight like that should come with a warning label," Stacey tried to laugh, but it came out strained.

"You're right." His agreement stung for approximately half a second as he reached for the shirt. "A warning label. It would read, Caution all heart patients and those suffering from premature ejaculation: seriously beautiful breasts ahead."

Rob held the shirt between them, blocking his view of her body. She stared up at him, unable to think, to move. He knelt.

"Put your hand on my shoulder and try to brace against it. I'll move up slowly until you're sitting again. Ready?"

She nodded.

"One, two, three."

The pain flared, but once she was upright again it settled to a much more manageable level.

"Thank you," she said, taking the shirt Rob handed her and covering her chest.

"If I promise not to look, can I help you get the shirt on?"

"Okay."

Together they got her dressed, and though the shirt was snug, as predicted, it did cover her. And the material was soft. Best of all, it smelled like him.

"If you lie back, I'll help you take your pants off."

She'd dreamed of hearing those words from a man as sexy as him, but never in these circumstances. She sighed. "There's not really a way around that, is there?"

"Not unless you want to sleep in them."

She didn't. She really, really didn't. But she also didn't want Rob to see her thighs. Her upper half had been bad enough, but at least he'd thought her breasts were okay.

"They're pretty comfortable, so I'll be okay staying in them. They didn't get too wet in the rain." She glanced around the room. It was obviously the master bedroom, with a walk-in closet to the right of the door they'd entered. Opposite was the bathroom. Inside she could see a large walk-in shower, tiled with slate and brushed nickel fixtures.

"Do you have a guest room?"

"Sure do," Rob said, pulling the covers back, "And Custard and I will be very comfortable in there. Here, lie back."

Rob gently let her down against the pillows. She watched him as he pulled the covers up over her legs, fluffed her pillows, and brushed her hair back from her forehead.

"You're really good at this," she said, as fingers of sleep reached up and curled around her consciousness.

"Nice of you to say."

"You were probably a nurse in a former life. Maybe Florence Nightingale."

Rob's laugh, velvety and warm, caressed her ears. "Maybe I was."

"Thank you for watching me." Her voice sounded small, faraway, like a child in a tunnel. "I don't have anyone else I could call tonight. My friends are all busy with stuff of their own. My family is far away and terrible. I was so lonely, but then, there you were, and I didn't have to worry."

"Sleep now," Rob said, his knuckles brushing against her brow. She closed her eyes and relished the sweet, simple touch. It was nice. Almost as nice as the kiss they'd shared. She said so aloud, not caring about being embarrassed anymore. She was too tired to care about that.

"It was a nice kiss." Was that a smile in his voice?

"Can we do it again later?"

He laughed again. God, she wished he'd keep doing that. "If you're feeling better, and still want to."

"I will always want to." She let herself descend into sleep then, the night finally over. She thought she felt a brief touch on her brow once more, but she couldn't be sure.

Soon, much too soon, an alarm was beeping in her ear.

"Gah," she grunted, and started to roll over to hit the SNOOZE button. The motion brought fresh, sharp pain in her leg, and the sensation ripped her breath away. Freezing, she waited for the wave to pass. Finally it had settled enough for her to manage movement. Carefully, slowly, she reached for the clock on the bedside table and slid the button to the *off* position.

Where was she? Oh. Right. Last night. The wreck. The hospital. The cop. Rob. Rob's place. Her boobs. Oh God.

She wanted to retch, but the thought of such a sudden, sharp movement made her whole body ache.

Staring at Rob's ceiling, she wondered what the hell she was going to do now. Forty-eight hours, they'd said at the hospital. She had to stay under observation for forty-eight hours. That meant staying here with him, unless she could find someone else to volunteer. But even if she could, did she want to?

She bundled the covers tight under her chin. He'd paid her a really nice compliment last night when he'd walked in on her changing. If things were different, she'd probably have been really flattered and maybe taken it as a sign he wasn't so indifferent to her. But with her situation the way it was, how could she?

Glancing at the clock again, Stacey groaned. It was nine thirty. The orthopedist was supposed to see her at eleven. That meant she needed to try to start moving soon if they were going to leave by ten thirty, as Rob had suggested. Besides, she really had to pee.

Moving the covers off, she gingerly scooted to the edge of the bed. A quick glance to gauge the distance, and a hand to brace herself on a friendly nightstand, then—

"Ah," she breathed as her weight went onto her good foot. There. She was upright. A little wobbly, her head a little bit spinny, but upright nonetheless. Now all she had to do was hop on one foot to the bathroom door. Once she was there, she could steady herself on the jamb before moving into the room.

Stacey stared toward her intended destination. It was a good plan. A pretty solid plan, as plans went. So, why couldn't she force herself to move?

"This is going to hurt," she said aloud. "You can do it. It's only what, six, eight feet?"

Nodding, she held her breath. Only one hop done before a knock came at the door.

"Stacey, I'm back, are you awake?"

She was gritting her teeth and trying not to fall over. "Uh-hnn."

"Are you okay? Can I help?"

Two more hops. Could she be a little lighter on her feet? It sounded like she was trying to stomp holes in his flooring. "Unn-nnn."

"I'm coming in."

Oh no, he couldn't. She was even with the door. Once he swung it open he'd . . .

She didn't fight it this time. There was no point. The door opened and she waited for him to catch her.

She wasn't falling, but that didn't seem to matter.

"Why didn't you call me? Christ, you could have fallen and hit your head again."

"But I didn't," she pointed out as he scooped her into his arms. Christ, she'd never thought she'd find a guy who could actually do that. Her arms wound around his neck instinctively and she held on tightly, trying to ignore how good it felt to be held this way. "You're going to give yourself a hernia if you don't put me down. I'm way too heavy for this."

"Let me worry about that. Listen. When you get some crutches, or a cane, you can hop around all you want to. But before then, ask for help."

"You going to put me on the toilet so I can pee?" She delivered the line coolly, pleased with her snappy comeback in the face of his proximity.

But when he didn't answer, just carried her toward the toilet, panic welled inside her.

"No, seriously, I was joking. Don't. Please, I'm humiliated enough." She didn't want to beg, but damn it, for this, she'd beg.

He gently set her down on her good leg beside the toilet.

"Go ahead. I'll be in the closet grabbing a few things, so if you fall or need help, yell and I'll be right here."

"Thanks," she said, her cheeks hotter than the desert sun. Thankfully, he closed the bathroom door behind him. The *snap* of the latch made her jump.

If ever she'd fantasized about a guy nursing her back to health, she'd been so very, very wrong. If she survived the next forty-eight hours with any dignity intact, she'd consider it a home run.

Chapter 13

The orthopedist's office was nice. Rob should know: He'd been cooling his heels in their ultra-plush lobby for about three hours now.

He sighed and picked a tiny piece of fluff from his jeans. If he'd thought ahead, he could have brought his laptop and made use of the time. As it was, he'd exhausted all the productive possibilities on his phone. He'd reached out to the gym, checked on things there, returned some e-mails, contacted clients. Hell, he was almost to the point of breaking down and checking Facebook. The situation was that dire.

Brandi had a good grip on the reins at the gym. He wasn't worried at all. But sitting still and not doing anything wasn't in his nature. He'd almost offered to go back into the treatment room with Stacey. Would have if he wasn't certain it would weird her out.

He smiled down at the toes of his shoes. She'd been funny that morning, so sure she'd won. But her squawking panic had totally wrecked her triumph. Custard was a fan, too. Once they'd had a longer introduction this morning, Rob wasn't sure whether his dog would ever leave the poor woman alone. Her wagging tail had threatened to dent the wainscoting in the hallway.

He still worried about Stacey. Her self-esteem had been in the crapper before this accident. And now? He still wanted to help her improve it. But he knew the challenge had just increased exponentially. Good thing he loved impossible odds.

The sound of the door opening broke his reverie, and he turned just in time to see Stacey, her leg splinted in a brace, hobbling through the door on crutches.

He rose from his seat and met her by the door.

"I need to come back on Friday," she said, raking her bangs away from her forehead. "There isn't a break that they can see, but they want to evaluate me after the swelling's gone down a little."

Rob nodded. "I can bring you."

She shook her head, looking pained. "I can't ask you to keep taking me everywhere. You're not running a taxi service."

"I've been meaning to look into it. Uber drivers can make good money. You can help me practice."

His light tease did the trick, and she made a face at him. "I don't tip."

He feigned offense. "The very idea. I'd never charge a dime."

"You'd make a crap Uber driver then."

"True," he said, holding the door for her. He watched as she navigated the crutches, her brow lined with concentration. He matched her pace, excruciatingly slow though it was, as they walked the short distance to the car. Thankfully there had been a spot open right in front of the entrance when they'd arrived.

"How's it feeling?" He nodded toward the brace on her leg.

"Not brilliant. And the crutches aren't exactly comfortable to work with, either." She leaned against the car as he opened the door for her and took her crutches. "But I shouldn't have to use them for long."

After tucking her crutches into the trunk, he slid into the driver's seat beside Stacey. Before he could crank the engine, his cell phone buzzed in his pocket.

"Sorry," he said as he pulled it free and glanced at the screen. Mom. "Excuse me one minute, Stacey. Hello?"

"Robbie, it's me."

"What's going on, Mom?" Rob kept his voice light, even though he was worried. It wasn't like her to call. She usually texted, or sent Facebook messages in all caps.

"Your father isn't feeling well. I've tried to get him to call his cardiologist, but he says he's fine. Can you talk to him?"

Shit. Rob shot a glance over at Stacey. "Of course. Give him the phone."

A moment went by, the sound of his mother walking through the house echoing through the tiny speaker.

"Richard? It's Robbie. He wants to talk to you about calling the doctor." His mother sounded faraway.

"Millie, I told you not to call him. I'm fine. What's he going to do anyway, tell me to do some sit-ups 'til it feels better?"

Rob's jaw tightened as he waited for their argument to end. This was becoming a much-too-common occurrence.

"Sorry, Robbie, he doesn't want to talk right now."

"It's okay, Mom. For now, just keep an eye on him, and if he gets any worse, call the cardiologist yourself. Let me know if I can help."

"I will." She sniffed, and the sound pierced straight through his heart. "I love you, Robbie."

"I love you too. Everything will be fine."

At least, he thought as he killed the call, he hoped it would be.

He cranked the engine and smoothly shifted into REVERSE.

"Is everything okay?"

He shot Stacey a glance.

"Yes. Sorry about that. Just trouble with my parents. My father's health isn't the best, and he's a damn stubborn ass at times. Refuses to listen to me because of my job."

"I can't imagine anybody disapproving of you owning your own business," Stacey said, her tone incredulous. "I mean, it's a really awesome gym, and it looks like it's doing well. There's nothing wrong with being a personal trainer."

"It's not an MD. That's what's wrong with it." Low-lying cloud cover blanketed the horizon, making Rob think of snow. "I swore up and down I wasn't getting a medical degree. That's why my undergrad was in business administration. My parents eventually forgave me once the gym started turning a profit and I never came crawling back looking for a handout. But Dad never misses the chance to point out what he feels should have been my career instead."

The car rolled to a stop at an intersection. Rob's hand rested lightly on the gearshift. He watched his thumb make slow circles around the silver button on the side. He wasn't sure whether he felt better or not. It wasn't a secret, but it wasn't like he went around telling everyone that he was a disappointment to his family.

"I understand."

The words were as surprising as the somber tone. Rob shot a look over at his passenger. "What?"

"About not wanting to stir the pot with your family." Stacey tucked a lock of strawberry-blond hair behind her ear. In the dim gray light of the winter day, her blue eyes looked almost stormy, like the sea. "I've kind of been the black sheep for a long time, too. Not as far as the career thing goes. But with looks? Yeah."

"What do you mean?" Rob didn't want to look away from her, but the light was green. He stepped lightly on the gas pedal.

"My whole family is genetically gifted. Seriously, they're the kind of people you hate on sight because they're just so damn beautiful. Well, like you." A mirthless laugh escaped her. "My mother's never dieted a day in her life. My aunt's even worse. My dad used to model in the early eighties. He met my mom at an industry party."

"Did she model too?"

Stacey shook her head. "She was trying to break into the business. But they hit it off, and then she got pregnant. So her career dreams were crushed, and then Dad had to get a more stable job. And then I came out looking like this."

Rob desperately wanted to look over at her, but he was turning into the parking lot of one of his favorite lunch places. "There's nothing wrong with the way you look."

"I've got my mom's coloring, but I've always had a weight problem. I tried to make up for it by being a really great student, by doing everything extracurricular I qualified for. But I've never been athletic. I tried out for basketball, volleyball, track. Never made a single team."

Rob cut the engine and finally looked over at Stacey. She was staring into her lap at the gray sweatpants he'd bought for her on an early morning Target run. He'd offered to grab her some clothes, and while she'd rather have had her own things, the thought of giving Rob free reign to rummage through her clothes made her cringe.

"I guess that's part of the reason I wanted to join the gym and finally get this weight thing figured out. So I could stop being such a disappointment."

He leaned over the center console and gathered her into his arms. This was good. The bandages were being ripped off, and the old wounds were getting a chance to breathe.

She didn't cry, just held on to him for a long, sweet moment. He closed his eyes. For a moment, he didn't think about her body, what he'd like to do to her once she was feeling healthy and whole again. He just held her.

Much too soon for him, she pulled away.

"Sorry. I didn't mean to dump that on you. We were talking about you."

"We were talking about common problems," Rob corrected gently as he reached for the door handle. "Let's go inside and continue this conversation over some lunch. Do you like Mexican food?"

"It's one of my favorites," Stacey admitted with a half smile that he was delighted to see.

Stacey settled into the chair that Rob helpfully held out for her. Damn it, she was really getting used to the gentlemanly way he treated her. Admonishing herself that he was just being kind, and that she shouldn't read into it, she began to peruse the menu the hostess had laid in front of her while Rob tucked her crutches in the corner beside them.

"What's good here?" she asked as Rob sat down across from her.

"Everything. This is where I come when I need a cheat day." He smiled and plucked a chip from the basket that had appeared in front of them when she wasn't looking.

"Cheat days. The concept is appalling."

Rob shrugged one shoulder, one muscled, impossibly broad, very sexy shoulder, and grinned. "It is what it is."

"I hate that expression."

Rob crunched his chip and continued looking at her. Her body grew warmer and warmer, and she fought to run a hand over the back of her neck to check for sweat.

"Don't you need to look at the menu?"

"Nope. My favorite's on special today. *Pollo ranchero*."

"I guess I'll get that, too." Stacey closed her menu and took a sip of water. Rob might be teasing her to help her deal with the emotions that their conversation in the car had stirred. She felt bad about that. Their talk had started because he was revealing things about himself, and she'd made it all about her. Rude, much? She cleared her throat. Time to make up for it.

"Do you mind if I ask you about your parents?"

His easy smile faded somewhat, but he shook his head. "No, fire away."

"Why did they want you to be a doctor so badly?"

Stabbing his salsa with a chip, Rob stared at the small brown bowl as he swirled around it. "My dad's an MD. Family practice. He's very old school, traditional gender roles, that kind of thing. My two sisters both went to nursing school, but since I was the boy, I was supposed to carry on the family tradition. My grandfather was a doctor, too. Dad really was gung ho over the third generation continuing the tradition."

His tone had soured a bit. Stacey fiddled with her napkin. "And you didn't want that."

He shook his head. "No. I thought about it, even planned to go premed for a while, but it wasn't me. I spent some time working in my dad's office when I was younger. Dad constantly complained about the people with chronic problems caused by their own actions. Like smokers with COPD and emphysema, and diabetics who refused to monitor their diets or keep up with their medications. I wanted to help people, and if I did his job, I would constantly be afraid of becoming jaded like he is."

A surprised, dry laugh escaped him then. "I'm sorry. But I've never really told anyone all of this."

"It's okay. I've never gone into that much detail about my family issues, either. I guess this is a mutually beneficial emotional-dumping day." Stacey twisted a slight grin in his direction. It was probably the pain meds talking, but what the hell. She raised her water glass.

"Here's to family. May we be a constant disappointment, a thorn in their sides, and the reason they regret procreating."

For a moment, she wondered whether her impromptu toast had offended him. He didn't raise his glass, but he did reach out and gently catch her arm by the wrist, lowering it gently to the tabletop.

"Let's change that up. May our families realize the treasures they have in front of them, and if they don't, may we have the strength not to give a fuck."

Her heart, which had stopped at the unexpected physical contact, restarted with a *thump*. She laughed and nodded. His returning smile made her belly flip-flop. To cover her nervousness, she reached for a chip and crunched it loudly.

"You've got—" Rob leaned toward her. "There." His fingertip flicked a crumb from her top lip. She stared, frozen. He didn't move his hand away, but his fingers trailed the line of her lips, softly, back and forth, as if he was memorizing their shape and feel.

His touch was so warm, so gentle. Her eyes fluttered closed, and she struggled to breathe. Her heart was pounding in her throat, just from that simple touch.

"Are you ready to order?"

The cheerful question from the waitress who'd appeared out of nowhere startled Stacey so much that she actually jumped.

Rob answered, ordering for both of them while Stacey gulped water like mad.

"Are you okay?" he asked once the waitress had gone.

"Oh yeah, I'm fine." No. She wasn't fine. What was that? Why had he been so sweet, touching her like that? Was he interested? That night in the locker room, had it been more than a once-in-a-lifetime shot? What would she do if he wanted more? What would she do if he didn't? It wasn't some weird experiment anymore, in which she practiced flirting with a ten so a respectable five would give her the time of day later. This was real life, in the middle of the day, and he had really made somewhat of a move there—hadn't he?

"You look like your brain is about to short-circuit. Care to share what you're thinking?"

"Bathroom," she managed to squeak out. "I need to go use it." She grabbed the crutches and scooted her chair backward with her good foot.

"Sure. It's just past the bar there, where that potted plant is."

She flashed a smile. "Thanks."

Hobbling toward the safety of the bathroom as fast as her battered body could carry her, she cursed herself for a coward. Why couldn't she just ask him if he was interested? Why did she have to be such a chickenshit?

Because it makes zero sense that he'd be into you. He's gorgeous. You're average at best.

Her inner voice was right, but damn it, she needed more reason than that.

In the safety of the unoccupied bathroom, Stacey perched atop the closed lid of the toilet, stretching her bum leg out in front of her. The cracked screen of her phone might not be the most attractive thing in the world, but it still worked well enough. Finding it in the bag of her belongings that had been scraped out of her defunct vehicle had been an unexpected boon. The call connected a moment later.

"Stacey! I've been so worried about you. I got the meeting postponed. How did the doctor thing—"

"Hannah, I need some advice, quick."

Chapter 14

Something had changed for him, and he wasn't exactly sure when it had happened. He frowned at the ring of condensation left on the dark wood of the table by his water glass.

He liked Stacey. Genuinely liked her. Not because she was a client he wanted to help. Not because they had shared an incredible encounter in the locker room. Not because she'd looked amazing in his T-shirt, the fabric stretched over her beautiful breasts. But something in the way she'd listened to him, really listened. She was kind. Sweet. A good person.

And he wanted to get to know that person much better. So, he'd indulged a bit.

He took a sip of his water. He'd startled her, but she didn't look like she'd hated the contact. On the contrary, she'd been closing her eyes, melting into his touch, when the waitress had interrupted.

Sighing, he glanced at the clock on his phone. He'd apologize, but he wasn't sure whether he should. Damn it, this wasn't like him. Normally he settled on a course of action and went for it with no questions asked. For some reason this girl was messing with his equilibrium.

"Two *pollo rancheros*." The server was back, and she presented their food with a flourish. "Can I get you anything else?"

"Some more salsa, please," Rob said with a grateful nod.

"I'll bring that and your lady friend some more water." The server winked at Rob before moving to the next table.

Stacey chose that moment to appear, hopping toward the table with the aid of her crutches. Her face looked pink, bright, as if she'd scrubbed it in the bathroom. The damp tips of her bangs seemed to corroborate that idea.

"This looks good," Stacey said as she approached. "You didn't have to get up."

But Rob was already on her side of the table, holding the chair for her and taking her crutches when she sat. "It's a pain in the ass to have to maneuver around on crutches like that. I don't mind."

"Thank you," she said. And then something flashed across her face, an expression so quick he couldn't really name it. Her hand shot out and grabbed his, a quick squeeze. "Really. Thanks."

He smiled, unable to help himself. "You're welcome." He squeezed back. Her hand was cool, soft.

The meal they shared was pleasant. As if by some unspoken agreement, they moved on to much more benign topics. The next upcoming *Star Wars* sequel, the latest on the new Braves stadium, it was all cordial and almost bland. They conversed easily, but Rob found himself missing the depth of their earlier chat. He wanted to know her more. Really know her, hidden wounds and all.

"That was too delicious," Stacey said, laying her fork down. "I can see why this is your favorite cheat."

"Go big or go home." Rob leaned back in his chair and laid a hand over his belly. "I could use a nap."

"Me too. I can't wait to crawl into your bed."

As soon as the words were out of her mouth, Stacey's eyes went wide and her cheeks paled. "That's not— I didn't—"

Rob didn't bother to hide his laughter. "You know, you're welcome any time you like. But sometimes that bed is occupied, so Goldilocks had better be careful."

A little smile curved the full lower lip he'd touched earlier. "If I'm sleeping in your bed, will the big, bad bear gobble me up?"

She was flirting. God help him. "Definitely."

He paid the check, trying to ignore the way his body had treated the idea of what she'd meant. His libido was sitting on "go," but his brain cautioned him to move at a much slower pace. He wasn't sure, at this juncture, which would win.

The ride back to his place was much quieter. Stacey's pain medication was wearing off, and she dozed in the passenger seat, the furrow between her brows deepening whenever there was a rough patch on the highway. His only thought was to get her home, and tucked into bed, with her next dose of medication safely on board.

"Samflynelly," she said.

"What?" Rob tilted his head toward her. "I didn't get that."

"Sam fly nelly, toboggan." She flapped a hand in his direction.

His guts tightened in alarm. Shit. He took the exit toward his house too quickly, glad they were so close. Thoughts of her recent concussion gripped him, made him drive quicker and more deftly. Once he'd pulled into the spot at home, he cut the engine and grabbed Stacey's hand.

"Wake up, Stacey. You need to talk to me." He patted the back of her hand, squeezing her fingers gently. "Come on, Stacey, where are we?"

She opened her eyes, frowning as she blinked. "Huh? We're at your apartment. What's the big deal?"

He didn't relax. Couldn't. Not yet. "How many fingers am I holding up?"

She sighed. "Two. I'm fine. I had a weird dream, but I'm fine."

"You were talking gibberish. I had to check. You're in my care, and I'm not about to let anything else happen to you."

He didn't let go of her hand and stared deep into her eyes. They were so close, such a deep blue, flecks of sky and silver dancing in them. Her brows winged delicately over them, looking so soft, fringed as they were by her bangs. The delicate skin was reddened at her temple by the contact with the air bag. Her nose, with a tiny line of freckles marching along the bridge, turned up at the tip. And her lips. They'd been so soft, so touchable earlier. Now he leaned closer, wanting to taste them, taste her, feel the way she responded to him.

And then she surprised him by closing the gap between them.

Her mouth took his, open, sweetly wanting. Her free hand touched his neck, threading upward to rub against his nape. He threaded his fingers through hers and laid his free hand gently on her hip. His tongue traced the line of her mouth that his fingers had explored earlier. She was sweet, so sweet, so open and giving as he kissed her more deeply. She matched him, movement for movement, her tongue swirling with his as they explored one another.

He wanted to kiss her mouth forever, but there were more places he longed to explore. The tiny taste he'd gotten of her seemed so long ago. Kissing his way down her jaw, he nuzzled at her neck, breathing in the sweet scent of her. Nipping gently at the shimmering pulse there, he smiled against her skin as she tilted her chin upward to give him better access.

She was loving this as much as he was. And the thought was damn heady.

Oh God.

His mouth was on her neck. His lips were pressed against the tender skin, his tongue laying sweet lines of sensuous fire on her throat. Her eyes were closed in bliss, and her hands wandered wherever they wanted.

They started in his sandy hair, rubbing the short length against her fingertips. Then lower, past the muscles of his shoulders, across the breadth of his strong chest.

His mouth moved to her collarbone, his teeth grazing it slightly. A moan escaped her then, a small sound that she hadn't meant to utter, but she could no more stop it than she could have stopped that truck from hitting her last night.

The truck. Her eyes flew open and she braced for impact with a gasp.

Rob stopped kissing her instantly, pulling back.

"Stacey? What's wrong, did I hurt you?"

She pressed a palm to her chest where her heart was thumping so hard against her rib cage that it sent waves of pain to her side. Her breaths were quick pants.

"Stacey?"

"No, sorry. I just, well, it was kind of a flashback. To last night. I suddenly remembered the impact and it freaked me out a little."

Rob reached for her, his arms going around her as if to comfort her. She'd just started to settle into them, grateful for the support, when he pulled away.

"I'm sorry. You're hurting, and tired, and here I am taking advantage of you."

"No! You're not taking advantage. Really. I was enjoying it." She looked down at her lap, hating the inadequacy she felt just then. Why did he have to be so far out of her league? He could have any girl he wanted, so why was he spending time with her? And why did she have to be so goddamn suspicious of his motives? All she wanted was to continue those kisses right where they left off. She'd been praying his mouth would drift lower, past her collarbone, down to the swell of her breasts where her nipples were tightening in anticip—

"Stacey." He broke her reverie. "Let's go inside. You should catch a nap."

She sighed as he pushed open his car door. "Okay. Even when you're not in the gym, you're bossy as hell. "

Making use of the mirrors, she watched as he pulled her crutches from the trunk. That had been unexpected, but incredible. Hannah had encouraged her to explore, to see just how far this thing could go, but disbelief still saturated her. Despite that one chance encounter, this kind of thing didn't happen to girls like her. She'd accepted the fact that she would be single well into her late thirties, and probably end up with someone whom she liked, but didn't necessarily love. A divorcé, probably, someone who was lonely, like she was. Someone willing to settle.

Wait a minute. What was it Rob had told her? Look in the mirror every day, and say something positive.

She reached for the rearview and twisted it toward her.

"I'm a nice person. We have a lot in common. So why shouldn't Rob like me?"

She smiled at her reflection, and was pleased to see that the woman smiling back at her didn't look as bad as she'd feared. Sure, she didn't have on a "stitch of makeup," as her grandmother used to say, and her bruises were darkening. Yeah, she was wearing the outfit that Rob had grabbed for her at Target before sunup. And maybe her messy ponytail wasn't the height of fashion. But her cheeks had color, her eyes were bright, and Rob was opening her door with the crutches.

"You okay?"

"Yeah. I'm good." She moved the mirror back into position and carefully swung her legs out of the car. Looking up at Rob, silhouetted against the wintry sky, she bit her lip.

"I don't guess you want to join me for that nap, do you?"

He tilted his head to the side, a puzzled smile stretching his lips. "What?"

She wanted to squirm, back down, laugh it off, pretend she'd said something else. She did none of that, though. *Nut up, buttercup*, she thought with a mental flourish.

"The nap. It's a big bed. Maybe we could continue a little bit of what we just started? I mean, if you want."

Reaching a hand down to her, his small smile broadened into a knowing grin. But his words took the thrill right out of her heart.

"That's really tempting. But you should rest. You were up almost all night, and your body needs time to recover. Come on."

She took his hand, trying hard not to let the sting of his rejection show on her face. He pulled her to her feet, and she tucked her crutches beneath her arms. They were already sore, unused to the way she had to walk. Her bruises and bumps were getting more noticeable now, the discomfort that had waned in the face of Rob's embrace buzzing toward the forefront of her consciousness.

Rob stayed beside her up the walk to his front door. She cast a glance around while he readied his keys.

It was a clean little neighborhood. If the tall shade trees in his yard were any indication, these condos had been here awhile. Hard to tell from the upkeep, though. The homes were all freshly painted, lawns kept well, but not too fussy. A picket fence ran across the side of Rob's yard, turning a right angle before shooting back. For Custard, she presumed.

The little visual excursion helped to distract her from the thought that she'd just been shot down. For a second, at least.

"After you," Rob said as he pushed the door open.

"Thanks," Stacey said, keeping her gaze glued to the ground as if to ensure she didn't trip over the threshold. It was really so she didn't have to look at Rob's face. What would she see there? Pity? Amusement that she'd tried to get him in bed? She didn't need to know. There were plenty of pillows in that bedroom. Maybe she could smother herself to death so she didn't have to face him at dinner.

"Get some rest. I'll wake you up in a few hours." Rob laid a gentle hand on her back as she stopped outside his bedroom door.

She stared at the bed for a moment, not moving.

"Stace?"

Without looking at him, keeping her gaze trained on that big, king-sized bed, its plush black comforter and soft gray sheets beckoning, she spoke.

This might be the biggest mistake she'd ever made in her life, but God help her, she had to speak the truth.

"Come to bed with me. Please. I want you."

Chapter 15

Her words wrapped around him and pulled mercilessly. Rob tried to resist them. He had to. It was sheer insanity to even consider it.

"Don't make me beg," she said, her voice low.

Christ, he was a bastard.

Wrapping his arms around her from behind, he pulled her close, resting his chin atop her head. Her ass pressed against his front, so soft. Her skin was warm beneath her clothing. He wanted to press her down into his bed and do what he'd promised to back in the locker room.

But that was insane. She wasn't healthy enough for that.

"Come to bed," he whispered against her hair. "I'll tuck you in."

She didn't respond, but let him lead her into the bedroom. He took the crutches from her and placed them against the wall by the bedside. When he turned to look at her, the sight punched him in the guts.

She'd sunk down onto the edge of the bed, her arms supporting her on the edge of the mattress. Her gaze was glued to the floor, her hair falling over her left shoulder in a sad strawberry curtain. The corners of her pink lips were down-turned, her teeth catching the edge of her bottom lip as she looked down at her toes. Shoulders hunched, spirit dampened; it was as if Rob's offer had been a blow to the back instead of the kindness it was meant to be.

Fuck.

He couldn't let it pass.

Reaching forward, he slid his hand into her hair, pushing the beautiful mass of thick waves back over her shoulder. Cupping the back of her head, he forced her to look up at him.

"You have to promise me."

"Promise you what?" she whispered.

"If you hurt, you have to tell me so I can stop."

"I promise," she said, then reached her arms up to him.

He couldn't say no. Wouldn't.

As he bent down to kiss her, the vision of the car accident passed in his mind's eye. Stacey was an incredible person, and in the span of a moment, she could have been gone. Of course she wanted the comfort and experience of being with someone. Life affirmation. That was what this was about. Sure, they'd been incredibly attracted to one another before this, but at the moment, Rob was fulfilling her needs. His own could wait—would wait. This was about Stacey.

Their lips met and he gently pressed her back onto the bed, lifting her legs up onto the mattress. She was hesitant at first, holding back. It was easy to imagine what was going on inside her head. Fear was written in each small movement, in the way her mouth parted for him, but not widely. The way her arms twined around his neck, but her fingers laced together instead of digging into his shoulders. The way her back arched to him, but she immediately drew back.

She was afraid of being rejected again. Only one way to stop the fear.

He stopped kissing her and lay down next to her, pillowing his head on his bent arm.

"Stacey, I want you."

She blinked. "Yeah?"

He nodded. "I do. Do you know what I want to do to you?"

"No . . ." She drew the word out.

He grinned. "I want to strip you naked and explore every last inch of you, starting with those beautiful breasts I got a glimpse of last night. Then I'll work my way down your belly, between your thighs, where I'll taste you again. I can't tell you how many times I've thought about licking your pussy ever since that night in the locker room."

Her cheeks went the most beautiful shade of pink. It should have clashed awfully with her coloring, but it didn't.

"Once you're screaming my name, then I'll kiss you and let you taste yourself on my lips while I sink my cock deep inside of you."

Her eyes fluttered closed and her body arched toward him, legs shifting against one another. There. He let himself grin. He had her now.

"I'll start slow, stroke after stroke, until you're panting and begging to come. Then I'll go faster, harder, pumping into you, stretching you, filling you, touching your breasts and ass, running my hands all over your body as my cock pumps inside your sweet, tight walls."

"Rob," she half-sighed, half-moaned, her tongue darting out to wet her lips. "Please."

"I'll slide my fingers down between us and find your clit. I'll rub it just how you like it, until you come. I'll come with you."

Her lips parted on a moan, and Rob's cock got so hard that it ached. He'd enjoyed teasing her past her inhibitions, and now it was time to put his money where his mouth was.

"If you want all of this, Stacey, all you have to do is say so."

"I want it," she said, never opening her eyes.

Excitement flooded him as he moved up onto his elbow to get closer to her. He leaned down, brushing his lips across hers as he spoke.

"I've got a condom this time. There won't be any need to wait, unless you're uncomfortable. Are you sure?"

"I'm sure," she said, then her eyes opened, nearly startling him with the brilliance of their color. "But there's just one thing."

"Anything," he said, bending closer again. "Name it."

"The lights off. And the curtains closed. I need both of those, if that's okay."

He stilled for a moment as his blood cooled and his brain engaged. *What?*

"You want it dark?"

She nodded, biting her lip again, this time in uncertainty rather than desire. "Please?"

He couldn't deny her, not when he needed this as badly as she did. And when the smoke cleared, he'd definitely want to discuss the reasons for it with her. But for now, he didn't want to force either of them to wait any longer than they had to.

Wordlessly, he rose from the bed and crossed to the windows, where he drew the blackout drapes closed.

* * *

Stacey tried to control her breathing as Rob let the curtains fall. Her palms itched as she watched him cross the room to the light switch.

Darkness fell, and the anxiety she'd been gripping inside loosened slightly. It wasn't the pitch darkness of the locker room, but the blackout drapes did a pretty good job of keeping out the light.

Was she a coward? Yes. Rob had seen more of her last night than she'd ever intended to show him. Her body was still a problem, even though some of the mystery was gone. Of all the things he could have seen, her breasts were probably what she was least ashamed of. And his reaction? Really good, actually.

But she couldn't chance the reality of showing him more. It would shatter the illusion that she could really do this—really be with him this way.

"Is that better?"

His voice seemed deeper in the dark, and it sent shivers of anticipation down her spine.

"Yes."

The aches and pains that had bothered her all day had faded to a dull buzz at the back of her consciousness, and the need to be with Rob was square in the forefront of her mind.

He moved toward the bed, and her stomach tightened, but he bent down beside her. There was a rasping sound of a drawer opening on his bedside table. A soft *rip*, like a foil wrapper, and Stacey bit her lip as she imagined what he was doing.

She turned away, unsure whether she should look at him through the darkness, or not. What were the rules? She didn't know, and she had no way of finding out.

She reached down and lifted the hem of her T-shirt up and over her head. In the dark, she could pretend she was alone. That no one could see her, could judge her, could find her wanting. The desire that Rob had stirred within her was still there, but her anxieties were beginning to overcome it.

"Let me."

She paused in unfastening her bra. "Let you what?"

"Undress you. I may not be able to see it all, but I want to touch it all."

Her hands fell away from the clasp, and she sat motionless as Rob's fingers took the place of hers. A knot worked its way into her throat as he unfastened her bra, and the straps fell down her shoulders. The bedroom air was cool, and it puckered her nipples as it brushed past.

At Rob's gentle insistence, she lay back, and his hands glided down her sides to find her waistband. He drew the pants down her legs softly, and she shuddered slightly at the touch of his warm, strong fingers. Her belly tightened as he brushed across her panties.

"You feel amazing," he said, his husky voice hovering just above her chest. "I wish I could see you."

"Just touch me."

He did as she asked, his hands starting at her shoulders, then making their way down to her breasts. She closed her eyes as he squeezed slightly, his fingertips finding her puckered nipples. Her blood heated within her veins, her fevered brain imagining all the delicious things he had mentioned doing to her.

She reached forward, unable to take the tantalizing torture. Her own hands itched to explore the planes of his body. At her insistence, he grasped the hem of his shirt, and together they removed it. As her fingers quested lower, she found that he had already unbuttoned his jeans, and they came down without a struggle.

Had he already put on the condom? She wanted to touch, to find out, but she was too afraid.

Why should she fear? She wasn't sure; she didn't like these feelings. She wanted to be bold, to take everything he offered without hesitation, but she couldn't. Not yet. Maybe one day she would have that kind of courage, but today was all about taking back the strength to believe again.

"Stacey"—he pressed her down against the covers—"Stacey."

His mouth covered hers then, and the hunger he had clearly been suppressing roared to life. His tongue was everywhere, tasting her, questing, searching for something, and she willingly gave up all her secrets to him. His hands roamed everywhere they could reach, and the shame she felt at her body's flaws could not withstand his passionate onslaught.

Her skin was on fire. Her pussy was burning, and her insides flipped and knotted with every touch and kiss he gave. Her fingers dug into his shoulders, rubbing down his back, and she moaned as she cupped his muscular ass to hold his hips tighter to her.

The heat of his skin was so delicious against hers. His deliciously hard cock lay against the softness of her belly, and she wanted it lower. Deeper. She parted her thighs and arched up against him, the throb inside her begging for what he had promised.

He lifted his head from her breast, where he had been nuzzling, kissing, and nipping. She gripped his hair.

"I could do this all night, but I don't think either of us would be satisfied with it."

"You're right." Stacey let her hand snake between them to find her hot, wet center. "I want you, Rob. I'm ready."

He reached between them and found her hand, smiling against her skin as he stroked the wetness on her fingers.

"It seems you're right."

She looked up as he braced his arms on either side of her shoulders. Even in the darkness, she could make out his features. The hunger in his eyes was plain, and it was a beautiful sight. Her body was tensed, coiled, primed, and ready. He had taken her further than she ever thought she could go.

"Look at me."

"I am."

He lowered himself until his forehead touched hers briefly. Then he lifted, once she was staring directly into his eyes. "Don't look away."

Staring into his eyes was the most erotic thing she had ever experienced, as the blunt, hot head of his cock parted her wet folds. She gasped, fighting the urge to close her eyes as he filled her, slid deep into her center. He was thick, and he stretched her. The delicious burn matched the heat of him, and her already pulsing desire ratcheted up to an eleven.

She shook, hips lifting upward of their own volition to encourage him deeper. Barely blinking, he looked down into her eyes, and began a slow, sensuous rhythm.

With every movement, he brushed against her clit. The slow, delicious sensation was driving her insane. She wanted more, faster, deeper. But he didn't relent. He kept up his even rhythm, not increasing his tempo even as she shuddered beneath him.

"Rob," she gasped, her nails digging into his shoulders. "I need . . . I want."

"I know."

His grin could only be described as demonic. The orgasm was building within her, slow, glowing coal that needed only a breath of his to encourage it to burst into flame. But he still went slowly, stroke after stroke.

She couldn't take this much longer. Her body could not withstand the torture. It was too slow, too good, he was so deep—but not deep enough.

With a twist and a cry, she reached down between their bodies and found her clit with her fingers. Rubbing it hard, she gasped his name, and in answer he quickened his rhythm. The sound of their flesh slapping against one another was loud in the otherwise silent room, and as the fire within her burned hotter and faster, she finally let go of the orgasm that had been growing within her.

Lights burst behind her eyes and her body arched wildly, spasms inside her unwilling to listen to reason. Rob pumped into her, his hips moving in and out, all restraint lost as she held on to him tightly, riding out the waves of her own orgasm.

Stacey's heart thudded hard against her ribs as she collapsed beneath him. Her ragged breath blew against his chest as he thrust into her two, three more times. His impossibly hot cock became even hotter when he came with a hoarse gasp. The pulses twitched within her, each movement felt by her sensitive inner walls.

He lay on top of her, and she wound her arms around his back, her cheek pressed against his chest. She could feel his heartbeat there, a loud, comforting sound.

Closing her eyes, smiling in the dark, Stacey let herself be happy.

Chapter 16

Her body was curled up against his, tucked closer than his heartbeat in the dark.

Rob rested his chin against her hair and breathed her in. She smelled good. Sweet, somehow, like a fresh beginning.

It was darker now, the last remnants of weak winter daylight having faded away. There was only the faint outline of light outlining the edges of the doorway. He'd left the hall light on.

Stacey's breathing was even and slow. She had fallen asleep soon after they came. It had been good. Better than he had anticipated, and he had anticipated quite a lot.

Rob pressed his lips to the back of her head. What was it about this girl? She begged him to sleep with her, when by all rights she should be feeling terrible after her car accident. Rob stayed still, keeping watch over her, his thoughts tumbling through his brain like towels in a Maytag.

This woman's self-esteem could really use a shot of adrenaline. But at least since their lunchtime conversation, he had a glimpse of what had caused her current situation.

A little sound, high and short, escaped her. He pressed his lips to her hair again.

For some reason, he was feeling very protective of Stacey Hough. Not to mention tempted by her. He was beginning to wonder exactly what he'd gotten himself into.

When she woke up, there was a delicious warmth pressed against her back. She kept her eyes closed and pressed closer to it. It was one of those dreams on the edge of waking that felt much too real.

The kind of dream that affected you with a profound sense of loss upon realizing that it wasn't actually true. She'd make this one last as long as possible.

A hand was splayed on her hip, a slight weight that pressed her into the softness of the bed. Scooting her hips back, she sighed at the feeling of a firm length pressed against her ass.

Warm air blew against the back of her neck in slow, rhythmic puffs. Her lover's breath. She reached down to her hip and threaded his fingers in her own, shifting to get even closer to him.

She winced. Damn, her dreams were detailed. She even remembered just how much her stupid leg was hurting. Shouldn't she get a free pass on that, just for the dream?

Pretend it doesn't hurt, and then it won't. It's a dream, after all.

Her subconscious was right. Besides, when was the next time she'd get a shot at getting a man in bed with her? The only guy she even wanted to try that with . . . was . . .

"Rob!"

She gasped it aloud as her eyes flew open. He gripped her hand tightly as if in automatic response.

"What's wrong?"

Collapsing against the pillows, she pressed her free hand to her chest in a fruitless bid to keep her heart from making a run for it. She'd forgotten it all. The way she'd begged Rob to come to bed, the gentle way he'd refused, then her eventual plea that wore him down.

She. Was. Pathetic.

"Stacey, talk to me. Are you in pain? Do I need to call someone?"

He let go of her hand and raised his body above hers, bracing himself on his arm so he could look down at her.

In this position she felt small, vulnerable. Desirable, even.

"No, I'm sorry. It was just a weird dream."

He didn't move, still looking down at her through the dim light of the room. It must be on the edge of sunset. His features were hard to make out clearly.

"Did it scare you?"

"A little," she said, not sure whether it was a lie or not. She'd been afraid, but not because of the dream. She was scared that he would regret kissing her. That he'd resent her for the fact that she'd wheedled her way into a "nap" with him.

She was scared of losing the closeness she'd just found with him. "Don't be afraid," he whispered, then lowered his lips to hers.

It was a sweet kiss, meant to comfort, not stir. Meant to take away fear, not build passion in its place. But no matter his intentions, Stacey's response couldn't be dampened.

Her arms wound around his neck and pulled him in closer. He braced himself on his forearms, not placing any of his weight on her. That was probably wise, since she was still so sore, but wisdom and passion didn't play nice. She wanted his body to press her down, the full length of him lying on top of her as he ravaged her mouth.

She opened to him, coaxed him on with small swirls of her tongue against his. A low groan escaped him as she nipped his bottom lip.

Maybe he wasn't as immune to her as she'd feared.

His kisses deepened, and she welcomed them fully. He had been holding back. She knew that now, because his control had nearly gone. He kept his weight off her, but his mouth showed none of that restraint. He tore his lips from hers and kissed a burning trail down her throat, past the collarbone that he'd begun kissing in the car, straight to the hint of cleavage left bare by the V-necked tee she'd pulled on before falling asleep.

His tongue dived in the cleft, and she gasped in response, tangling her fingers in his short hair. His lips and breath and teeth and skin overwhelmed her, the touch of him short-circuited her brain, and nothing existed but him and her and the pain.

Her positioning was awkward. She was halfway turned toward him, trapping her good leg with the heavy brace atop it.

She tried to ignore it, tried to ride the tide of passion rising in her brain, the delicious burning tingle of lust that tightened her belly and prickled her skin, but it was a losing battle.

In one last attempt, she rolled toward him to ease the pressure on her leg. Her muscles clenched in violent protest.

"Ah!"

"Jesus Christ, I'm sorry." Rob moved away immediately, ripping the covers off and turning on the bedside lamp almost in the same motion. "Is it your leg? Your ribs?"

Damn it all to hell.

"No, I just moved the wrong way. I'm sorry." She repositioned herself by using her hands to move her bum leg. "There. Seriously, I'm fine."

Rob sighed, standing at the foot of the bed with one hand rubbing through his hair.

"We shouldn't have started that. You're hurt."

"I'm fine."

"You're not fine. You've got an injury to your leg, and you've had a concussion."

"Can you let me decide what I can and can't handle? I'm not a child, or an invalid."

"You're a guest in my home, you're in a vulnerable position, and I don't want to take advantage of you."

"Why the hell not? What's so wrong with me?"

"You're too damn trusting, that's what!" He yelled it, and the sound stunned both Stacey and Custard. The dog jumped up from her bed by the closet, and Stacey might have jumped up, too, if she hadn't been lying down.

"Trusting? I shouldn't trust you? You're the perfect guy, Rob, it's obvious. Even your deep, dark secret is admirable. That's why I felt so safe practicing on you."

Rob shook his head. His mouth was pulled down at the corners, and an angry furrow knitted his brows.

"'Practice'? What the hell do you mean?"

She pushed herself upright, wincing at the discomfort. "You're out of my league, and I know that. I'm not good at this." She gestured between them. "But being with you is good—practice—"

"I'm not someone you can just 'practice' on, Stacey. I can't— you—Jesus, fuck."

He left the room, leaving a stunned Stacey staring at the door and wondering what the hell had just happened.

Rob paced through the kitchen, anger spurring him faster with each step. The workout shorts he'd pulled from the laundry room made soft *whish*ing sounds as he paced.

Custard, who'd followed him—although she left much greater distance between them than usual—sat in the hallway, her big, wrinkled face turning to follow as he went back and forth.

His hands were clenched into fists at his sides, and his insides felt like they were made of overstretched bungees.

Why did she have to be so damn honest? He could have pretended that she was as into him, the real him, as he was into her. But now he knew that he was just a project to her. A test run. And for some reason, that made him angrier than anything else could have.

A soft *whuff* from the hallway made him pause.

Custard had lain down, and her big head was pillowed on her front paws as she looked up at him with huge, sad brown eyes.

He took a deep breath.

"You're right. I'm sorry."

He knelt beside his dog and scratched her behind the ears. "I'm mad at myself for hurting her. I should apologize."

Custard said nothing, just pawed at his hand when he stopped scratching, encouraging him to continue. He obliged for another moment, then gave a peace offering of a dog biscuit to ease his parting.

With Custard crunching away at her prize, Rob headed back to the bedroom. The door was still open, so he stepped inside.

"Stacey?"

There was silence, at first. She wasn't in bed anymore, and her crutches were gone. The bathroom door was closed.

"Be out in a minute," she called. Her voice was small, uncertain. Damn it. He'd done it again. It seemed like he was destined to constantly misstep with this woman.

He sank down on the edge of the bed to wait for her, when the front doorbell sent Custard barking down the hallway.

"Be right back," Rob said toward the closed bathroom door as he followed his dog down the hallway. He looked through the window beside the door. A cop stood there, in full uniform, with a distinctly unpleasant expression on his face.

Oh shit.

Tightness spread across Rob's shoulders, but he forced himself to take a deep breath before opening the door.

"Can I help you?" Custard bristled beside him, a low growl coming from deep in her chest. She was pretty particular about the people she didn't care for, and Rob trusted her judgment. It had never steered him wrong before.

"Is Stacey Hough staying here?"

"Why do you need her?"

The cop's face grew even more serious, which was impressive. Frowning any harder would look almost comical on anyone else, but on this guy, it was intimidating. He and that cop from the hospital could have been brothers.

"Please ask her to come to the door."

"She's on crutches, and has been told by her doctor to remain off her feet." Rob pitched his voice intentionally loud as he blocked Custard with his leg. But behind him, a telltale *thump* told him that his statement had come too late.

"Rob? Is it for me?"

The cop's frown eased a little as Stacey appeared.

"Ma'am, this is for you." He held an envelope toward her, and she took it reflexively.

"What is—"

"You've been served. Good evening." With a tip of his hat, the cop turned and walked down the front steps.

Shit. Rob shut the door, easing Custard back. She wagged her tail, nosing at Stacey's thigh, but Stacey didn't respond to the dog's plea for attention.

"What does he mean, I've 'been served'?"

Rob took the paper from her nerveless fingers and steered her toward the living room. "Come on. You need to get off that leg."

She sank down onto the couch, and he moved the coffee table over to prop her foot on top of it. Then he opened the envelope and handed her the papers. They shook a little as she read them. He didn't ask any questions, just moved into the kitchen, keeping an eye on her as he poured her a glass of water. On his way back, she looked up.

"I'm being sued. The guy who hit me, he's coming after me for the damage to his car, for his injuries, everything. How could he have gotten this together so quickly?"

Rob took the papers and laid them on the table by her foot, then he grabbed her hands and looked directly into her wide, blue-eyed stare.

"Don't worry. Everything's going to be okay."

"How? He blows through a red light, he nearly kills me, but I'm the one who's supposed to pay for all this? How is this even fair!"

"Stacey, come on. This has no chance of going anywhere. The police report will show that he was in the wrong, and—"

"But that cop last night thought I was on my cell phone. That's why they're doing this, isn't it? They're trying to pin all this on me, when I didn't do anything wrong!"

He'd thought she was about to cry, but he'd been very, very wrong. Her cheeks were bright with anger, and her jaw was tight. Her brows had lowered to a dangerous level, and he began to feel very sorry for the punk who'd decided that Stacey Hough was a good target. He had no reason to be proud. After all, they weren't really anything other than trainer and client to one another. Well, maybe at this point, "friend" would be closer to the truth. Potential lover? Maybe once she'd healed, if he could convince her that her "practice" idea was crap.

"Where's my cell? I need to make some phone calls."

"You know it's after eight, right?"

She snapped a look at the wall, looking for a clock. He pointed helpfully at the opposite wall.

"Damn. A list. I need pen and paper."

He rose without a word and grabbed what she needed from the front bedroom he used as an office.

With the clipboard he'd handed her, Stacey began scribbling furiously atop the paper. He watched for a moment as a numbered list appeared.

Not wanting to snoop, he moved toward the kitchen.

"I'll find you something for dinner, okay?"

She didn't respond, wholly absorbed in her angry, driven scribbling.

He gave a wry smile as he pulled open the refrigerator. Angry Stacey, driven Stacey, Stacey with a cause and a plan, was much sexier than a woman on crutches had any right to be.

Chapter 17

Stacey had a love affair with lists. Her projects at work lived and died by her lists. She had about seven to-do-list apps on her phone that she relied on every week. But as nice as the technology was, nothing beat her old, tried-and-true, trusty lined paper and pen.

She'd been working on this particular list for quite a while now, but something was missing. Nibbling on the end of the pen, Stacey read over it for what seemed like the tenth time.

Number one—Call lawyer. Number two—Set up meeting and plan strategy. Number three—

"Hey, dinner's ready. Can you take a long enough break to eat?"

Stacey looked up and her heart was suddenly in her throat.

Rob stood there, in the doorway to the kitchen, wearing an apron. An honest-to-God apron. He was still wearing his T-shirt, cut tight enough to show off his ridiculous shoulder and arm muscles, but for some reason the domestic addition amped up his sexiness to eleven. His hair was more tousled than usual, he was holding a wooden spoon, and unless he was offering her a nice, healthy bite of him, she wasn't sure whether she could tear her eyes away long enough to eat.

He gave her a quizzical look. Oh God, had she made a face at him? Her breath caught in her throat, almost feeling solid, and she coughed. Damn, that didn't feel good to her ribs.

"Sorry. Yes, that would be awesome."

"Sit right there, I'll bring you a bowl."

Rob disappeared back into the kitchen, and Stacey took advantage of the moment to look up at the ceiling and pray.

"Listen, I know I owe you for the whole not-dying-in-the-accident thing. And I appreciate that more than I can say. But if you've got any leftover goodwill for me, can you please help me not to make a giant ass of myself in front of Rob? He's incredible, and I can't stand the thought of him thinking I'm some desperate loser."

There was no answering clap of thunder, so Stacey figured she and the higher power must be okay enough.

"Something smells good," she remarked when Rob reappeared. He'd shed the apron, sadly, but he was carrying a tray. He set it down on the end of the coffee table that wasn't propping up her bum leg.

"Just a quick chicken and rice soup. They say that chicken soup has medicinal properties." He handed over her bottle of medication and waited while she took her dose with a sip of water.

"How's the pain?"

She shrugged. "Not as bad as it could be."

He leaned toward her, his hand hovering over the edge of her splint. "May I?"

Curious, she nodded.

His fingers descended and gently probed her thigh at the edge of the brace. A shiver went through her, but she fought it as best she could. She didn't want him to know just how much his touch affected her, not after their eventful "nap" from earlier. He set up a gentle massage, and she leaned her head back against the couch, closing her eyes.

He found the knotted places, the tenseness in her muscles from the awkward way she'd been holding her leg all day. Then his hands moved to her other leg, and with long, smooth strokes, he soothed the tiredness there, too.

She wasn't sure if it was the power of his touch or the medication kicking in that sent her brain reeling. Maybe it was both. Maybe it was the fact that his hands roamed her body freely that made her imagination run wild.

She'd love it if there were no clothes between them. No injuries to hinder their desire. Just him, and her, and this couch. His hands moved higher, up to her hip. She moaned aloud as he found a particularly intense knot.

"Too much?"

"No," she hissed between her teeth. "Ah, it hurts so good."

"You're all knotted up from the difference in your gait. The medication will help, but this will too."

She imagined that his voice was a little too low, a little too gravelly to be normal. In her fantasy, he wasn't as unaffected by this as he'd pretended to be. She smiled, keeping her eyes closed as Rob's strong hands roamed to her other hip, echoing the same ministrations there.

Too soon, much too soon, a light scratching on her arm signaled that he was done.

"You should eat before it gets cold."

"I'm a big ball of mush right now, and you expect me to chew?"

At his chuckle, she cracked one eyelid open. He was stirring one of the bowls of soup on the tray.

"You won't have to chew much. Come on, you need nutrients to heal."

She took the bowl from him with a word of thanks, and as she spooned up her first bite she watched him.

There was a lot she'd done wrong with him. Being too bold, being too honest, being too forward. She'd tried so hard with him, and she kept falling on her face. Any other guy would probably have run for the hills by now.

She took a bite. So unfair that a man so gorgeous could cook, too.

But Rob? Rob . . . He'd stepped up for her in a way that was shocking, honestly. Even her friends wouldn't have dropped everything to care for her the way he had. Hell, her parents didn't even know about the accident yet. Of course, Sabrina would have—

Shit. Bree was going to kill her.

"Too cold? I can reheat it for you."

"No, it's good," Stacey said, stirring her soup with a frown. "I just thought about how dead I'm going to be when my cousin Sabrina finds out that I didn't call her right away."

"Do you need to use my phone?"

"No, mine still works okay. I just didn't want to bother her on her honeymoon." Soup dripped from the end of Stacey's spoon, and she sighed. "I nearly ruined her wedding ten days ago with a trip to the emergency room, I don't want to do the same with her honeymoon."

"Wait, you were just in the emergency room ten days ago?"

"Twelve," she corrected, realizing exactly how little difference it made. But the semantics mattered to her. "It was a stupid incident and it's all over with. I was fine, no real injury."

Rob set his own bowl on the coffee table and pinned her with a stern look. "What happened? And did you bother to tell the ER doctor that you'd so recently been injured?"

Well, shit. So much for a peaceful night.

Rob killed the call with a heavy breath.

Stacey had tried to assure him that her trip to the ER last week had been a nonevent, but her description of it made it clear that the doctor should have known what had happened. Since she hadn't been able to talk about it when she came in, it had flown under the radar.

The nurse he'd spoken to had told him that Dr. Calhoun was coming in soon, and that she would pass along the message.

Of course, the fact that she'd had a suspected concussion so recently would be clinically significant. He just hoped that the second injury hadn't done her more permanent damage.

"It's bad, isn't it?"

He turned. Going to the guest room to make the call had seemed like the best idea, so that he wouldn't worry Stacey, but she'd followed him, obviously unable to stand the wait.

"I told the nurse, and she's going to contact the doctor when he comes in. It's just another piece of the puzzle, that's all."

"What does it mean?"

"I don't know much about brain injuries, Stacey." He kept his voice pitched low, gentle. She leaned against the doorjamb, her head making a soft *thump* as it connected.

"But you know a little bit more than I do. We don't deal with brain trauma much in the city planning department."

"All I can tell you is what I think. I think the doctor needs to know. And I think we have to watch you more carefully. But as far as it changing anything for your diagnosis or prognosis? I can't say."

Stacey stood upright again, adjusting her crutches beneath her arms. "I guess worrying about it won't change anything. I need to call some people myself. First, I guess I need a lawyer. I don't know anyone who'd be good for this kind of thing, so I guess hitting the Internet is my only option."

An idea bloomed, and Rob held up a finger. "Maybe not. I've got a client who's a lawyer, and he's pretty good. I could call him up in the morning if you want."

Her half smile, wan, but honest, warmed him slightly. "Really? You don't mind?"

He shook his head. For her? He wasn't sure why, but he'd do more than a simple phone call. Hell, he already had. "Nope, don't mind at all. Tony's been a regular at the gym almost since we opened. I'm sure he could give some advice, even if he can't take the case."

The cell phone buzzed in his hand. He glanced at it. Unfamiliar number, but it looked like the ones from Charter Memorial. He looked back at Stacey. "I think this is the hospital. Sit down, okay?" He gestured to the bed and answered the call.

"Hello?"

"Rob Liston, please." The deep, almost brusque voice was easy to recognize.

"Dr. Calhoun, this is Rob." Rob sank down on the edge of the bed beside Stacey and put the phone on speaker. "I've got you on the speakerphone, and Stacey's right beside me."

"I'm glad you called back. This is definitely information that changes things. Do I have permission to speak about your care to Mr. Liston now, Miss Hough?"

"Yes," Stacey said, glancing over at Rob. He held the phone a little closer to her. The heat from her body kissed his arm, and he tried not to think about it. She was either nervous, or cold, because she shook, just a little. Putting his arm around her might be what he wanted to do, but he didn't, for her sake. No need to muddy the already-turbulent waters.

As Stacey recounted her fall and trip to the Hawaiian ER, Rob stayed silent. What was he doing here, really? As soon as she'd walked through those gym doors the other day, he'd been tied up in her, to the exclusion of all else. His gym, his paperwork, hell, he hadn't even called his dad back to grill him about the cardiologist appointment. What was it about this woman that drew him in, made him want to help her, protect her, hell, just be near her?

She was pretty, but not beautiful. She was funny, but too self-deprecating. She had drive, but she was fearful. All in all, it wasn't like she was perfect.

But neither was he.

He'd worked hard, but he did it to bury his feelings of inadequacy. He was pursuing his dream, but he was still fighting against his family's expectations. He had a life he loved, but he'd never met anyone he'd be willing to share it with long-term. Even Rebecca, whom everyone had thought was his perfect match, hadn't worked out.

Maybe that was why. Maybe somehow, this funny, sad, energetic, wounded woman matched up with the parts of him that were missing something. Maybe she'd been onto something when she'd flirted with him.

He liked her. Really liked her. Custard snorted at his feet, and he patted her hip to shush her.

"All in all, I think the prognosis is still pretty good. But I do recommend some further precautions. I want you under someone's supervision for the next couple of weeks. No driving. For the next three days you need to be awakened every four hours. Mr. Liston?"

"Yes," Rob said.

"She'll need to answer some questions for you, and make sure to check her pupils. You've got the discharge instructions with the warning signs. If you see any of those, she needs to come back in immediately. As it is, I do want to run another CT scan in a week to make sure there aren't any changes. I'll transfer you to the nurse for that appointment."

Rob thanked the doctor, then waited while the call was put on hold.

There was quiet between them in the room.

Two weeks. Another two weeks of Stacey in the house with him, of her constantly near him. The idea was a little bit like a giant dessert that he'd hate himself for eating. She tempted him, but was it really the best idea to pursue her, with her in such a vulnerable position?

Of course, she might run screaming to someone else's house. Two weeks was a long time. Her family might come down, or another of her friends might insist on putting her up.

"Two weeks?" She said it aloud, breaking the silence. "What am I going to do?"

He reached over and took her hand. "Don't worry—" he began, but the nurse picked up right then. Any more reassurance would have to wait.

Chapter 18

The ball *thump*ed against the hardwood floor, and Custard lazily trotted after it.

Stacey sighed as she watched the big brown dog set herself down on her plush doughnut-shaped bed and gnaw on the unsuspecting green tennis ball. The TV was on, some random reality show that Stacey hadn't really been watching. The clock on the mantle ticked lazily.

This was torture.

The vast majority of her normal life was spent at work, or thinking about work, or planning for what to do next at work. Her job was something she felt confident in, and she did it really well. But convalescing? Staring at the TV for hours on end, scrolling through Facebook, talking to the dog? This was stuff she didn't know how to handle.

Her brain was screaming for something positive to do, something productive. But all that was impossible for the moment.

For four days now she'd been trapped, for lack of a better term, in Rob's house. After that conversation with Dr. Calhoun, he'd been less of a paramour and more of a nurse/warden. He'd awakened her every four hours, as promised. He constantly checked her pupils. He asked her her name, what day it was, all the typical questions. She'd started answering them incorrectly just to get a rise out of him. His growls were fun, but his kisses were "funner."

Stacey sighed again. "Funner" wasn't a concept for her right now. All of that had gone right out the window. He hadn't so much as held her hand in the days since their afternoon encounter in his bed. She'd begun to believe that she'd dreamed it up.

After all, it was unbelievable on the surface. She wasn't the kind of girl that a man like Rob would pursue. It had been a one-off event—even though it had happened twice. She was sure of it now. He might have put her up in his bed, but he wasn't interested in her.

"Serves me right for wondering, doesn't it, girl?"

Custard thumped her tail at Stacey's question, a line of drool connecting her mouth with the ball between her front paws.

At least her leg wasn't broken, and she'd been cleared to walk on it now. Those crutches had been a literal pain.

The faint *thump* of a car door closing met Stacey's ears, and she glanced toward the front windows.

Rob. He was back from the grocery store. He opened the trunk and began loading bags onto his forearms.

Her stomach tightened as she watched the breadth of his shoulders shifting with his movements. He was such a pipe dream. She'd been insane ever to think something could really happen between them.

But he had invited her into his home. He'd taken care of her tirelessly over the past several days. Hell, he'd given up his bed for her. She frowned, picking at the edge of the throw pillow on her lap. He'd met Hannah at her apartment, watered her plants, picked up her clothes.

The sound of the key in the lock interrupted her mental list.

"Just me," Rob said as the front door swung inward. Stacey pressed the POWER button on the TV remote to kill the screen, sitting forward as she watched Rob set the grocery bags down on the floor of the foyer.

"Can I help?"

"No, I've got it. Just one more trip."

"I'll take those into the kitchen," she said, pushing off the couch to stand.

Rob frowned, the sunglasses covering his eyes making the expression more severe. It was fucking sexy. "Take it easy."

She rolled her eyes so hard she was afraid they'd pop out of her head. "I have been. This couch has a permanent groove from my ass. I need to get up and move a little bit. I'll be careful."

He hadn't been able to completely hide his amusement at her snark, but he just shook his head. "Do what you want." He turned and pulled the door shut behind him, not quite able to completely muffle his, "You were going to anyway."

Victory. She smiled to herself as she crossed the living room to the hallway.

Moving felt good now. She'd been stiff and sore for a few days, but now the pain was fading and her body was definitely craving some movement. She glanced longingly at the bedroom as she passed it on the way to the kitchen.

Well, since that kind of movement wasn't really an option right now, putting up groceries would have to do. On her return trip to the doctor, she'd put the kibosh on the idea of any sexual activity.

If she was lucky—and she hadn't been recently—she'd give Stacey the green light when she returned to the office later this afternoon.

Milk and eggs went into the fridge. Canned goods she lined up on the kitchen island, paper grocery bags folded neatly into a pile beside them. The front door squeaked open again.

"I got some more of that salad dressing you like," Rob said as he set the rest of the bags on the kitchen table. "Thought a spinach salad would be good with the salmon tonight." He turned, and she had a hard time pulling her gaze away from his muscular ass.

"Sounds nice," Stacey said as she opened the cabinet where Rob kept his spices.

Her heart tripped over itself. This felt—weird. *Good* weird, but weird. She hadn't had this kind of interaction in a long time. It was almost like they were dating.

The pepper box she'd been putting away slipped out of her nerveless fingers and hit the floor with a sharp *thunk*.

"Hey, you okay?"

Rob was suddenly there, taking her hand, looking down straight into her eyes. The steely gray wrapped around her and pulled her close. He wasn't concerned about what she'd dropped; he was concerned about her.

Damn him to hell and back.

She jerked her fingers away and bent down quickly to scoop up the pepper box. "Yeah, I'm just klutzy today." Turning her back to him, she busied herself with the spices in the cabinet.

Why was she doing this to herself? Why did he have to be so goddamn chivalrous all the fucking time? It was screwing with her head big-time.

"If you're not feeling well, you need to tell me."

"I'm fine," she said, her voice coming out much more shrill than she would have liked. She tossed a quick smile over her shoulder at him as she moved toward the table and the other bags. "Just glad to be able to have something to do."

He took a step toward her, but then an insistent chime came from his pocket. She watched as he pulled his cell free from his jacket and frowned at the screen.

"Sorry, I've got to take this."

He moved from the kitchen as his finger swiped across the screen. "Hello?"

His footsteps faded down the hall, and a door *click*ed closed behind him.

Sinking into a kitchen chair, Stacey cradled her head in her hands. A slight pounding behind her temples was the only indication that her head had had a bad month.

She had to get out of here. If the lust didn't get her, his kindness would surely do her in. It was too much for any woman to resist. And she was so, so weak where he was concerned.

Resisting him would take much more strength than she had.

The guest room door closed behind Rob before he was able to get a word in edgewise.

"Mom, slow down. What's wrong?"

"Robbie, he's not listening to me. He's all out of breath, and he's swelling in his legs, and I want him to go to the hospital."

Rob tensed, his hand gripping the phone tighter. He hadn't wanted to leave Stacey right then, but he'd only considered letting the call roll to voice mail for a split second. He'd made the right decision. "How long has this been going on?"

"Since early this morning. He didn't sleep well, went out onto the couch in the middle of the night. But he wouldn't come to breakfast, even though I made his favorite omelet. Then he admitted he wasn't feeling well, but he won't let me call anyone."

Fuck. Rob jammed a hand through his hair as he paced the floor. "Give him the phone, Mom."

"Please make him listen," his mother pleaded.

"What is it?"

Richard Liston's voice was gruff, but it had less *oomph* than usual.

"What are your symptoms?"

"Why should I tell you? You're not a doctor."

"No, I'm not. But I can bench-press twice your weight, and if you keep upsetting my mom like this, I just might have to come up there and pound some sense into you."

The begrudging laugh was encouraging. "It's not as big of a deal as she's making it out to be, son. I'm just a little tired today."

"And short of breath. And swelling."

The admiration in his answer was easy to hear. "She's not a bad clinician, your mother."

Rob smiled halfheartedly. "You should know that. You taught her. Now, come on, I have a lot going on here. As much as I would love to run up there and kick your ass into going to see your cardiologist, it would really be helpful if you would promise to go on your own."

"Don't talk to your father like that. I wiped your ass before you were even old enough to know you had a father. I know when I need to see a doctor, and it isn't now."

Irritation and worry twined together in Rob's chest, making it hard to breathe evenly. He closed his eyes for a moment. Calm. He couldn't let himself get riled up. His father was just as stubborn as Rob himself, and they had clashed enough times for Rob to know what worked and what didn't where his father was concerned.

"I will call 911 myself if you do not promise to go or at least call your cardiologist. Mom wouldn't have called me for no reason, and I will get this done if you don't agree."

The sigh that came through the line was one of irritated defeat. "Don't call those EMS bastards. I can get wherever I need to go on my own with your mother's help."

"So, you'll go somewhere?"

"Yes, you stubborn jackass. It's not a big deal, I know exactly what it is."

"Then, what is it?"

A muffled sound happened then, as if his father was adjusting the phone. "My cardiologist and I have been discussing it. It's nothing new, and it's being managed."

Rob lost the tenuous grip he'd had on his temper. "For fuck's sake, Richard, just tell me you'll see the goddamn doctor."

"Fine." The answer was snapped in equal temper. "I promise, you happy now?"

Rob nodded, even though his gesture couldn't be seen over the phone. "Perfectly. Let me talk to Mom."

Rob sank down on the edge of the bed as the sound of the phone being passed met his ears.

His mother's voice was slightly shaky. "Robbie?"

"He promised he would go somewhere, or at least call someone. Let me know if he doesn't."

Her voice was slightly hushed. "Are you sure he will? I hate to ask you, Robbie, but if you could come up here and convince him in person . . ."

"I would feel better if I could, but there is a lot going on here right now. He'll do what he needs to do, and if he doesn't, let me know. We'll go from there."

As if on cue, a *beep* came through the phone, and Rob pulled the screen away and glanced at it. The gym. Of course. "Mom, I need to go. But promise me you'll let me know if he doesn't call someone within the next hour or so. I'll do what I have to do to make sure he gets taken care of."

"Thank you, Robbie. I love you."

"I love you too, Mom. Go take care of him, and take care of yourself too."

Rob pressed the button to switch calls, and rubbed a hand across his abdomen. "Robert Liston."

"Rob? It's Brandi. I really hate to bug you, I know you said you're busy, but we've got kind of a situation developing here."

A scratch at the door signaled that Custard wanted to join him, but Rob ignored it. Could anything else fall apart at the moment?

"What's going on?"

"Well, you know that new Krav Maga teacher we hired? I think one of the students said something to him that made him angry. And there was kind of an altercation, and now the cops are coming, and I—"

"Shit. Okay, I'm on the way. Hold down the fort until I get there. Christ, I'm sorry this happened."

The relief was evident in Brandi's quick answer. "Yup, on it. Thanks. Sorry to bug you."

"No, thank *you* for taking care of everything while I'm away. I should've vetted that guy better. His résumé looked so good that I didn't call everyone on it, just the first reference on the list. My laziness is biting me in the ass now."

As the call ended, Rob surged to his feet. There was way too much going on. This was the absolute worst time for him to become tangled up with Stacey. But he couldn't help himself.

He pulled open the door and strode down the hall. Every time he laid eyes on her, he was reminded of not only the incredible way she felt against his body, but the way she had taken each challenge thrown her way. He couldn't help but admire her, and he wanted to inspire greater confidence in her. Also, he couldn't wait for her to be cleared medically so he could yank those pants off of her one more time. Keeping her at arm's length had been almost impossible, but after that one interlude, he couldn't afford the temptation of kissing her again. Not until it was safe to take things as far as he wanted to take them.

Stacey was seated at the kitchen table, her cheek resting on her palm as she stared down at her smartphone screen.

He shouldn't. She really needed to stay here and rest. But he didn't know how long this was going to take, and having her with him would ease his worry about her.

He held his keys up in the air. "Hey, Stacey, want to come with me? There's some shit going down at the gym, and I have to take care of it. We should be done well before your doctor's appointment."

She glanced up at him with a wan smile. "Really? The jailer is letting me out of my cell? What, am I being let out on good behavior?"

Rob shrugged. "You don't have to come if you don't want to. I can come back and pick you up afterward."

She jumped out of the chair faster than she should have, and winced as her bad leg bore too much weight. "Oh, I want to. Just try to stop me now."

He laughed as she hobbled quickly down the hallway. At least she didn't need the crutches anymore. It was a lot easier to check out her ass without the distraction.

Things might be going to hell in a handbasket, but at least there was Stacey to share the ride with him.

Chapter 19

Rob explained the problem on the way to the gym. Stacey gripped the armrest as he wove expertly through traffic. He was a good driver, but the thick of the Atlanta rush hour meant there was much more traffic than she was comfortable with so soon after her recent traumatic experience on the road. Her knuckles were only a little pale, though, and her stomach had tensed only halfway.

"So, this teacher hauled off and hit a student?"

"As far as I understand it, yeah." Rob checked his mirrors before hitting his turn signal and easing into the left lane. "Brandi didn't have time to get me the details. This Flowers guy came highly recommended, and I know the guy he used to teach for. I just don't understand how he could have lost his cool like that."

"It sucks," Stacey agreed as he took the exit off the highway. "I hope the gym doesn't suffer because of it."

Rob sighed as he stopped at the end of the ramp, waiting for the traffic to clear so he could turn. "We've got enough problems without this happening."

"What do you mean?"

He shot a quick glance her way before easing off the brakes. "I shouldn't bother you with it. Not when you've got so much stuff of your own going on."

She didn't deny it. "My project is on hold, yeah. It's ready to go, but unless the city council gives me the green light, I can't do much of anything but twiddle my thumbs. Dr. Colt won't release me back to work for another week and a half. I'm going insane without my job to keep me occupied. So, help me out and distract me. Tell me about your problems."

"Sounds kind of tough to be away from something you're so passionate about." He evaded her question.

His unwillingness to talk stung a little, but she brushed it off. "It is. But my CT scan was clear, the awesome lawyer you found for me is convinced that this case won't ever make it to trial, and my bruises are turning a beautiful shade of mustard yellow now. Oh, and I've got the sexiest nurse this side of the Mississippi. Yup, things are pretty hellish for me at the moment."

As a move, it wasn't particularly bold, but damn if it hadn't taken all the guts she had to lay it out there for him. She was rewarded by a crooked smile as Rob pulled into the parking deck near the gym.

"You think I'm sexy, huh?"

"You fishing now?"

"Depends," he said, pulling his keys from the ignition. He slid the sunglasses up, revealing the amusement in his gray eyes. "Are you the bait?"

Jesus Lord. Her stomach flipped as she daringly leaned toward him. "I'd like to be."

Her heart thumped so hard against her ribs she was afraid he could hear it. Her tongue darted out to wet her lips and she held her breath, praying, hoping, waiting for him to close that gap between them and brush her lips with his own.

But just then, a cop car pulled to a stop across the street, its red and blue lights flashing against the building.

Rob moved back, and Stacey's sense of loss was palpable.

"To be continued," Rob said as he opened the door.

"It better be," Stacey said under her breath as she pushed her own open.

Rob moved much more quickly than Stacey could with her bruised leg. He came back to walk with her, but she waved him toward the doors.

"Go, I'm fine. Promise."

He frowned, but walked quickly toward the entrance anyway, leaving her to follow.

When Stacey pushed through the front doors, the sight that greeted her was definitely tense.

Rob was standing in front of the counter, toe-to-toe with a guy at least four inches shorter, fifteen years older, and thirty pounds heavier than him. The man was red-faced, his gray-streaked hair frazzling around his head as he gesticulated wildly. "Come on, man. How do you expect me to do my job if you don't respect my methods? That kind of attitude doesn't belong in my class, and I won't tolerate it!"

"I don't give two shits what kind of attitude he gave you. You do not ever—*ever*—lay a hand on a client of this gym. And the fact that you have means that you are no longer employed here. So get your shit, and get out, and do not ever come back." Rob's voice was as cold as liquid nitrogen and stronger than steel. Stacey shivered a little as she sank into one of the chairs by the smoothie bar, glad it wasn't her that he was mad at.

There was a police officer talking to a young guy in a sleeveless shirt and basketball shorts, along with Brandi, the woman who was supposed to have been Stacey's trainer. She couldn't quite make out what they were saying, but there were obvious red marks on the guy's arm. Shit. Had the teacher done that?

Another cop entered the building then, and he pulled Rob and the angry teacher aside. A small group of people were gathered outside the front glass windows. Stacey watched the scene unfolding with a sickening feeling in her stomach.

This wasn't good. No wonder Rob had been so cagey about it. The gym hadn't been here that long, and this kind of thing wouldn't exactly endear it to the neighborhood. A business's reputation could get made or broken so easily.

She pulled her purse into her lap and looked down at it, tracing the curved edge with her finger. She'd been so preoccupied with getting back to work, to her projects, that she hadn't considered what Rob was doing about his time off work. Was this partly her fault? Rob had taken off so much time to be with her, to watch her, to nurse her back to health. Hell, he hadn't even asked her for a dime. She'd offered to chip in for groceries, for takeout, but he'd insisted on doing it all. How was she supposed to feel about all of this? His business needed him, and all she could do was think about her own shit.

A sound from the people outside drew her attention, and she examined the crowd with a critical eye.

Maybe there *was* something she could do.

Rob lifted his hands in the air, and stepped back several paces as Dylan Flowers, the Krav Maga instructor, lunged for him. The man was beyond all reasoning, and had started screaming after Rob had informed him for the fifth time that he was fired.

"Settle down, or I'll put the cuffs on you right now." The officer stepped between them, his hand splayed as he warned Dylan off. "I need information, and I need it now. Who is in charge here?"

"I am. I'm Robert Liston. This is my gym, I'm the owner."

The officer pulled a small notebook from his upper pocket and flipped it open. "Can you spell that for me, sir?"

Rob nodded. "Liston. *L . . . I . . .*"

Something out of the corner of his eye caught his attention, and he turned his head to see as he continued spelling. Stacey. She was outside, and the small crowd of lookie-loos were gathered around her as she spoke. She was making large, sweeping gestures, and though her back was to him, he could almost see how animated her features were. What the hell was she up to out there?

"Mr. Liston, I'm going to need more information from you later. For now, I need to talk with this gentleman here. Is there somewhere quiet we could go?"

Rob tore his gaze away from Stacey's antics, and nodded. "There's a classroom right here off the hallway on the left side. You're welcome to use that for as long as you need it."

The officer nodded, and escorted Dylan away from the milling onlookers at the front of the gym.

Standing alone for a moment, Rob took a deep breath to ease his frustration. There was no one working out now; everyone who wasn't standing around waiting for more sparks to fly had already gathered their things and left. The machines were empty, with the exception of one lonely ambler on a treadmill in the corner, whose headphones were on; he seemed not to care if the roof was falling down around him.

Healthy Living did not need this. They were just starting to make some strides, to get membership numbers up where they needed them to be. If this little incident cost him his business, he would be sorely tempted to murder Dylan Flowers. The teacher hadn't even had a good reason to go after the student. All the student had done was to mention how one of the moves Flowers had modeled looked like a sexual position. It was a harmless joke, and Dylan had taken it completely wrong and then tried to throttle the guy.

Rob shook out hands that he just now realized had been curled into fists. A *buzz* in his pocket distracted him momentarily, and he pulled his phone free.

At the cardiologist's office now. Thank you, Robbie.
Will keep you posted.

The text from his mother was a welcome relief, at least. He didn't have to worry about his dad for the moment. One issue off his plate, and the cops had Mr. Flowers's anger management issues in hand. Just one more thing to worry about: Stacey.

He turned on his heel and walked out the door, just in time to hear someone ask Stacey, "So, the whole thing is a police exercise?"

Stacey nodded, her smile bright. Rob's melancholy began to lift. Hell, that was an incredible idea. It might even work.

"Yes, in coordination with the Atlanta Police Department, the city planning department has implemented a strategy planning session with local businesses. To help them respond to an emergency, we've got actors and other professionals in to help employers prep their staff for incidents that can pop up." She turned and saw Rob standing there, and grabbed his arm. "Rob, I mean, Mr. Liston here, agreed to be our first 'guinea pig,' and he's quite pleased with how his staff has handled this little exercise. Aren't you, Mr. Liston?"

She pegged him with a stare. The message was clear in Stacey's brilliant blue eyes. *Lie. Lie your ass off, and you might just get out of this unscathed.*

"Yes, it has been a really enlightening event. My staff has handled the exercise with aplomb, and they will each be receiving great feedback on their performances. They responded to the threat with calm and clear heads."

A woman at the back of the crowd, who had been looking through the front windows while Rob was speaking, piped up with the question, "Do you guys do Pilates here?"

The relief that blanketed his shoulders nearly caused his knees to buckle, it was that strong. He shook off the feeling and pinned on his most pleasant expression. "Yes, we offer yoga, Pilates, and several other classes here, including some MMA classes."

He mentally crossed Krav Maga off the list. It had been hard enough to find Dylan Flowers, and it would be a long time before he trusted himself enough to hire another teacher for that particular class. Too bad, because the Krav Maga class had had one of the higher initial enrollments.

"How much does it cost to join? This is a really nice place."

"I like how they're so prepared for an emergency. I mean, I work at a gun store, and we've never had any kind of training like that. It would be helpful, with some of the crazies we get in there."

Rob fielded each question, his incredulousness and relief growing with each one. This whole disastrous situation had just turned into the best membership drive he had ever had. He glanced over at Stacey, whose calm expression fed his ever-growing gratitude toward her.

She was incredible. He had just wanted to keep her close, so he could keep an eye on her, protect her, and what had she done? She had protected *him*. She had done her best to save his business while he was in there trying to keep from killing the idiot who'd started this mess. He owed her big-time.

"Yes, once the exercise is over, we will be more than ready to accept applications. As a matter of fact, I'll gather up some information packets for each of you who are interested and you can bring them by later once you've filled out the forms. Thank you."

Stacey hobbled inside, and Rob followed. As he gathered up new member information packets, he nodded toward the bank of tables by the smoothie bar.

"Thanks for that. Now, please sit down, you need to rest some. You've done an amazing job, you've earned a break."

Stacey's smile wrapped around his heart and tugged. "I just wanted to help a little bit."

"You helped a lot. Now, go and sit. I need to finish this dog and pony show before we lose our audience."

Rob returned to the thinned-out crowd, and handed out packets to the prospective new clients. And as he returned, and saw Stacey with her back toward him, he had to fight the urge to wrap his arms around her.

Weird. Who would have thought?

Chapter 20

Stacey's legs dangled off the edge of the doctor's table, and she took a deep, steadying breath.

Rob had offered to come back into the examination room with her, but she'd shaken her head with a smile and a word of thanks. He'd been extra-sweet to her since she'd taken over the crowd control at the gym. Tender, even, as he put a hand at the small of her back to help her to the parking deck, pushing a lock of hair back over her shoulder as they talked in his car.

She wished he wouldn't do that. It was becoming very hard to keep the idea that they were just friends at the forefront of her mind.

The paper beneath her crinkled as she shifted her weight and crossed her ankles. Hey, it didn't hurt as badly now. The swelling and bruising in her leg was improving every day, and her limp was diminishing too.

She couldn't have Rob back here with her. One of the questions she had would have been much too embarrassing to ask in front of him.

A brisk knock at the door made her turn, but the doctor was inside before Stacey had a chance to answer.

"Hi, Stacey," the bright, blond woman said with a smile. Her white coat billowed out behind her as she breezed into the room, heels clicking on the industrial-tiled floor. "How are you feeling?"

"Better than I was, Dr. Colt," Stacey said. "The headaches are much less now, and I haven't had any double vision or anything."

"Excellent," Dr. Colt said as she typed on the small laptop she'd set on the flip-down desk.

Her examination was quick and thorough. Stacey opened her eyes when told, looking straight ahead as the doctor shined a bright light beside them. Turning her head this way and that, looking up and down, answering questions, it was a familiar routine at this point. She'd seen Dr. Colt three times now.

When she was done, Dr. Colt sat on the rolling stool once more. "You can stop waking up during the night for checks now as long as you don't have any worsening symptoms. You can gradually start adding more normal activities to a day, but keep it very limited, and make sure you're always supervised. Do you have any questions for me?"

Stacey took a deep, steadying breath. Time for her questions.

"When can I go back to my apartment? I'm staying with a friend, for now, because his place is one level and due to the whole supervision stuff."

"I'd recommend you have someone around for the bulk of the day for the next week to ten days. Sometimes these things take a while to really show if you're going to have problems, so while I'm encouraged by your progress, I wouldn't rush into staying on your own just yet. Think of it as a vacation if you can."

"Okay. And driving? Work?"

"Same. Give it another ten days or so. I'll clear you for driving at your next appointment if you're still improving. And from what you've told me, your job can be high-stress at times, and the last thing we want to do is derail your recovery."

Deep breath. One last question. She fought the urge to squeeze her eyes shut as she spoke. She could do this—it wasn't a big deal.

"And . . . sex?"

Dr. Colt didn't even bat an eye. "Sexual activity is no problem, as long as you don't bang your head against a wall. Keep it low-key for the next week or two, no swinging from the rafters."

Stacey's relief was huge. "Thanks."

With orders to return in two weeks, Stacey was set free. She walked tall—well, limped a bit—to the checkout desk.

Rob was there waiting for her at the door.

"All clear?"

"I don't have to come back for two weeks."

"Well, that's good news," he said as he followed her outside. "Anything else?"

"You're still stuck with me, unless you'll let me relocate to Hannah's house."

"Not a chance," Rob said as he opened the car door for her. "I need to repay you for that incredible stunt at the gym. I owe you big-time."

"No, I owe you for putting me up and taking care of me for the last week."

"You took care of that and more with the way you saved my bacon today. Come on, let's go get dinner. My treat."

It had been his treat for days now, but she'd learned that arguing with him really didn't get her anywhere. Stacey just shook her head and buckled her seat belt securely.

The late afternoon sun was weak in the western sky, falling quickly this time of year. She missed the sun, but the person sitting to her left did a lot to ease her winter blues.

Dinner was at a Japanese restaurant that Rob recommended. It was delicious. He had sushi, and she had udon noodle soup. Rob told her more about the teacher who had caused the incident at Healthy Living. Apparently Rob had discovered that the guy had been let go from one of his former positions because of anger management issues, but he'd managed to keep his nose clean for the last few years. Too bad for Rob, and for the gym, Flowers's rein on his temper had frayed through at the wrong moment.

"I feel like dessert tonight, what do you say?"

Stacey looked down at her bowl, which was mostly empty. "I don't ever turn down dessert. Of course, I should probably say no, but since the whole training thing is down the crapper at this point, why not?"

Rob frowned, lowering the dessert menu. "What do you mean?"

"Just that I've got no idea when I'll feel up to returning to the gym. I'd barely gotten started when all this happened, and now?" She shrugged, laying her spoon down on the white tablecloth beside her bowl. "Just seems pointless to even think about continuing."

"It's never pointless to invest time and energy into bettering yourself."

"That sounds like a commercial."

"It's not a commercial; it's what I truly believe. You had made a commitment to getting healthy, to taking control of your life. Why stop?"

"Why continue? It's more than I can focus on right now. Hell, right now I can't even think about my job, let alone how many miles I could walk on the treadmill whenever walking doesn't hurt like hell." Her chest was getting tight, and her skin felt prickly and hot.

Rob stared at her, the softness in his gray eyes going steely. "You're going to let this knock you down, aren't you? You've already made up your mind that this means you've failed."

"No, I haven't! It's just too hard, Rob." Her fingers curled into her palm, and her tone climbed higher. "I can't go to work, I can't drive, why should I keep chasing the idea of getting my weight under control?"

"If that's all you think your training was about—your weight—then I've failed you utterly." Rob slid his wallet from his pocket and plucked some cash free as the waitress arrived at their table side. "Here, I don't need any change. Thank you."

The waitress accepted it with a smile and thanked them as Rob rose. "You ready?"

Feeling like she'd somehow ruined what had been a very good day, Stacey stood. Damn it, why should she feel guilty? Everything *had* fallen apart! And he was mad because she didn't want to keep throwing herself at the brick wall of change?

Well, screw him.

And, as she watched his gorgeous ass move as he pushed the door open for her, she sighed. She wished she *could* screw him. But despite what the doctor had said, it was probably not happening.

Damn it.

Rob kept silent on the way home from the restaurant. Stacey, beside him, didn't say much of anything, either.

It wasn't for lack of things to say. There was plenty he wanted to say to her. But what right did he have to chastise her for falling off the wagon after the traumatic experience she'd just had? He'd probably screwed that up royally. He should have been more understanding, more gentle with her. But when she'd said she didn't even want to try? All he'd heard was that he'd failed her, and that fact pissed him off.

Stacey deserved to be healthy and happy, and proud of herself. And the fact that this had knocked her confidence back further, and that he had done nothing to stop the slide?

God, it made him want to punch something. Normally, feeling this way, he would work out his frustrations on the heavy bag in the gym, or by running an extra five miles. But as it was? He'd have to settle for sit-ups in his guest room with Custard looking on. If Custard would leave Stacey's side long enough, that was. Even his damn dog wasn't on his side.

As the car drifted onto the off-ramp, Stacey finally broke the silence.

"Listen, I'm sorry if I pissed you off back there. I just don't see how I can keep working out with all of this going on."

Rob dragged a deep breath in through his nostrils as he flipped on his turn signal. "You don't need to work out with all of this going on. I wouldn't let you even if you wanted to right now."

"Then why are you so pissed? This makes no sense at all."

He shook his head. They needed to have a long discussion, and at the moment, he wasn't exactly in the best frame of mind to lay his points out like he needed to. This was important, and he needed to get it right. He needed to think it through before having a talk with her.

"Stacey, let's talk about this in the morning. It's getting late."

She stared pointedly at the dash as he cut the engine in front of his house. "It's quarter to nine."

The winter wind howled as he pushed open the door, the cold breeze swirling into what had been a pretty warm interior. He caught her shiver in the corner of his eye, and felt like a bastard. Again. Damn it, how could he possibly keep making her feel bad? That was the last thing he wanted to do. Hell, she'd stuck her neck out to save the gym today. She was his client; her health was his responsibility to an extent. He owed her an explanation, even if it wasn't the perfect one he needed it to be.

Hustling around the car, he caught the passenger door before the wicked wind could knock it into her as she exited the car.

"Thanks," she said, catching her hair in her fingertips and pushing it away from her face. Her cheeks and nose were getting redder from the cold by the second.

"Come on, let's get inside," he said, reaching out and grabbing her hand without a second thought. Her cold fingers curled into his and he led her toward his house.

It felt good to hold her hand. He didn't let go as he put the key into the lock. When the door had shut behind them, and Custard had wagged and kissed her way around them, Rob finally relented and let go of her hand.

His felt cold and empty when her fingers fell away.

"Come with me," he said, and turned to walk into the living room. He didn't wait to see if she'd follow, just bent down in front of the fireplace to switch the knob on his gas logs to ON. The pilot light clicked, and blue fingers of flame ran across them. The dancing flickers of fire chased a bit of the chill from his bones, and he held his hands out toward the welcoming heat as uneven footfalls announced Stacey's entrance into the room.

He smiled, since his back was to her, and she couldn't see. Amazing how the simplest action from her could make him happy.

"What is it?"

Turning then, he took in the sight of her.

She'd removed her jacket, and was leaning slightly against the doorjamb. Her gray top and black pants accentuated the brightness of her hair and her wind-reddened cheeks. Her arms were folded across her middle, and she looked down and to the side, as if she was unwilling—or unable—to meet his gaze.

She looked uncomfortable. Sad. He had done that, and he was a bastard.

"Can you forgive me?"

His question seemed to startle her out of her funk. Her arms fell, and her wide blue gaze was directed straight at him. "What?"

"I was a dick to you. In the restaurant, and all the way home. I shouldn't have pressured you or made you feel inadequate, but I did, and I'm man enough to admit that I was a total fuckhead. Can you forgive me?"

She smiled a little, bemused, but no less beautiful for the confusion. "I forgive you. Thanks for the apology."

With a motion, he invited her to sit on the couch. When she did, he sank down beside her and covered her hands with his.

"This definitely is a setback. I know you've got some recovering to do, physically, emotionally, and mentally. What I should have said in the restaurant was that I understand you've got some more things to overcome, and that I'm ready, willing, and able to help you through these additional challenges. This doesn't have to be the end of this journey for you, if you don't want it to be. You had made a commitment to like yourself, Stacey. And the thought of you giving up on that? It made me angry."

"Angry?" Her echo was questioning.

He nodded, keeping his gaze trained directly on her eyes. "I was so angry at the thought of you never seeing the woman I see when I look at you."

She trembled slightly, and he tightened his grip on her hands to steady her. Her lips parted, her pink tongue darting out to wet them. "And who do you see when you look at me?"

His body warmed, and it had nothing to do with the fire cheerfully casting shadows on Custard's blanket just in front of the fireplace. "I see a woman who's strong, who's capable, and who doesn't understand how intensely beautiful and desirable she is."

Her eyelids fluttered closed. "You—see that in me?"

Instead of words, he let his kiss be the answer.

Chapter 21

Stacey didn't know what was happening. She'd been so mad at him, he'd been such a standoffish prick in the car, but then he'd delivered the most sincerely sweet apology she'd ever heard, and now his mouth was on hers.

His tongue swirled against her lips sweetly, beseeching, and she couldn't help but part her lips to him. He breached her defenses with such sensuous fervor that she had no way to resist.

She didn't want to resist.

Leaning into his kiss, she sighed, winding her arms around his neck. He was so warm, so big, so strong as he gently pressed her back into the cushions of the sofa. He teased her tongue, her lips, her teeth, his kiss at once strong and so sweet it made her want to weep. Her blood heated, her body rising to meet him as her skin prickled with fire.

He deepened the kiss, and she opened further, her tongue meeting his as his hands began to roam her body. Finally, she wanted to breathe as his fingers quested across her collarbone to brush the tops of her breasts. She'd dreamed of this for days, had longed for it. In the shower she'd closed her eyes and imagined that they were together, the soap cascading down their bodies, him pressing her against the cold tiles as the hot water rushed over their nakedness. Her nipples peaked, tight and tingling, as the backs of his knuckles brushed over them.

More. She wanted so much more.

He lifted his head, brushing light kisses over her cheeks, her chin, even her nose as she wrinkled it in a smile.

"Stacey," he whispered against her throat, the sensation sending goose bumps trailing in the wake of his breath, "I have to stop this."

"No, you don't," she whispered back, lifting her hips as his hand brushed the front of her jeans.

"You're not recovered yet. I can't take the chance of hurting you. I've kicked myself so many times for what we did days ago, I can't take that chance again." He nibbled the delicate skin of her neck, and she shuddered.

"The doctor said it was okay."

He lifted his head, and she almost wept from the loss. "What?"

Now it was her turn to befuddle him. "You heard me. The doctor said it was okay."

His grin, when it came, was almost wolfish. "That Dr. Colt is my favorite person in the world right now."

"Mine too."

He kissed her heartily then, and she clung to him. He ravaged her mouth with all the pent-up hunger she herself had been feeling over the past several days. It had been torture having him so close without indulging the desires he stirred inside her. She had been unbelievably tempted every time he walked by, and it had seemed so unfair that he could be near her without having to struggle through similar feelings.

It seemed life was a bit fair after all.

He kissed his way down her neck, and her head fell to the back of the couch to give him access. More. She wanted him all over her, everywhere. She wanted to kiss him, too, make her way down from where the dark stubble was just beginning to show on his strong jaw to his broad shoulders, kissing and nibbling on his tanned skin. To rip his long-sleeved tee away and reveal every bit of his toned, taut body. To watch how the firelight danced across his muscles and let her itching fingertips bump across the 3-D landscape in front of them.

But her fervid imaginings disappeared as he grasped the hem of her shirt and began to lift.

"No," she gasped, yanking the hem of her shirt down.

He froze in place, not moving as she scrambled backward.

"What's wrong?"

Her heartbeat was in triple time, and it was hard to breathe with how quickly it was moving.

"Sorry," she said, her knuckles turning white as she gripped the hem tighter. "Just . . . let's move to the bedroom, okay?"

"Stacey, what happened? Talk to me."

How could she? How could she possibly tell him that she was embarrassed to let him see her in the light? That, despite the fact that he'd been so kind and wonderful and sexy as fucking hell to her, that she was terrified he would be disgusted at her body?

She couldn't ruin this. Not by telling him the truth about her fears and not by letting him see.

"We can stay here," she said, glancing around the room. "But the lights have to be off."

Rob wasn't a man. He was an angel. He closed his eyes for a moment, but he didn't say a word. Just rose and crossed to the lamp at the end of the couch and switched it off.

Stacey looked around the room. Light from the hallway was spilling through the doorway. The firelight was flickering across the floor. It wasn't pitch-black in there like she wanted it to be.

"Is that better?"

Better? Yes. Enough? She bit her lip.

"It's fine, but can you turn off the hall light when you go get a condom?"

Rob frowned. It wasn't dark enough to hide his reaction from her, and that was exactly the thing she was afraid of.

She shook her head. No, this was all wrong. She was all wrong. How could she still be doing this? Rob was too good for her.

"I'm sorry. I—I'm sorry." She stood and began to limp past him out of the room, but he caught her arm.

"Don't go," he said, pulling her into his arms. She fought his grip for a hot second, but then melted into him. How could she not? He was breathing against her hair, his broad, warm hands rubbing her back.

"Don't run away from me, Stacey."

She closed her eyes and buried her face in his strong chest. He'd taken such good care of her. All she wanted was to be the kind of girl who deserved someone like Rob. But for now, all she could do was pretend. Was that enough?

"Let's go to the bedroom," he said, lacing his fingers through hers. He shifted his hips forward, and she caught her lip between her teeth as his erection pressed against her belly. "You're beautiful, and I want you."

She wanted him, too, so she led him to the comforting darkness of the bedroom.

He wasn't stupid. It was patently obvious why she wanted the lights off.

She was embarrassed. He understood her reluctance. After all, she hadn't come to the gym because she was super-happy about how she looked. This whole relationship—well, situation—wasn't exactly normal. She didn't know how to react. Despite the fact that he'd done everything he could think of to make sure she was happy and comfortable with him, she still had some walls up.

That was okay. He could tear them down, brick by brick. He was patient.

When the bedroom door *click*ed shut behind them, Rob reached over and flipped the light switch on.

"What are you doing?" Stacey turned and looked at him.

"Just give me a second," he said, moving to the bedside table. He slid the drawer open and removed a condom and some water-based lubricant. She sank down on the edge of the bed as he reached for the hem of his shirt.

She stayed quiet as he pulled off his shirt. His skin prickled with the cool air of his bedroom. Then his hands went to his belt.

Her nostrils flared and she shifted her weight, moving her hands beneath the crooks of her knees. She wet her lips slowly as he drew the end of the belt through the metal buckle.

Rob moved slowly, deliberately. He wanted her to take this in, memorize his every movement. He wanted her gazes, her reactions, hell, he wanted her to help. And eventually, he wanted her to do this for him. He'd witness her confident striptease one day. It was inevitable in his mind. No matter what happened between them, whether or not this was a few weeks of heaven or something more long lasting, it was a goal of his that Stacey gain the confidence to let him see her nude.

And Rob always reached his goals.

The jeans fell away, and he laid them in a neatly folded square on the foot of the bed. His socks followed. When he stood in front of her with nothing but his form-fitting black Calvins on, he was pleased to note that her gaze was glued firmly to the front of his briefs. He gave a half smile.

"Like what you see?"

"Yes," she said, her cheeks coloring, but she didn't look away. His cock hardened further under her perusal, straining the elastic. His body grew warm, his need to strip her down and touch her growing apace with his erection. But he wasn't quite finished.

"Want to see more?"

She nodded, her white teeth catching her lower lip.

Hooking his thumb beneath the waistband of his briefs, he began to drag them downward, revealing the base of his cock, nestled in neatly trimmed hair. She made a half-strangled sound deep in her throat, her hips twisting a little. The devil sitting on his shoulder urged him on, and he pulled the waistband a little lower, just enough to give her a glimpse of his turgid shaft.

Her eyes were bluer now, as if the desire he was stoking inside her was affecting her in ways she couldn't control. It was only fair. She'd been driving him crazy with lust for days now, by doing nothing other than being herself. Now it was his turn.

"Wait here," he said, then turned and walked across the room. He reached for the light switch, but glanced over his shoulder before he hit it.

She was staring at his ass as if he were a steak and she was a starving woman.

Oh well. Memorable lessons were sometimes painful.

The room was plunged into darkness as soon as he flipped the switch.

He waited there, one heartbeat, two.

"Your timing sucks balls," Stacey said, her voice a bit husky.

"Hmm, it might," he agreed, shucking his briefs and tossing them aside. "But the question is, did you change your mind? Want me to turn the light back on?"

"Yes . . ." she said, the word trailing off. He waited. She sighed. "No."

He was patient. He could wait. It would happen.

"Then close your eyes and feel instead."

He knelt on the bed beside her, pushing her back onto the plush comforter. She went willingly, her arms reaching up and playing across his shoulders and back.

Her touch felt so good. *She* was so good. Stacey, soft, willing, eager, and beautiful. If only he could help her see herself the way he did.

He kissed her, and together they rolled toward the center of the bed, Stacey lying halfway on top of him. She tried to lift herself away while maintaining the kiss, but he stopped her. She had to get out of her own way. It was the only way they would both enjoy this the way it should be enjoyed.

His hands wandered beneath her top, and she sighed in surrender. Her skin was so hot, so soft. Her bra's catch fell away beneath his fingers, and their kiss stopped long enough for the offending garments to be tossed away.

Rob rose onto his knees and felt his way down her body. From her beautiful breasts down to her waist, which flared to her generous hips. Every bit of her skin was precious, delicious, and made him hunger for her. She fit against him, her height, her softness, all of it designed to perfectly contrast and complement him.

When he wasn't out of his mind with lust, he'd have to examine the idea, but for now, it was more complex than he could manage. All he could think about was removing the last barriers between them and feeling her body against his.

His fingers delved beneath her waistband, and she lifted her hips for him. Her pants and underwear slid down her legs, and he tossed them aside, all the while thinking about the way her skin felt. His hands couldn't get enough of her. His mouth following soon after, he rained his kisses over every patch of available skin.

She tried to pull away when he kissed the fleshy part of her hip. The soft rise of her belly. The sweetly dimpled patch on her outer thigh. He wasn't having any of it. Why couldn't she see that every square centimeter of her was beautiful to him?

"Rob," she said as he pressed his lips to her inner thigh.

"Yes?" He blew a breath over her labia, gratified as she shivered.

"I want to kiss you and explore you the way you've done to me. Can you lie back for me? Please, Rob?"

His cock jumped at the way his name sounded when she said it that way. Pleading, sweet, beseeching.

How could he possibly deny her?

With one last kiss to the sweet lips that hid her most precious place from him, he moved away to lie back onto the pillows.

If Stacey wanted to explore his body, who was he to stop her?

Chapter 22

Stacey felt bold as the darkness surrounded her, cloaked her, as she crept up Rob's body to settle between his legs.

He lay there at her mercy, a beautiful, sculpted piece of humanity, hers to explore, hers to kiss, lick, touch, and possess.

Even if it was just for this moment, she intended to enjoy every last inch of him.

It had been so hard to lose the sight of him. When he'd killed the lights, she'd had to bite her tongue to stop herself from asking that he turn them back on. She wanted to see him—and who wouldn't? He was incredible. Sculpted, toned, he was everything that a guy who owned a gym should be. But that was the problem. He was everything Stacey wasn't.

But she refused to think about that anymore for the moment. He was here at her mercy, and she wanted to touch what she'd seen before the lights went out.

Leaning down, she kissed him, only catching the corner of his mouth in the darkness. He smiled into her kiss, and she adjusted her aim.

He opened his mouth when her tongue traced the seam of his lips, and she delved inside. He tasted so good. She deepened the kiss, leaning down and pressing her breasts against his chest. The slight tickle of his hair excited her nipples, hardening their tips. The room was a little cool, and that made the heat of his body even more tantalizing.

As she kissed him, she braced her weight on one hand and let the other run over his shoulder, feeling the play of smooth muscles beneath the skin. He was so strong. He'd lifted her so easily the other night, and she couldn't pretend that the sensation wasn't wonderful. He was tall enough to make her feel small, strong enough to make her feel slight, and wonderful enough to make her feel desirable.

What kind of magic was he made of?

She broke the kiss, only to begin her sensuous survey of his body. Starting at his shoulders, she pressed a line of kisses across each of them.

"That's nice," he said, and she smiled against his skin.

"You're nice." She pressed her lips to the center of his chest, his light sprinkling of hair tickling her nose. She breathed him in. God, he smelled so good.

Her hands played downward, over the abdominals that he help-fully tensed for her, allowing her to bump her fingertips across them. She sank back onto her heels, allowing her hands to wander down over his hips and onto his strong, tensed thighs.

His breathing was harder, more ragged in the darkness. It was nice to hear that he wasn't unaffected by this. Her own body was wound tight, tensed, throbbing, and ready for him.

Maybe it was time to take matters into her own hands.

Her mind made up, she rose onto her knees and pressed her lips to his toned, ridged belly.

"Stacey," Rob said on a deep growl as her lips dragged downward, toward the velvet heat of his cock.

"It's only fair," she whispered, letting her breath blow by the weeping tip of him. His hips lifted toward her, and she felt a surge of satisfaction at the involuntary movement.

Now he knew how she felt.

Starting at the base of him, she cupped his sac with one hand while kissing the thick base of his cock. The soft sounds of fabric rustling beside her indicated he was fisting his hands in the sheets. Good. Bolder now, she licked up the thick vein on the underside of his shaft. He was all velvet-covered steel, and as she sucked the broad head of him into her mouth, his hungry gasp made her jump.

"Damn," he bit out a soft curse as she took him deeper, all the way to the back of her throat. Mouth working, she swept her tongue across the broad, smooth head on the upstroke.

Deep and shallow by turns, she sucked him, her hair falling around them. He threaded his fingers through the hair at her nape, gently tugging as she quickened her rhythm. He tasted good, sweet and earthy, and so very male.

"I'm not going to last much longer," he groaned as she gagged slightly on a particularly deep draw.

Feeling like a sex goddess, she lifted her head. He reached over to the bedside table and grabbed something. A soft *rip* sounded, the bed bouncing slightly as he rolled the condom on. When he stilled, Stacey straddled his hips.

"Are you ready?" Rob asked as she positioned herself over him. "God, Stacey."

She was already sinking down onto his hard cock. She closed her eyes as the delicious, hot, stretching sensation slipped through her. For a moment she stayed still, letting her body adjust to his girth. His hands gripped her hips, and he trembled beneath her, as if stopping himself from thrusting up into her.

Her hands slipped down her body to rest atop his hands, and staring down into the darkness, she began to move.

Rob did not lie still. He lifted her and snaked his hips against her, the twisting and grinding hitting her clit at just the right angle. Gripping his wrists, she rode him, tilting her head back. Her hair fell around them, tickling her back as she gasped.

Harder and deeper, quicker and quicker, her movements became frantic. Rob moved against her, steadying her, hips churning beneath her as skin met skin. Her belly clenched, muscles quivering, as she strained for that peak.

"I can't, Stacey, I need more."

With that hastily worded and less-than-clear statement, Rob lifted her off him and laid her down on the bed. She blinked into the darkness, and his form was suddenly silhouetted above her.

And then he was everywhere.

His mouth, hands, body—there was nowhere he wasn't touching her. He kissed her breasts, her nipples, her hips, her belly, his fingers rubbing down her arms, beneath her to cup her ass, over her thighs, parting them. The blunt head of his cock slipped inside her with barely a half a second's warning.

"Ah," she gasped, wrapping her legs around his hips. "Oh God."

He was so much deeper than before, nudging against her heart, it seemed. She clutched at his arms, relishing the way his muscles stood out as he braced his upper body above her. He lowered himself, clutching her close, and began a quick, steady rhythm, continued from their earlier dance.

"Rob," she gasped, when his mouth tore from hers and the thrusts came quicker, harder. "Oh God, please."

He lifted up then, just enough to reach down between them and find her clit. Biting against the scream that started to build in her throat, Stacey arched into him. Deeper, and harder, his hand and cock falling one after the other in a quick dance of sensuous insanity. She couldn't fight it any longer.

In the dark, she held him as she shattered into a million pieces. Clinging to him as her orgasm rocked her, she barely registered his groan, and the heat that built inside her as he came. Her eyes were open, but it didn't matter. The darkness surrounded them, covered her, gave her the courage she needed to relax into this moment with him.

As the flames quieted, and Stacey finally came back to herself, she realized exactly what was going on.

She had fallen for Rob.

Not that it was much of a surprise. She'd done a shitty job of holding him at arm's length. And who could blame her, really? He'd taken care of her, made her feel beautiful, and given her some of the best orgasms she'd ever had. What woman could resist him?

She buried her face in his chest. Certainly not her.

The sense of comfort, of completion, that blanketed him was incredible. He pulled Stacey closer, rolling to his side so his weight wasn't crushing her.

This woman had crawled into his heart, and he couldn't have dislodged her if he'd wanted to. He didn't want to.

What he wanted was to sleep with her by his side for an hour or two, then lead her into the bathroom and shower with her. Soap up every inch of her, watch as the rivulets of foam outlined her every curve, and then bend her over the edge of his tub and go for round two. He could lean forward, cup her beautiful breasts as he entered her from behind . . .

Christ, he was getting hard again.

She shifted, rolling onto her side, and he spooned her with his chin atop her head, her sweet ass pressed back against him. Her body fit him so wonderfully, soft where he was hard, sweet and giving and just so—Stacey.

Suddenly the sleepiness left him, and he smiled. He was about to open his mouth and suggest they head to the bathroom for that shower, when the realization hit him.

The lights.

Stacey wouldn't agree to the shower, because she was too embarrassed to let him see her.

Some of his joy dimmed, and he closed his eyes.

How was he going to help her fix this? He cared about Stacey, was caring more for her every day, but how could he consider being with someone who wouldn't even let him see her in her underwear?

They'd had sex several times now, but the only reason he'd ever even seen her breasts was because he'd walked in on her changing.

His heart, so recently glowing and happy, turned cooler inside his chest. Damn it. Things had been going so well, and now reality was pissing all over his parade.

Pressing a brief kiss to her bare shoulder, Rob slipped from the bed. He needed to take some time, think this through. No, he hadn't made plans for the future where Stacey was concerned. How could he? There was so much competing for his attention right now. The gym; his family; hell, even his accountant had been hounding him for some late paperwork for two weeks now. But with every minute he spent with her, it was getting harder and harder to imagine a life without her.

"Rob? Where you going?" Her voice was sleepy, and the bed creaked as if she'd lifted her head to look toward him.

"Just grabbing a shower," he said, his hand on the knob of the bathroom door. For a moment, he considered, then threw caution to the wind. "Want to join me?"

Silence fell, an awkward, ugly thing. Seconds ticked away. Eventually, the answer he'd been expecting came.

"I'll grab one later."

Pursing his lips together, Rob nodded. The bathroom door *click*ed shut behind him.

With his palm on the door that separated them, Rob closed his eyes.

He'd made a promise to help her with her self-image. It went much deeper than helping her get healthy, and he'd realized that pretty early on in their association. But that was before. Before he'd fallen in love with her.

With a heavy breath, he pushed off the door and flipped on the light switch. He tossed the condom in the garbage can and flipped the water in the shower on.

Bracing himself on the counter, he looked into the mirror. Facing himself critically, he listed his flaws.

His abs could use some more definition. He needed a shave. There was a mole on his shoulder, a scar on his left pec from where he'd fallen out of a tree when he was ten, and his arms weren't where they should be, either. There was more. If he stayed there, he could find any number of things to be unhappy about. But what did Stacey see when she looked at him? Could she not see any of the things that were wrong with him? Did she think they were so mismatched?

Or maybe she just didn't want this to go anywhere.

Rob adjusted the temperature and stepped into the shower. Steam clouded the glass walls, and he soaped up quickly, methodically. Putting the whole Stacey situation out of his mind was difficult, but necessary. He needed to work on other things. Calling his mom to check on his dad was high on the list, as well as contacting the clients he'd missed appointments with over the past week. Scheduling makeup sessions with the ones who'd opted to wait instead of work with his fill-in. Doing payroll, which was coming up over the next few days. Reviewing the list that Silvio had made for restocking the smoothie bar. Tasks on top of tasks on top of tasks. He didn't have time to try to figure out what to do about Stacey right now.

But she never left his mind. Not while he rinsed his hair, not while he dried off, not while he shaved. Not even when he pulled on clean briefs and loose-fitting track pants. And then, when he'd run out of things to do in the bathroom, and he had to go out and face her, he was met with darkness and the soft, even sound of her breathing.

She was asleep.

He wanted to go over to her, place his hand on her hair, bend down, and kiss her awake. Pull her into his arms, and show her exactly how beautiful he found each and every part of her.

What he did was walk softly to the door and open it quietly so he didn't disturb her. A shaft of light fell onto the bed, illuminating her face for a moment. A furrow appeared between her brows, but she didn't stir. Her strawberry-colored hair was spread out around her, a cloud he'd love to feel falling over him once again.

With a shake of his head, he let the door close behind him.

It was up to her. He couldn't force her to love herself. He couldn't force her to love him. He couldn't beg her to give them a chance. It was all up to her.

Padding barefoot down the hall, he retrieved his cell phone from the pocket of his coat. Patting Custard on the head, he sank down onto the couch beside the dog and dialed his mom.

He wished he could unload all of his problems on someone—on anyone—but he was the fixer. He was in charge of keeping everyone healthy, happy, and thriving. So, for now, he'd do his job. He'd fix his own problems later. If they were fixable.

Chapter 23

More than a week later, Stacey leaned closer to Rob's bathroom mirror to neaten up the wing on her eyeliner.

Finally getting back to work had been amazing. She was full of ideas and energy, ready to attack her solar panel project with renewed vigor.

Over the past few days, with her doctor's permission, she'd even gone to the gym with Rob and done some simple workouts. Nothing strenuous, just light weights for her upper body and some steady walks on the treadmill. Her limp was gone, but the soreness still lingered, so they kept it brief.

Honestly, she was only doing it to have more time with Rob. Her drive to improve herself had been totaled just as completely as her poor Jetta, which her new lawyer friend, Tony, was fighting with the insurance company about. The lawsuit from the other driver was shaping up to be a long, messy affair, with unfounded accusations and unreasonable requests flying. It was a major source of anxiety, but fortunately Rob had connected her with one of the best lawyers in town.

Stacey paused halfway through her application of lipstick.

Rob. He had confused her thoroughly over the past week. They'd had sex several times, but when she'd asked for the lights to be off, he hadn't argued, but he had hesitated. It was almost as if her request was hurting him somehow. He was always pleasant, kind, his usual self, but somehow there was a bit of distance that hadn't been there before. Even the simple Thanksgiving dinner they'd shared had been quiet, almost stiff, before they'd gone back to the bedroom and shut off the lights. She didn't like the disconnect, but how could she ask him about it?

Hey, is something wrong? Because you're being super-nice and taking care of me, but something is off and I can't tell what it is, but did I make you mad?

Pfft. Yeah. That would go over well.

Stacey capped her lipstick and tucked it back into her makeup bag. Stepping back, she eyed her reflection.

Not bad. Her face was a little thinner, but there weren't any obvious marks remaining from her wreck. The bruise on her leg, still a sickly yellow beauty, was covered by her slacks. Her headaches were gone now, and her limitations on driving and working had been lifted as of the day before. After her workday today, instead of coming back here to Rob's house with his big, goofy dog and the bed they'd begun to share every night, she would return to her cozy one-bedroom, third-floor walk-up. With her houseplants. And no Rob.

There was an inexplicable lump in her throat, but she coughed to clear it and checked the contents of her bag. Pajamas, clothes, toothbrush, it was all there.

Stepping back, she looked at the counter. Rob's stuff was still there. His deodorant, razor, toothbrush, all lined up in neat order. The counter had taken on a much friendlier appearance over the past week. Her stuff had mixed with his. Her toothbrush kept his company in the gray ceramic holder. Her deodorant had sat alongside his. Her contacts case and eye solution had lined the space beside his razor and aftershave.

It looked so lonely now.

"Stacey, are you almost ready? I'm going to start the car and let it warm up."

"Yes, I'm coming," she called back, jumping a bit at the sudden noise. She turned to walk out of the bathroom, but glanced over her shoulder one last time.

She was stupid. Foolish. Insane. But she jammed her hand into her bag and pulled her toothbrush from the case it had been in. Without a second's hesitation, she placed it back in the holder beside Rob's. Then she turned and left the bathroom, killing the light switch on her way out.

A quick cuddle with Custard later, she pulled on her coat and left through the front door. She didn't want to look back. For some reason, the thought of seeing that big, goofy dog staring after her and knowing she wasn't coming back tonight crumpled her insides like an aluminum can that had just been stepped on. So she kept walking, the heels on her boots clicking their way up Rob's front walk.

"Sorry to keep you waiting," she said, putting her bag in the trunk Rob had opened for her. Her breath fogged out in front of her in the cold. "Had to say 'bye to Custard."

"It's okay," Rob said, shutting the trunk. "I'll lock up and be out in just a second."

She sank down into the passenger seat and shut the door behind her, watching as Rob trotted down the walk to the front door.

Her phone pinged with a new text message.

> Hey, sweetie! How are things? I am dying to talk to you. The honeymoon was nice, but it's so great to be back home. Catch up soon?

Bree. Stacey smiled at her phone. Her cousin really did have incredible timing.

> Most definitely. I'm finally going back to work today, and then I get to move back into my apartment.

The reply came as Rob was rounding the car.

> Get to? More like have to, LOL. How is Big Guns? Declared your undying love for him yet?

The door opened, and Stacey jumped and killed the screen like a kid caught doing something they shouldn't be doing. Fortunately for her, Rob didn't seem to notice.

"Ready?"

"Yes," she said with a tight smile. Rob put on his shades—it was a fairly sunny morning for early December—and shifted the car into REVERSE.

Her phone *ping*ed again.

Oh, come on, honey, you know I was just kidding.
Don't be mad.

Sabrina would have seen that she'd read the text without respond-ing. She was tempted to keep ignoring it, but Bree wasn't the type to give up easily. Stacey unlocked the screen and began typing out her response.

"Back to work already?"

"No," Stacey said, "it's just my cousin. She's back home now."

I'm not mad, just in the car with Rob. I'll text you later.

The engine purred louder as Rob accelerated to merge onto the highway.

Okay. I want details, though! ;)

"She was the one on the honeymoon, right?"

Stacey tucked her phone into her purse as she replied, "Yeah, they stayed in Hawaii. It was nice, but definitely not the kind of trip I would have picked. Suited Bree, though."

"What kind of trip would you pick, if not a tropical island?"

She turned her head so fast to look at him she was afraid she'd given herself whiplash. Seriously? Her heartbeat quickened. The thought of being on a vacation with Rob—much less a honeymoon—sent her imagination sailing right off the edge of fantasyland's cliff.

He glanced at her past the edge of his sunglasses, and she realized she'd taken much too long to respond.

"Oh, Europe, I think. I mean, beaches are beautiful, but I think a honeymoon should be a once-in-a-lifetime experience. So, Paris, London, Florence, Madrid, I'd want to do a whole tour of Europe."

The way his smile slowly curled his lips made her melt into her boots.

"Makes sense."

Her fingers worried the toggles on her coat as she debated. Well, he'd asked first, so why not her?

* * *

"Where would you go on a honeymoon?"

The question shouldn't have surprised him, but it did.

After the week they'd just had, he had wondered if things were stalling out with Stacey. He'd tried to give her some space to heal, to come to grips with what had happened to her. But he'd never stopped wanting her, and showing her that he desired her. They'd slept together in the same bed, only becoming intimate in the dark. He'd initiated things in the light, but she never agreed unless it was dark. He had tried to show her in a million small ways that she was beautiful to him, but none of his efforts had paid off. So for her to ask that question? Confusing, but he'd play along.

"Europe would be nice," he agreed, settling into the right lane as traffic moved along at a decent clip. "I went to London in college, but it wasn't a long stay. It would be nice to go there again, and see more of Europe."

"Never thought about anything else?" she pressed. Her cell phone chirped again, but she ignored it.

He had, but the answer wasn't one she was looking for.

"Machu Picchu," he said. "I'd love to see it, do some hiking."

Her blanch was easy to see even from the corner of his eye. He didn't shake his head, even though he wanted to.

Of course she'd take that as a sign they weren't compatible. But hell, what did that idea have to do with the thought that they could be together if they wanted to? He didn't want to end up with someone who was a copy of him. He wanted to be with someone who complemented him. Who was soft where he was hard. Who would think of a solution while he was busy being bullheaded and sticking to the wrong way of looking at a problem. Who would help him challenge himself in other areas of his life.

Someone like Stacey.

All too soon, he was winding through the streets of downtown. He thought about what to say to her, how to communicate the idea that he liked her—really, really liked her—and that he was going to miss her in his house tonight. In his bed. Having her to come home to was a luxury, a commodity he'd not expected to enjoy quite so much.

But he didn't have time to craft the perfect "I'll miss you" speech.

They were there in front of her building, and there was only the empty loading zone.

"Can you pop the trunk for me?" she asked as she unbuckled her seatbelt when he came to a stop.

In response, he hit the button, and the trunk popped open.

Her hand on the door latch, she turned her head to look at him. He stared into her eyes, so impossibly, beautifully blue. Her pink lips, perfectly complemented by the shade of lipstick she wore, were turned down at the corners. That furrow was back between her brows, and without thought he reached over to smooth it out with his thumb.

"I guess this is good-bye?"

"See you later," he corrected. "You're coming to the gym tomorrow, remember?"

She nodded. Her eyes began to look suspiciously wet. Wait a second, was she going to cry?

"See you tomorrow," she said, her tone too bright, and she shoved the door open.

For a second, he sat there looking at the space she had just occupied. What should he do? Damn it, why wasn't the correct answer coming to him? He'd tried pushing; he'd tried pulling back. But none of it had worked to get through to her. He just wanted her, for fuck's sake. He wanted her to come to him and share everything with him, but she couldn't. She was too afraid. And no matter how hard he pushed, he couldn't push her through the fear.

His trunk slammed shut and she stepped onto the sidewalk with her bag hanging on her shoulder. Rob set his jaw and waved back at her when she lifted her hand.

And then he shifted into DRIVE and maneuvered his way onto the street in the gap in traffic. When he glanced in the rearview, she was turning to walk into her building.

"Fuck," he said aloud, slapping his steering wheel. The sting of his palm felt good, but it didn't solve the problem. Did that problem even have a solution he could supply? He didn't know. There wasn't exactly a carton of self-confidence he could gift her from Amazon.

He shook his head as he waited at the next stoplight. How long should he keep torturing himself like this? It hadn't been that long, but he'd shown her who he was. What he was. He hadn't hidden anything from her, but she couldn't trust him at all.

His cell phone beeped as he pulled into his space at the garage. The screen revealed that it was Brandi.

"I'm here," he said when the call connected. "What's up?"

"We've got problems," Brandi said, sounding out of breath. "Flowers is back and he won't leave. Silvio is keeping him out of the classroom, but he's insisting he teach his class."

"Fucking hell," Rob said, yanking his bag from the backseat and slamming the door in one quick move. "I'm coming right now. Have you called the cops?"

"Called them first. They're starting to get loud." Brandi, normally unflappable and tough, was sounding just a teensy bit nervous.

"Try to keep everyone away from them. Let Silvio handle him until the cops get there. I'll be inside in twenty seconds." Rob killed the call and shoved his phone into his jacket pocket.

He'd been toying with the idea of a restraining order on that nut job, but his shortened schedule at the gym had kept him playing catch-up everywhere, and that particular task had slipped through the cracks. Damn it. His idiotic pursuit had put his business in jeopardy—again.

Goddamn his horny ass. Stacey was incredible, but if she didn't want him in the same way, why was he risking everything for her? It didn't make sense.

But even as he shoved his way through the front doors of his gym, he knew it didn't matter. As long as she was around, he would have to try. She was too precious to give up.

A crowd was starting to gather near the hallway that led to the classrooms, Brandi doing her best to keep them back. Rob tossed his bag behind the counter and shed his jacket before heading that way and rolling up his sleeves.

He hoped Stacey started to trust him soon. If she didn't, he just might lose everything.

Chapter 24

Surrounded by her project lists, files, her focus playlist playing through her computer speakers, Stacey could almost pretend things were back to normal. Hannah had greeted her with a huge hug and gushing praise on how great she looked. Stacey had filled her coffee cup in the break room, said hello to the interns who were working at a table in the copy room, even skirted by the double whammy of Vance and Walter. The sun was out, shining through her windows, and the responses she'd gotten from her inquiries to the solar panel companies were encouraging. The numbers were adding up, and her proposal had all the finishing touches.

So, why did she feel like shit?

Every time she turned her chair to pull a page off the printer or grab her stapler, she caught sight of her overnight bag in the corner of her office. Enterprise was delivering her rental car sometime this afternoon. Hannah was bringing her lunch, and they'd have a quiet one here in the office to catch up. Things were back to normal—well, as normal as they could be considering Stacey herself was completely different.

She couldn't stop thinking about Rob. He'd looked sad this morning as he'd driven away. That expression didn't belong on his handsome face. But she didn't know what else to do. She'd tried to make it clear that she was interested in him, without coming right out and asking him to be her boyfriend.

Heat climbed into her cheeks, and she pressed a palm to one to cool it. God. She couldn't do that. Her fear of rejection was much too real. But it was maddening to think that she was this close to someone she cared for this much and she didn't have the guts to come out and tell him that she wanted to be with him.

"Stupid," she muttered under her breath as she thunked proposal pages together on the desktop to straighten them into a neat stack. "Just be honest with him. It'll work out."

Despite her words, she wasn't so sure.

A knock on her office door drew her attention. "Come in."

Her boss, Ed Cramer, poked his head inside. "Welcome back."

"Thank you, Ed," Stacey said, smiling at the director. "I'm very glad to be back."

"I need to go over some things with you. Do you have a minute?"

"Sure," she said, putting her pages aside in the notebook she'd laid out for them. "Want to come in, or should I go to your office?"

Ed came in and shut the door behind him. Stacey tilted her head in question. Her boss was normally a loud, jovial kind of guy. Shutting the door wasn't like him.

He sat down across from her, an unusually serious expression on his face.

"I hope your recovery is going well?"

"Yes," Stacey said, trying to calm the butterflies that were banging against her rib cage. "I'm slowly getting back to normal."

"Are you ready to present your project to the city council tomorrow?"

Hannah, bless her efficient and well-connected soul, had performed a miracle. She'd managed to convince Ed and his boss to call a special meeting of the city council to consider the solar panel proposal tomorrow.

"I'm putting the finishing touches on the presentation right now."

"Good," Ed said. He nodded. "It will be nice to have that project in the works. You've done an excellent job on it."

"Thank you," she said, his praise making her smile. But something was still off. "Was there something else?"

He nodded, his expression inscrutable. "I wanted to let you know that I received a few very interesting e-mails and phone calls while you were away, about our partnership with the Atlanta Police Department."

The floor fell out from beneath Stacey, and her mouth went desert-dry. "Oh. Um . . . Yes. I can explain that."

"Please do," Ed said, propping his elbows on the arms of the chair and steepling his fingers.

She launched into the story of the fight at Rob's gym, glossing over the fact that she'd been staying with him. Let Ed think she was there for physical therapy. It wasn't pertinent to the discussion anyway. As she spoke, her palms went clammy, and she was certain a flush was climbing up her neck.

It was bad. She hadn't stopped to think about how bad it could be when it happened; she'd just wanted to help. But to have lied like that?

"So, in the interest of helping a local business, I let the onlookers believe it was a training exercise."

"So, you lied." Ed stated the fact calmly, without any anger.

"Yes. I did, in fact, lie." She could have said more, tried to point out that she'd been an exemplary employee, that she'd come up with more projects than anyone else this year, had streamlined the department, but she didn't. It wouldn't matter. At the end of the day, she had to answer for her actions.

"Well, you might have lied, but it was a damn good idea."

Her heart flopped over like a dying fish. "It was?"

"Yes. The police chief and I are already coordinating on it. I contacted him on the off chance he'd been thanked like I was. He hadn't, but when I explained the premise as I understood it, he was on board. It's a great publicity tool for the city and the police."

Relief made her sink back into her chair. "Oh good."

"That being said, you're not off the hook for this, Hough." Ed sat forward, his sharp green eyes pinning her like a butterfly to a corkboard. "You stuck your neck out pretty far, and you could easily have been fired for this kind of stunt."

"I know. Thank you." Stacey crossed her legs at the ankles, wincing as her boot brushed up against her bruise. "I promise I won't do anything like that again."

"As for your punishment," Ed said as he stood, hiking up his khaki pants, "you'll be working with Vance Farmer to head up this project."

"With . . . him? Vance? But he hates my guts—you can't . . ."

Ed grinned, his usual levity returning. "Gotcha. You're on your own. Draw up the ideas and have them on my desk by Tuesday morning. I'll see you tomorrow at the city council meeting."

"I wouldn't miss it for the world." Stacey smiled as Ed turned to leave her office.

Well, that had gone much better than expected. Stacey hummed to herself as she turned back to her proposal. If—when, she mentally corrected herself—the solar panel project was approved tomorrow, she would definitely have time to dedicate to the police project.

And maybe, with a couple of major career successes under her belt, she could find the courage to just come out and ask Rob if he wanted to make things more official between them.

Maybe she'd do that. Soon. She nodded as a sense of confidence filled her. Yeah.

Maybe things could really work out after all.

It was late. The gym was empty, other than Rob. The only sounds were the rhythmic pounds of his footfalls on the treadmill's deck. He ran, staring straight ahead, trying to clear the cobwebs from his brain.

It had been a hell of a day. The cops had come, and there had been no Stacey to distract from what was actually happening. Three of his regular clients had canceled their contracts. If things kept going like this, he would lose the gym. It sucked.

Maybe he had made a mistake in taking time off when he did. No, he definitely had. But taking care of Stacey had shown him a glimpse of what life could be like with someone like her. Someone caring, funny, who shook him out of his normal comfort zone and helped him see things in a new light.

But he hadn't been able to make that work, either. For some reason, despite his best efforts, Stacey still didn't trust him.

Over and over his feet hit the deck, his steady run taking his breath, making him sweat. The televisions were off, and everything was quiet, but why was the noise inside his head so loud?

He would see her tomorrow. But until then, how was he supposed to distract himself from what was going on inside his head and heart?

He should tell her that he loved her. He should ask her to share his life somehow, to explore what they could be together. But he knew that would scare her even further.

When he glanced down at the treadmill's readout, he was surprised to see that he had gone nearly ten miles. It hadn't felt like that long, but apparently it had been. He slowed the deck to a walk, and placing his hands on his hips, he looked down at his toes as he began his cooldown lap.

"You're not supposed to look at your feet. You'll fall."

He jerked his head up and nearly stumbled at the quick movement. But he righted himself, and stopped the machine dead.

Stacey. She was standing there in front of him, a shy smile on her beautiful face, wearing her coat and holding her overnight bag.

"Sorry, I shouldn't have come in, but you didn't answer your cell phone."

"I left the front door unlocked, huh?"

"Yeah." She unhooked the strap from her shoulder and set the bag down on the floor. "Hate to bother you, but I need a ride. Enterprise flaked out on me, and I don't have a rental car until tomorrow."

"Sure." Rob stepped off the machine and closed the distance between them. "You know I'll give you a ride."

Without thinking, he reached out to pull her into his arms, then stopped. Had the intimacy between them just been for the time they had spent together? What if everything was different now? Besides, he was sweaty from his run, and she was still wearing her professional work clothing.

But she didn't seem to notice his hesitation, and she went into his arms willingly. He closed his eyes and squeezed her tight.

"I didn't know how I was going to sleep tonight without you." Her voice was muffled against his T-shirt. "The thought was not nice."

"Well, you don't have to sleep without me if you don't want to."

His offer made her look up at him, blue eyes wide. "Really?"

He nodded, not bothering to stifle his smile. "Custard won't mind."

She sighed, and pulled back a bit. "I really should get back home. I've got a major presentation tomorrow, and I really need to polish it up."

His sense of loss was deep, but he nodded. "Yeah, I guess it's for the best. We had to get back to reality sometime."

"Yeah."

He clasped his hands behind his back, just to do something with them. The awkward feeling was definitely not going over well with his insides. "Well, if you want to hang out for a second, I'll get my coat and shut everything down. Then we can head out and I'll take you home."

"Thank you, Rob, seriously. I can't tell you how much everything you've done has meant to me."

"Well, you have to prove to me how grateful you are when you show up tomorrow for your training session."

She laughed, and the sound lifted his spirits a little. "You bet."

Rob left her standing in the front lobby while he went to his office to shut everything down and gather his things. As he went, he debated internally. What was his best move here? He wanted Stacey. He wanted her in his life, and he wanted to help her gain the confidence she needed to be his partner. It seemed like he had tried everything, but maybe just being direct with her was the best approach.

As he shrugged into his coat, he debated. Yeah, it might make her run scared, but then again, it might actually boost her confidence to know that he sincerely wanted to be with her. He wasn't used to talking about his problems. Sadly, that was one aspect of his father's character that he had inherited. You didn't talk about problems; you just put your head down to solve them. But this wasn't a problem that his usual approach had been able to solve.

He killed the lights in his office and headed out to meet Stacey. His mind was made up. He was going to do this, and hopefully it would work out.

Stacey smiled when he met her, and he couldn't help but notice how the expression lightened his spirits. Yeah. This was the right thing to do.

As they walked across the street to the parking deck, he reached over and caught her hand. She looked surprised, but didn't pull away, a small smile curling her beautiful lips.

With her directions, he drove to her apartment. It wasn't far, but with the cold, the car was a definite necessity.

He killed the engine in her assigned parking space, and they sat there for a moment in the quiet.

"Thanks again. I don't know what I would've done without you over the past two weeks."

"I do. You are smart, you're incredibly resourceful, and you would've been fine regardless. But I am happy that I was able to help in some small way." He took a deep, steadying breath. For some reason, he was nervous. Well, there wasn't any way to prepare better for it, so he'd just have to swallow his pride, say a little prayer, and throw it all out there.

"Stacey, I—"

"Wait, can I say something first?"

Well, so much for that. He nodded.

She took a deep breath, and closed her eyes. "I like you. Well, you know that. What I mean is, I think I'm falling in love with you."

And just like that, he realized he'd worried for nothing. She continued.

"I don't know if you feel the same way. It's been amazing to be with you, and if you're interested, I'd like to continue to see you. Romantically, I mean."

Something swelled in his chest. A lightness penetrated his heart, spreading and lifting him higher than he'd ever imagined he could feel. The emotions pulled him forward, directly toward her. Leaning across the console, he took her in his arms and pressed his lips against her eager mouth.

She was his now. And he had every intention of keeping her.

Chapter 25

They stumbled into her apartment, barely breaking the kiss long enough for Stacey to toss her bag down on the floor of the living room.

Weak light from the streetlights outside spilled through the window, giving just enough illumination for them to avoid colliding with the coffee table on the way to the couch.

Rob pressed her down into the cushions, and she shoved his jacket down his arms, desperate to touch his skin again.

It was stupid. It hadn't been that long since she'd seen him. Hell, they'd had longer times apart when she was staying in his house. But for some reason, their separation today had seemed much more distant, more final. And to now be with him again? Stacey was overcome with both love and lust.

He lifted up long enough to yank his shirt over his head, and she made use of the time to do the same. His lips took hers once more while his fingers desperately fumbled with the front catch of her bra. She arched her back while reaching down to slide the elastic of his waistband as far down as she could reach.

"Fuck, I can't. It's dark."

"Here, let me," she said, sitting up, and took over the bra while he removed his track pants.

With her bra sliding off her shoulders, she stopped stock-still.

He was silhouetted in the small, silvery beam of light there, his cock hard and standing proudly. Her mouth watered and her belly tightened at the thought of his hardness against her, inside her again.

She had missed him so much. She wanted him so much.

He turned to her then, and the darkness took his features from her.

"Stacey? Can I turn on the light?"

She wanted to say yes. Her heart ached with the need to see him, to lovingly trace all the parts of his body she had only felt, not seen. She wanted to look into his eyes when he parted her, pushed into her, set up that delicious rhythm that had her screaming his name.

But the thought of him turning away from her, disgusted at the sight of her far-from-perfect body made her stop. She was scared. Too scared to lose him, too scared to risk it.

"No need for that. I'll grab a condom," she said, and raced from the room.

In her bathroom, she paused by the sink with her hands braced on the countertop. Though it was right in front of her, she didn't dare look in the mirror. She knew what she'd see. Her half-naked body wasn't anything to write home about, and if she really thought about it, she would chicken out of this whole relationship when it had just barely gotten started.

Her heart was beating too fast. She stared at the tiles between her still-booted feet. *Breathe, Stacey, calm down.*

She reached into the cabinet and pulled out the stash of condoms that had been there for quite a long time. Quick check of the dates . . . Thank God. She'd need to grab some more in a couple of months, but for now, this would do.

Pulling off her boots, she timed her breaths. Counting as she breathed in and out forced her to calm, and by the time she'd removed the rest of her clothing, there in the privacy of her bathroom, she was feeling a bit better.

With condom in hand, she killed the lights before opening the door. "Rob?"

"I'm in here." His voice came from her bedroom, but the apartment was still dark. She shook her head slightly as she padded barefoot down the hall. He had asked for light, but he hadn't argued once. What had she done to deserve this man?

"Your bed is more comfortable than the couch would be, I figured."

She hadn't closed the curtains in her bedroom, so a faint glow illuminated the bed where Rob lay, naked, his head pillowed on his arm. Shifting to the side quickly to be out of the beam, she bit her lip before answering.

"It might be."

He was out of the bed and by her side faster than she could say anything further. He gathered her into his arms and breathed against her hair. "If you're not comfortable with this, I need to know."

"No, it's not that. It's— I— Damn it Rob, just kiss me."

He did, bless him. She opened her mouth at his gentle urging and leaned her naked body into his, so grateful for the warmth of him, the smoothness of his skin, the taut muscles that rolled and moved under his skin as he scooped her into his arms and gently laid her on the bed. It wasn't possible for a girl with her body type to feel dainty. But somehow, Rob made her feel that way.

He laid full-length on top of her, his erection brushing against her thigh. The touch of him made her whimper; his kisses made her sigh with want. Her belly was tightening and warming with the sensations he built with kisses and touches and ever-heightening need.

She kissed him fervently, rubbing her hands down his shoulders, his back, his arms, his ass, everywhere she could reach. And then it wasn't enough. His mouth was on her nipple, sucking, drawing her in, and her fingers were twisted in his hair, but her body screamed for more. She parted her thighs and lifted her hips, the moisture making her inner lips cool as they parted.

Seeming to understand her silent plea, Rob moved his thigh higher, between her legs. As he moved to her other nipple, she shifted and moaned aloud when her slick pussy made contact with his strong, warm thigh.

"There, honey," he said, tweaking her wet nipple while he plied the other with small kisses. "Ride me."

And she did. Slow at first, she relished the feel of her sensitive skin gliding up and down the firm muscles he tensed for her. He rolled her nipple tighter, the combination of pleasure and pain stoking her fires hotter. Her movements came quicker, her tension building. A slow, burning, throbbing ache had set up shop between her thighs, and only an orgasm could cure it. Rob lifted his head and eased his body forward.

The move brought her clit into deep contact with his leg, and her cry came from deep inside.

"There, Stacey, that's in the right spot, isn't it? Come for me, honey. I want to hear you scream my name."

She bucked, she twisted, she clawed at his shoulders as the heat built in her lower belly. It was a fire that he stoked, and he did it so masterfully, so incredibly, that she knew she'd be incinerated and she didn't give a good damn.

"Ride me, Stacey. Ride me 'til you come."

It was good, so good, but it wasn't enough. There was a yawning ache inside her, and though he was so close, touching her nearly everywhere, it wasn't enough. But he had what she needed to get there.

Without another thought, she reached down between them and grasped his hot, throbbing, naked cock. Spreading her thighs wide, she guided him home.

He'd only thrust twice when she lost all control, her body shattering into a billion pleasure-soaked pieces. She did scream his name, clinging to his arms like he was the last solid thing in her world.

Because he was.

When Stacey's orgasm had finished, Rob fought for the last shred of control left inside him. It was all he could do to thrust three more times, then force himself to leave the sweet warmth of her body.

He reached down, and with two smooth strokes, finished the orgasm he'd been holding at bay for the last five minutes. She'd been so damn hot, grinding on him and twisting and moaning like her life was dependent on the way he touched her.

Spent, he lay beside her in the dark, listening to her breathe. She was drifting off to sleep.

Just then, a rhythmic buzzing began, along with a cheerful, chirping ringtone. His mother's ringtone. Rob's stomach dropped, and he shoved off the bed and onto his feet. Where?

"Rob, is that yours?"

He felt around for the clothes he'd brought into the room, but he couldn't find them. They must have fallen off the bed while he and Stacey were rolling around.

"Yes, it's mine, and it's important. I'm sorry, I can't find my phone. I'm going to have to turn the lights on."

He was already reaching for the wall by the door as he spoke, but her frantic squeak made him pause.

"Wait! Just a second!"

Fabric rustled, and then an out-of-breath Stacey said, "Okay."

He flipped on the light. A glimpse toward the bed revealed that she'd clambered under the covers and was using the sheet as a shield against his gaze. He'd think about that later. Right now he had to grab the phone that was about to ring out.

"Mom?"

"Robbie . . ." She was crying, and his heart stopped. "It's Dad. We're at the hospital."

"I'm on my way," he said, scooping up the clothes. "Where?"

"Fairfield General. The doctors are with him now. I'm so afraid it was a heart attack. We were out Christmas shopping, and he said he had some indigestion, so we were heading back to the car, and he just fell over. I didn't know what to do. The store manager called nine-one-one, and the ambulance got us."

He'd known it before he even answered the call, but the confirmation made him feel physically ill. "Just hang tight, Mom. I'll be there as soon as I can. Have to wrap up some things at home and then I'll jump on the highway. Are Greta and Marla coming?" His sisters lived much closer than he did, and he wanted his mother to have some company as soon as possible. Just in case of— Well, for moral support. He refused to think of the worst-case scenario.

"Greta is. I called her from the ambulance. I think she called Marla, but I wanted to call you."

"Okay. I love you, and we'll be okay." He hoped and prayed he was right.

"I love you too." His mother sniffled, and then the phone went dead in his hand.

He was standing naked at the foot of Stacey's bed. His clothes were scattered at his feet, where he'd tossed them while digging for his phone. A still-wrapped condom was lying on the bedside table, and peeking out from beneath the covers was a tousle-haired, wide-eyed Stacey.

What should he say? He had to go; there might not be much time. But this thing between them was so fragile, so new, so terribly uncertain. Could it survive his leaving right then?

Whether it did or not, he had no choice. His family needed him.

"I have to go," he said, pulling on his briefs. "I'm sorry."

"Is everything okay?" She sat up straighter as he pulled on his track pants, but she kept the sheet clutched tightly to her chest.

"No, it's not. My dad's in the hospital."

"I'm so sorry. Is there anything I can do to help?"

Before he could answer, his phone rang again. He swiped the ANSWER button. "Hello?"

"Rob, it's Greta. I'm here at the hospital."

"How's it going?" He tucked the cell phone in the crook of his shoulder and flipped his T-shirt right-side outward.

"Talked to the doctor. It's not good, Robbie. He had a heart attack. They're doing the angioplasty now to see the extent of the damage."

"I'm getting ready to leave right now. I've got to get Custard over to Silvio's, if he's home, and toss some stuff into a bag. I should be on the road within the hour."

Greta sighed. "Okay. Just—drive safe. Don't fly on the roads. They may be transferring him to a hospital with a better cardiac unit, so keep your phone nearby."

"Will do."

When the call with Greta disconnected, Rob dropped the phone on the foot of the bed and pulled the shirt over his head. His body felt like a live wire, all restless energy that had no outlet. His skin prickled, and everything inside him was screaming to fight, to run, to somehow escape the nightmare that he was caught up in.

His father—his overly critical, much-too-demanding hero of a father—was sick. Maybe dying. And he could do nothing to help.

"What can I do?" Stacey's small voice broke into his world of darkness.

He looked over at her, and for that moment, he couldn't hide a damn thing even if the thought had occurred to him.

"Come with me. My father—well, his heart isn't good. I don't know if he's going to pull through." Though his heart was breaking, his voice was steady. "I have to be there, for him, for my mom, and for my sisters. I have to be strong for them. But it's my dad."

He hated this. Hated the feeling of weakness, of vulnerability. He wanted to wrestle this problem, tackle it head-on, like he'd always done. But that wasn't possible this time.

"I—I can't." Stacey looked down at the covers as she spoke. "I want to, I really, really do. But my project—my job . . ."

She trailed off, and Rob stared at her for a long moment.

"I understand." He reached down and scooped his jacket up from the floor. "I'll give you a call sometime, yeah?"

"Wait!" she called after him as he moved toward the bedroom door. "I can fly out tomorrow night after work."

"I'll be okay. I'd hate to put you out."

"No! I want to." She scooted toward the edge of the bed, keeping that damn sheet tucked around her like a shield.

He tightened his fist and stared at the ceiling. Not like this. This wasn't what he'd wanted. His pain was so great, and she couldn't let her guard down even now?

"Seriously. I'll fly out on the first flight I can get. Will you text me the name of the hospital?"

His treacherous heart screamed at him to accept her offer. His brain told him to leave it, to figure out the whole mess some other day. But he was short on time. His heart won out.

"Okay," he said, then walked toward her. Bending down, he kissed her firmly, longingly, and with the lingering taste of sadness that was clouding his mind. With his hand at the nape of her neck, he tilted her head up to look at him.

"I love you."

The words were unbidden. She blinked, and her eyes looked misty as she replied.

"I love you too, Rob."

He turned and left the room, hoping like hell that she would keep her word. He needed her at his side. If he had to do the one thing he'd been dreading for so long, he'd need someone to lean on.

Not just someone. He needed Stacey.

Chapter 26

She'd slipped into her robe as he left the bedroom. Belting it quickly, she stepped out into the hallway.

The front door shut behind him with a *click* that seemed to leave a bruise on her heart.

Leaning against the wall, she stared at the closed door. This had been the most wonderful and most terrible night she'd had in a very long time.

Rob loved her. She loved him. They'd sort of come to an understanding about their relationship, but then that terrible news had come.

Of course, she wanted to drop everything and go be with him. There was nothing that would have made her happier than to support him through his time of need. He'd done so much for her when she'd been injured—hell, she still owed him and the debt would probably never be repaid. But her job. Her project. She had poured so much of her heart and soul into it, and tomorrow was her big chance to prove that she deserved the promotion she'd been given all those months ago. How could she just abandon that chance?

But how could she let Rob go through this painful time alone?

"God," she moaned, letting her head thump backward against the wall. If only the answers were more clear. She needed to figure things out. She needed clarity. She needed a friend.

She needed Bree.

Her bare feet made soft slapping sounds against the hardwood floor of her hallway as she went to fetch her purse. With her cell phone in hand, she went into the kitchen. Her "favorites" list popped open, and soon Bree's face was smiling up at her from the screen.

"Hey there beautiful! What's up?"

Stacey propped the phone up against her cookie jar and yanked open the fridge. "I know you're a newlywed and you probably want to shoot me for Skyping you at eleven o'clock on a Thursday night, but I need to talk. Are you busy?"

Bree shook her head. "Nope. Greg is out playing pool with his buddies. I was just about to finish watching *Sixteen Candles* for the umpteenth time."

"Oh man, I want an eighties movie night with you so bad," Stacey groaned as she poured herself a glass of wine. "We haven't done that in a billion years."

"It's been way too long," Bree agreed, straightening her messy blond topknot. "God, I look hideous. I should really look in the mirror before I answer a video call."

Stacey snorted as she set her glass down on the counter. "Bullshit. You couldn't look hideous if you tried. Those glasses are cute, your jammies are fun, and if I looked half as good as you when you're"— she made air quotes—"'hideous', I would be doing great."

"You look amazing. I think you've lost some weight." Bree wagged her finger at the screen. "So, stop being mean to my favorite cousin."

Stacey fought the urge to shake her head and scooped up the phone. With her glass in hand, she moved to the living room.

"So, it's not like you to want to talk like this. I'm the one who usually comes after you to get things figured out." Bree rubbed her hands together and grinned almost evilly. "Come on, what's going on?"

Tucking her feet beneath her, Stacey propped her phone on the arm of her oversized chair and took another sip of wine. "It's complicated. It's long, and involved, and I think I've screwed it all up."

"Is it about Mr. Big Guns? It is, isn't it?" Bree was practically bouncing with joy. "You guys are an item."

"Yes. No. Well, I don't know."

Bree's smile lost some of its glee. "Wow, this is complicated, huh. Why don't you start at the beginning?"

So Stacey did. She filled Bree in on details she'd only barely sketched in texts. From the way Rob had made her feel during that first ill-fated workout session, to that incredible session in the locker room, to the way he'd run straight to the hospital to be by her side. Stacey talked, and Bree listened, never judging, never laughing, just taking it all in as Stacey bared her soul. Her feelings, her confusion, the sweet way he'd wooed her during their stay together.

And then tonight. How she'd admitted her feelings, and he'd reciprocated, and then how her need for the dark had seemed to hurt him. His father's sudden illness, and her refusal to go with him.

When she was done, Stacey was raw inside. Her voice was hoarse, and her cheeks burned from the slow track of her tears. Her glass of wine was nearly empty, and the slight buzz wasn't nearly enough to dull the pain and confusion swirling inside her.

"I love him. And I want to be with him. Am I screwing up totally because of this project? But my job is so important to me, and I really believe in what I'm doing. This project could help a lot of people, and it will actually save the city money in the long term. If I can do both, shouldn't I?" Stacey took a long, ragged breath, and waited.

Bree bit her bottom lip and furrowed her brow. "Wow. That's a lot to take in, honey. You love this guy?"

Stacey nodded.

"And right now he's hurting."

She nodded again.

Looking down, Bree tucked a lock of hair that had escaped her topknot behind her ear. "I can't tell you what to do. I mean, yes, your job is important to you. And you've worked a really long time on this project. And if you miss that meeting tomorrow, the whole thing might go down the pipes." Bree cleared her throat, then looked straight at Stacey. "But this guy is important to you. And he put his whole life on hold to help you heal after the car accident. He asked you to go be with him. I just— I mean, I can't say what you should do."

"What would you do? If you'd just met Greg, and you had something really important going on, and he needed you? Would you drop everything and go?"

A little laugh escaped Sabrina then, and she shook her head vehemently. "Oh no, that comparison isn't going to fly here."

A niggling feeling of doubt lodged in Stacey's stomach. "Are you not happy with Greg?"

"We're talking about you and Rob, sweetie. Greg and I are fine, or we will be." Bree turned her head quickly. "Shit, that's the door. He's home."

"But I don't know what to do yet," Stacey said, the panic welling up in her throat. "I need your help."

"I can't make this decision for you. But I'll tell you this. If I cared for anyone, or anything, the way that you seem to care for Rob?" Bree smiled, a little sadly. "It would take a lot more than a major work project to keep me from his side."

"So, in conclusion, this project would ensure that the tenants of Lawson Meadows would always have the power they need, and save the city a considerable amount of money in the long term." Stacey smiled at each of the city council members. There. She'd done it. Presentation finished.

"I think we're ready to vote on this proposal," Councilwoman Tanner said, looking at the other council members.

Stacey held her breath as the votes were cast. Four yea votes, one nay. It had passed.

The councilman adjourned the meeting, and Stacey almost fell backward in relief as Hannah squeezed her arm in celebration. Ed was grinning from ear to ear.

"Stace, you did it! Oh my God, I knew you could do it," Hannah said, her voice an excited whisper as they walked sedately out of the council chambers, members of the local news media milling around them. "This is the best!"

"I knew it would pass. You did all the research, had an incredibly compelling presentation, and the savings to the city is considerable. They would have had to be insane to pass this up."

"Thankfully, they were not insane." Stacey laughed, her relief making her shaky as she walked through City Hall with her boss and Hannah on either side of her. "I'm just glad they saw the potential. And after Lawson Meadows is finished, then there's a good chance the other housing projects could benefit from the same kind of updates."

"Ms. Hough."

Stacey turned at the sound of her name. She smiled, a bit puzzled, but tried to keep her face pleasant. "Councilman Pendleton, what can I do for you?"

"We'll go on ahead," Ed said quietly, and with a polite nod at Councilman Pendleton, he and Hannah excused themselves.

The elderly councilman had been the one nay vote on the council. He had a reputation for being a hard-ass, and he'd certainly grilled her during the Q-and-A section of her presentation. But she'd been able to counter each of his questions with facts and evidence, so he hadn't taken her off her game. Thankfully.

"I just wanted to tell you that you did a good job in there." He nodded back toward the chambers. "We hear a lot of proposals that aren't anywhere near that polished and professional. Excellent work."

Well, that was unexpected. And confusing. She rubbed her suddenly sweaty palms on her slacks. "I don't understand. You voted against the proposal."

"I did."

"So, why are you telling me this?"

He laughed, a wheezy, rusty sound that made it seem like his mirth was a rare thing. "I didn't vote against the project because of the proposal. I did it because I think the city should be spending its money and time in other ways. But I respect a person who does a good job, and you did that." He bobbed his graying head. "Have a good afternoon, Ms. Hough."

"You . . . too," she said, watching as the elderly man sauntered off.

She wanted to be flattered, but the whole exchange had just left her confused. Oh well. In the end the nay vote hadn't mattered, the project had passed, and she had done a good job.

She glanced down at her cell phone's screen. Two thirty. She had two hours before her flight to Charlotte. Just enough time to get back to her office and pick up her bags, then grab a cab to the airport. She'd texted Rob several times that morning, but she'd only received one reply from him.

He'd arrived in Charlotte at four in the morning. His dad was being transferred to Carolinas Medical Center. It didn't look good.

She'd read that text probably a hundred times, and each time she wanted to go back in time and convince herself to drop everything and go with him. To hold his hand as he went through this painful time. To ease his pain and heartache and somehow make things better.

But she couldn't desert her career goals, even though she loved him. They were so new as a couple. Hell, she'd only told him she loved him that night! She couldn't throw away her entire career on a whim, could she?

She'd wrestled with the question so long that the decision was eventually made for her. When she looked at the clock, her plane ticket booked, it was nearly half past one in the morning.

"Doesn't matter," she said to herself as she gripped her briefcase tighter. "I'm on the way there now."

Her heels *click*ed on the polished tile floors, and she joined the crowd of people waiting for the elevator. Hannah and Ed must have gone down to the lobby already. She'd join them there and catch a ride back to the office with Hannah.

It seemed to take forever for the lift doors to open, and she squeezed in the corner with the rest of the people. She closed her eyes and took a deep breath.

She hated tight spaces like this. It always reminded her that she was a big girl. Someone was always invariably brushing up against her, making her feel self-conscious. If she wasn't so chubby . . .

What would Rob say if he heard you say that?

She smiled to herself at the thought. He'd probably remind her that she wasn't supposed to bully herself.

She'd see him soon, and then her worries would lessen. They had to.

The elevator doors opened, and Stacey filed out into the milling crowd. Gosh, there were a lot of people here today. Sure, there'd been some interest from local newspapers and bloggers about the special city council meeting, but this number of people wouldn't all be here for that. A chorus of giggles to her left drew her attention, and she noticed the set of risers in front of a holiday display. Oh yeah, local high schools were doing a winter concert in the spacious lobby. Well, another day she might have stayed to listen. But she had things to do today.

"Where the hell are they?" she said under her breath as she scanned the crowd. Ed and Hannah had to be around here somewhere. But when she'd looked in all the obvious places and they were nowhere to be found, she sighed and pulled out her phone.

Where are you?

Her text to Hannah sent, she stepped through the revolving front doors to look out on the front walk. She got Hannah's response text almost at the same time she clapped eyes on her dark-haired friend. She didn't bother to read the message, just walked down the sidewalk to the benches where Hannah and Ed were standing.

"Hey, there you are!" Stacey moved her briefcase to her other hand. "I was looking all over for you."

When Hannah turned to face her, Stacey's stomach dropped at the expression on her friend's face. "Wait, what's wrong?"

"Did you read my text?"

"No . . ." Stacey unlocked her phone screen, and when the words on the screen registered, she wanted to throw up.

Walter just called Ed. We've got major problems.
Lawson Meadows is on fire.

Chapter 27

The waiting room of the cardiac intensive care unit was the most comfortable version of hell that Rob could imagine. Seriously. It was nice.

There were soda and snack machines in the corner, along with a complimentary coffee bar that he and his sisters had utilized heavily over the past fourteen hours or so. The couches, while made from that heavy-duty vinyl material that was easy to wipe down with industrial cleaner, were surprisingly cushy. The lamplight was soft, and the art on the walls was generic, but done in calming colors. They'd even decorated a small Christmas tree in the corner.

He hated every last fucking square inch of the place.

Beyond those double doors, his father lay dying. He was in desperate need of bypass surgery, but his condition was too poor for them to attempt the operation. The heart attack had done a lot of damage. How much? Difficult to determine. Would he recover?

It wasn't looking good.

"Robbie, come sit down."

He'd been standing at the windows, looking out over the city of Charlotte. But at his sister Greta's voice, he turned and faced her. "I don't think I can sit right now."

Frowning, Greta set her coffee cup down on the corner table. "You need to rest. You haven't slept in way too long."

She was right. He'd gotten that phone call and bolted straight home. Custard went to Silvio's place to bum around with his big mutt, Max, and Rob had taken his hastily packed duffel bag and driven straight through the night to get to the hospital. The only thing that had given him pause was when he was in his bathroom.

He'd grabbed the wrong toothbrush. As soon as his fingers curled around it, his heart had sunk into his belly. Stacey. She'd left her mark here, and on his heart, and now he had to do this without her.

At the hospital, he'd paced, he'd watched, he'd waited. But he couldn't rest. Not now. Not while things were so . . . uncertain. At any moment, things could go sideways. At any moment, he might have to be strong for his mother, his sisters.

He turned back to the large window, watching as the night sky grew darker and more bleak. "I'm fine."

Greta didn't say anything else, but he could feel her concern and disapproval. How could he not? It was almost impossible to miss.

The mood had been tense. His mother refused to leave Dad's side, even for things like going to the bathroom, or showering. Marla was with her now, because the rules of the unit stated that only two people could be in the room with the patient at a time. That meant some pretty long, unbearable stretches in the hellish waiting room.

Rob sighed, raking his hand through his hair for what seemed like the thousandth time. He was so antsy, full of nervous energy. He wanted to pace the floors. There was a walking track outside, but he couldn't leave the unit. He was too afraid that something would happen and he wouldn't be here for it.

Dad was on a respirator, not able to speak. To see the man Rob had idolized his entire life—had fought with, clashed with, loved so much—lying there so helpless? It had torn something inside Rob's heart irrevocably.

There was one ray of hope, and he clung to it with everything inside himself. Stacey. She had promised him that she would be here tonight. She had sent him her flight details early in the morning, and he pulled his cell phone from his pocket to check the status again.

The plane was in the air finally, and if there were no delays, she would be here and in his arms within two hours. He couldn't wait. The one thing that would ease some of this pain was the knowledge that she was there for him.

Shoving the phone back in his pocket, he turned back to Greta.

"Sorry. I know you're just trying to look out for me." He sank down into the seat beside her, and she reached over to grab his hand.

"I know. You're so much like Dad. If the situation was reversed? He would be doing the exact same thing you're doing."

"I know."

They sat in silence for several long moments, hand in hand, like they were small children needing comfort. It was nice. Greta was only three years older than Rob. When they were small, they had been best friends, but when Greta went off to college they'd drifted apart. Things were different now, but it was nice to know at moments like this that their bond could reignite at a moment's notice.

Rob pulled his phone from his pocket to check the flight's progress again. Greta looked over at him with a quizzical expression.

"You expecting an e-mail or something?"

He killed the screen with a tap of the button. He almost felt like he'd been caught doing something he shouldn't, and that was stupid. This was something, this was real, and in just a couple of hours his family would meet Stacey for the first time. He wasn't ashamed of her, so why the need for secrecy?

"My girlfriend. She wanted to come with me last night, but a major work project was happening today, so she got on a flight after work. She's on the way here now."

A genuine grin lit Greta's face for the first time since he'd seen her early this morning. "Girlfriend? Really? Well, that's awesome. I was wondering if you were still hung up on Rebecca, since it had been so long. How long has this been going on?"

Rob smiled, feeling a little sheepish. "It's pretty new. But she's amazing, and I think you're really going to like her."

"Well, if my picky baby brother thinks she's special, then I'm sure she is. It's really nice of her to come here to be with us." The end of her sentence was much less joyful, and the memory of why they were here at all dimmed Rob's excitement. It should be a joyful event to introduce his family to the woman he had fallen in love with. Instead? She'd be coming to wait with them—or mourn with them.

Rob stood. "I should go check on things. You okay? Need anything?"

Greta shook her head. "No, I think I'm just going to call my husband. Check in with him, see how the kids are. Seeing you all mushy and in love has reminded me of my family and home, and I really wish they could be here too."

Greta's kids were much too small to enjoy hanging around the waiting room for any length of time, so the separation was necessary, but Rob kind of understood the feelings that his sister was having right now. He was chafing at the separation from Stacey, and they had only been together a short while.

"Okay. Love you, sis." Rob leaned down and brushed a kiss on her cheek.

"Love you too."

Rob walked down the hall toward the nurses' station. He had taken the last shift with Mom, but Marla had been in there for an hour and a half now, so she might be ready to get out and stretch her legs a bit. He wished Mom would leave the room, take a walk, get some fresh air, just do something. But he couldn't blame her. He wanted to be in there with his father, and given the chance, he wouldn't have left Dad's side, either.

"Hi, I'm Richard Liston's son. I was wondering if there's any update on his condition?" Rob propped his arms on the high counter of the nurses' station as the woman checked the computer.

"No change. Would you like to see if someone wants to switch places?"

Liking to and having to were two different things. He should give Marla and Mom this time together. "No, they'll come out when they're ready. I'll just be in the waiting room if anything changes."

The nurse gave him a small smile. "Okay. We'll definitely update you."

He backed away a step, then turned and shoved his hands in his pockets. His fingers closed around his phone automatically, and he pulled it free. Only a few minutes had gone by since he had checked the flight's progress, but he couldn't stop himself from doing it again. There, in a little image, was the tiny icon of the plane hovering above a map of the United States. Rob let his finger tap the icon, wishing it would speed up the plane and bring her here to him faster.

But the screen lit up under his fingertip, and he glanced at the notification bar. A text. From Stacey? Must have gotten in-flight Wi-Fi . . .

He opened it immediately, and his heart shattered at the sight of the words that greeted him.

> I am so sorry. A major disaster happened at work, and I missed my flight. I'm trying to grab another one, but there isn't a seat available until tomorrow afternoon. I am so, so sorry. I love you. I'll be there as soon as I can.

His arm fell, taking the hateful words with it, and he closed his eyes.

She wasn't coming. She had promised, and she wasn't coming.

By the time Stacey finally got back to her apartment, it was nearly nine.

The fire at Lawson Meadows had started from faulty wiring. Wiring that should have been replaced years ago. Wiring that was standard throughout every single unit in the housing project. Wiring that would cost money to fix. Money that had—just that afternoon— been earmarked for the project Stacey had crafted. Money that was no longer available.

The solar panel project was dead. It had burned up in the flames of three apartment buildings that very afternoon.

Stacey collapsed on her couch, kicking her heels off and staring at the ceiling. It had been hell. They'd had to do media interviews, talk to the city council, coordinate with contractors to get estimates on the repairs. She'd been numb through it all. As the minutes ticked away, and her chances of making her flight diminished, Stacey had gone into automatic mode just to cope.

But it was over now. The flight had long since landed in Charlotte, without her on it. Her call to the airline had been less than helpful. And her stupid rental car still hadn't shown up. She had no plane to fly to him, no car to drive to him, and the reason she'd stayed behind hadn't even been successful.

A hot tear rolled down her cheek. The ceiling had gone blurry. No surprise, since the pain in her chest was growing with every ragged breath she took.

All she had wanted was to be there for Rob like he had been there for her. Should she have sacrificed what she'd been working on in her career for him? Well, since things had panned out the way they had, maybe. But she still believed in the solar panel project. For months she had lived and breathed that effort. To have skipped out on the crowning moment? To gas out on the last lap? It had been unthinkable last night. But it had gone up in smoke, quite literally.

Rubbing her cheeks, Stacey sat forward. It was late. She hadn't eaten anything since that muffin that Hannah had shoved at her between interviews this afternoon. She'd been too nervous for breakfast, so that little blueberry morsel had been her only food of the day. But the thought of cooking was completely intolerable at the moment. Just . . . no.

Yanking her laptop from her bag, Stacey sniffed. No harm in checking, was there? Maybe something had opened up.

A quick scan of the airline's website proved to be a waste of time. No, there weren't any seats available. And the agent had promised to call her if there had been. But she couldn't quite give up hope that maybe, just maybe, something would work out in her favor tonight.

Fat chance.

With a heavy sigh, she closed the lid of her laptop and stood, stretching toward the ceiling. As she moved, her waistband slipped down low.

Wait, what?

She lifted the hem of her shirt and looked down.

Holy shit. Her stomach was . . . not flat, but definitely less fluffy. Or was it? Was it the angle she was looking at her body?

She rushed down the hall to the bathroom, whipping her shirt off as she went. In strict opposition to the way she normally did things, she stared straight in the mirror at her half-naked body.

Her breasts were still large, framed by her plain nude bra. Her stomach, though . . . it was different. She turned to the side. Holy shit, it was true. There was less of her now. Not a lot less, but a definite difference.

She looked in the mirror, and oddly enough, she smiled.

"I'm not as ashamed of how I look."

The words echoed against the tiles, bringing her voice right back to her. Rob had told her to look in the mirror and say something positive, and today, she could actually do that.

Looking at the reflection in the mirror, she made a decision.

Next time she and Rob were together, she would ask him to leave the lights on. She might have failed him by missing the flight today, but she still wanted him to know how he had helped change her life for the better.

Her cell phone buzzed in her pocket, and her stomach flipped. She pulled it free and walked into her bedroom. Sinking onto the edge of the bed, she looked at the screen. Rob.

"Hello?"

"It's me," he said, his voice low, tone inscrutable.

"Rob, I'm so sorry. I can't tell you—"

"Don't worry about it," he cut her off, and she pressed her lips together. She couldn't blame him for being upset. She'd promised, and then circumstances had made her into a liar. Someone he couldn't trust. And that made her feel like a total bitch.

"I just wanted to call and tell you not to fly out here tomorrow. We'll be fine. I'll let you know when I get back to Atlanta."

Her heart, already crisscrossed with breaks from the hell that had been today, cracked a little further. "But I want to be there for you."

"Things are—" He stopped, cleared his throat, and started again. "Things are on hold here. He's on a respirator, and they need to do surgery, but his condition needs to improve a bit before they can risk it. I don't know how long it will take for things to change. There's nothing to be done here but wait, so just stay there."

The pain was clear in his voice, and she hunched forward, hugging herself with her free arm. Would there ever be a pain greater than seeing the man she loved in distress when she had no way to ease it?

God, she hoped not.

"Please, promise me you'll let me know if you want me there." She fought to keep her tone steady, her voice even. He didn't need to hear how upset she was. Didn't need to know her hurts, because then he'd just bear those too. "I want to be there for you if it helps you."

"I'll let you know," he said.

Her lids drifted closed. In her mind's eye, she could see him. Standing in a hospital hallway, surrounded by white floors, neutral walls, the acrid smell of antiseptic clinging to everything. Beeps of machinery and low voices making a blanket of sound around him. His hair, tousled from repeated brushes of his fingers, curling around the edge of his phone as he held it to his ear.

And his broad shoulders? Rounded. Bowed. Strained from the emotional weight of the situation that she had been powerless to prevent, but had failed to share.

A single sob escaped her, and she clapped her hand over her mouth.

"Stacey?"

Breathe, idiot, don't let him hear you. One breath, two, and she'd regained control of her emotions.

"Sorry, had to cough."

"It's okay. I need to go. Marla wants to go get some dinner, so I'm going to take her down to the cafeteria."

Stacey nodded, glad that her tears this time were silent. "Sure. Keep me posted."

"I will."

Silence on the other end of the line, and she wondered. Would it hurt to say it this time? Would he even want to hear the words, when nothing she'd done could prove they were true? Should she—dare she—tell him again how she felt?

He beat her to it. "I love you."

Her tears flowed faster, and she couldn't stop the break in her voice as she answered. "I love you, too."

Chapter 28

"Robbie."

The sound seemed to come from far away, and he paid it no attention. Wrinkling his brow, he squeezed his eyes shut tighter.

"Robbie." An insistent push to his shoulder. "Rob!"

"What?" he barked, his eyes popping open as he pushed himself upright. He blinked, trying to get his bearings. Oh yeah. The waiting room. The couch, which he wanted to set fire to, along with that damn Christmas tree and the soda machine whose cooling apparatus had an insistent whine that couldn't quit. These four walls that had stopped closing in on him three days ago, when his world couldn't possibly get any smaller. And his baby sister. Marla. Her dark brown hair falling in a mass of unruly curls around her shoulders.

"Mom wants to talk to you." Marla reached a hand out to him, and Rob took it, gaining his feet. He walked with her past the double doors and past the nurses' station.

"Is everything okay?"

Marla glanced at him, her dark brown eyes serious. "No change. I think she wants to tell you to go home."

He was already shaking his head before the sentence was completely out of her mouth. "Not happening."

With a sigh, Marla stopped in front of room 824, a set of digits he was afraid would always be burned into his memory. "Just listen to her. It's been almost two weeks now, and you've barely left the hospital. It's not good for you, Robbie."

"It's not good for her, either, and she hasn't left," Rob countered.

"Save your arguments for Mom. I'm going to head home for the night." Marla shouldered her purse strap and patted him on the arm.

"Your life doesn't stop just because of this, Robbie. At some point you're going to have to decide what to do."

Rob didn't answer, just watched his little sister walk away.

She was right. At some point, he would have to leave this hospital, with or without knowing what his father's fate would be. It had been the longest eleven days of his life. There hadn't been a great amount of change. At one point they thought he was improving enough to attempt the surgery, but then his test results had regressed again, and so they were still stuck in the never-ending hell of waiting. Waiting for him to pull through, or waiting for him to die.

Rob took a deep breath, staring down the closed door in front of him.

How was he supposed to keep doing this? He'd been as stalwart as he could be. He'd shoved his mother out of the hospital room for showers and meals. He'd kicked Greta out of the waiting room, so she could be at home with her kids. Even the normally impervious Marla had been force-fed breakfast for the entire week. But his steam was running out. His heart was broken, and shattered, then crushed again. With every improvement, he gained a tiny shard of hope, and with every disappointment, that hope shoved another crack into his soul. He hadn't even allowed himself the comfort of Stacey.

He closed his eyes for a moment. Stacey. At first she had texted him constantly. Encouraging messages, notes of love, things to try to make him laugh. But he couldn't respond. Didn't know how. He was angry, disappointed, and so, so sad. The texts had grown less frequent. She'd only texted him once the day before yesterday. Then yesterday, not at all. He might have finally succeeded in driving her away.

Not sure how he could ever face Stacey again, he had called Brandi and told her to take over training Stacey if she came back to the gym. He hadn't gone into details, but he had let her know that things had gotten personal between them. Eventually he'd have to sort it out, but for now? He'd let Brandi handle it.

With a sigh, Rob grabbed the latch on the hospital room door. Knocking softly, he pushed it open.

"It's me," he said, easing his way into the room.

The rhythmic beeps of the cardiac monitor greeted him, and

the sight that lay spread out before him was no less painful for its familiarity.

His father lay motionless, tubes and wires running from his body to the bags and machines at his bedside. His face was covered by a ventilator mask, and his steel-sharp eyes were closed. His skin looked pale, pasty, so unlike the vivacious and ornery man whom Rob loved.

His mother sat in the armchair at the bedside, her normally perfect hair in slight disarray. Her clothing, always pressed and neat, was wrinkled and askew. She looked dazed, like someone who'd just been through a horrific event with no idea where to turn.

And, in a way, she was.

"Mom," he said, and she turned to face him with a small smile.

"Robbie." She held her hand out to him and he grasped it. "I want you to go home."

"I can't do that," he said, easing down into the small chair beside her without letting go of her hand.

"You have to. He could stay this way for months." She delivered the line matter-of-factly. It was something they'd heard days ago from the medical staff, and as time had worn on, it had proven true. "I don't want your business to suffer any more from your absence. It's important to you."

"And so are you."

"Robbie, I've never doubted that." His mother sighed, and released his hand. "I know what you're doing. You're trying to fill his shoes."

Damn, she was sharp. Rob looked down at the toes of his athletic shoes. He supposed, in a way, he had been. Dad was the strong one, the one who held everything together when it was falling apart. And since Dad was now the one falling apart, Rob had done his best to keep things in order.

But nothing was in order, because he couldn't fix this.

"You aren't your father. I know we were hard on you for not going to medical school. And I know how you want your gym to be a success so your father will see that you made the right decision. But, honey, I want you to know, despite how he acted?" She sniffed, and Rob felt his chest tighten. "He has always been so *incredibly* proud of you."

She cried softly then, and he put his arm around her shaking shoulders. They had spent so much of the last week crying, praying, begging whatever deity would listen to heal him. But there had been no answer. Rob just held her, wishing that the purgatory would end. Of course, he wanted his father to be better, but the uncertainty was stretching them all too thin, and his returning home would leave his mother to deal with this all on her own.

"I'm sorry," she sniffed, dabbing at her cheeks with a tissue. "But it's true. We are both so very proud of you, and all we want is for you to be successful. So, please. Go home for now. I promise, if there's a change—"

"But what if I miss it?" For a moment, he wasn't strong. He was a little kid again, sad, uncertain, and needing comfort. "What if he gets worse, and I don't make it back in time?"

His mother smiled. "He would be happy to know that you were off chasing your dream. That always made him smile, how single-minded you were about your goals. How you wouldn't take no for an answer. He roared, he complained, he needled you, but he never stopped telling people about your successful business."

The news rocked Rob on his moorings, and he sat back, staring at the still and silent man on the hospital bed.

His dad was . . . proud of him?

"No, no, *no*." Stacey slammed the white mouse down on top of her desk. Her fingers curled tight around the white plastic in disbelief. "That isn't even close to correct. How do they get away with printing this crap?"

"I told you, you need to stay off the Internet." Hannah set down a large mocha with extra whipped cream on top of Stacey's desk. "They're having a field day with this. It's best just to let them have their fun, and not get upset about it."

"How am I supposed to stay calm about this? They're acting like this department practically set fire to those apartments ourselves. We're the ones trying to fight to upgrade them, and—"

"I know that. And you know that. But the truth doesn't grab any-where near as many page views." Hannah sighed and took a sip of her own coffee. Hitching one hip on top of Stacey's desk, she continued, "It's all about sensationalism. Don't worry, something else will happen soon, and all this will be just a memory."

Stacey pushed back from her desk, staring at the ugly headline once more. CITY PLANNING DEPARTMENT FAILURES MOUNT AS HOUSING PROJECT BURNS. It was so ugly, and so untrue. Just because her project had died in its infancy didn't mean the whole department had failed. It hurt, and she was fucking sick of it.

"It's been almost two weeks now. Why hasn't someone printed the truth? I've given tons of interviews, there are a million sound bites they could use. I just . . . I don't know. Just really freaking tired." Stacey propped her chin on her hand.

Hannah gave her a knowing look. "This isn't just about the housing project, is it? You still haven't heard from him?"

Stacey shook her head sadly. If not for Hannah and Bree, she probably would have gone insane with worry over the past few days. At first, she had clung to Rob like an anchor. Texting him, checking on him, thinking about him kept her distracted from the maelstrom of her career problems. But his responses had been few and far between. She began to second-guess herself, and decided maybe she was just bothering him. So, she slowed down her texting. When he hadn't responded after two days, she'd given up altogether.

When he came back—*if* he came back—then they could reevaluate whatever they were to one another. For now? She didn't know what else to do but cling to her last threads of sanity.

"I haven't heard anything from him. Last he said, his dad was still on the ventilator. No idea when he's coming home, or if he will ever forgive me." She barked a bitter laugh. "And I'm so stupid I still want to text him."

Hannah pulled her cell from her pocket. "Well, if you feel the need to text someone, you can always text me. I'm not guaranteeing that my four-year-old won't try to text you back, but at least you have somebody."

Stacey smiled. "Thanks, Hannah. You're the best."

"Now, you'd asked for my help. What was it that you wanted me to help with? The police project?"

With the Lawson Meadows project obliterated, and the media fallout hopefully slowing down, Stacey had decided to throw all of her energy into the impromptu small business–police training project.

With everything that was going on, the city planning department definitely needed the good publicity. If she could hit all the right notes with this project, maybe things would even out for them.

The feelers she'd put out in the community were positive, so far. She just had to compile the data, iron out a few bugs that were cropping up with the force, and then hopefully be able to present the project to the city council in the next couple of weeks.

She and Hannah were poring through her project spreadsheet when a sudden knock on the door jerked Stacey's gaze upward. Ed stood there, his brow furrowed.

"Hannah, Walter said he needs your help with something in the copy room."

Hannah rolled her eyes where Ed couldn't see, and gathered up her coffee. "Yeah, okay. I'm on the way. Stace, you let me know if there's anything else I can do to help with this, okay?"

Feeling more and more grateful for her friend, and really reluctant to let her leave, Stacey nodded. "You bet. Talk to you soon."

Ed stood in the doorway as Hannah passed him and exited through the hall. Stacey stared, unsure of what to say.

She knew that Ed had had a meeting yesterday with his superiors. It had gone late, and she hadn't been able to find out what had been discussed. But she was afraid she might have an inkling of what had gone on.

"Stacey, do you have a minute? We need to talk."

Oh boy. She gulped. "I guess if I said no, it really wouldn't change anything, would it?"

Ed shook his head. Was she imagining the sadness that painted his features? "Let's go to my office."

Stacey followed him down the hall to the corner office, her sense of foreboding growing with every step. It wasn't fair. It was not her fault that this had happened. But, as was so often the case in a large machine like the government, when something got screwed up, someone had to pay. And though she had no proof, at this moment, she was pretty sure that the head on the chopping block was hers.

"Have a seat." Ed rounded his desk, an old, beaten-up wooden affair. He sank down into his scuffed leather chair and looked at her.

She crossed her feet at the ankles, unsure of what else to do. The clock that hung on his wall ticked loudly, a sound that reminded her of a bomb about to go off.

"Stacey, you know that I think you are a wonderful employee. Your work on the Lawson project was beyond what I could've asked of you. But, with the way the media is howling over this, I wasn't able to sway the decision."

"You have to fire me."

Even though she hadn't phrased it as a question, Ed nodded. "Yes, I'm afraid so."

She closed her eyes, and wished with all her heart that this was a bad dream. But even though she pinched her arm as hard as she could, she just couldn't wake up.

Chapter 29

The next three hours were a blur of tears, good-byes, and packing. Ed had done Stacey the favor of keeping her dismissal quiet, so she didn't have to worry about being chased down by local reporters or overeager news bloggers as she prepared to haul her belongings from the office.

With each pen and personal item that landed in the cardboard storage box, a little bit of Stacey's heart crumbled away. The picture of her and Ed from their first project together. The little figurine of a sea horse that Hannah had brought back from her trip to the beach last summer. The pen that she'd claimed from the grand opening of her favorite coffee shop on the corner.

The same coffee shop that Rob had cornered her in to convince her to give Healthy Living—give him—another chance.

It was all gone now. The job, the man, her chance at making her life everything she wanted it to be. Circumstances had taken it all away. Could she have done something different? Probably. But the might-have-beens didn't do anything to ease the pain she was going through now.

She closed the box.

Hannah was inconsolable. Stacey had had to talk her out of quitting at least three times before she finally agreed to stay on the job, and then only on the condition that Stacey would try to find a job somewhere on the same block so they could still lunch together. As she walked through the front lobby, she was happy to see that Hannah wasn't at her desk. She couldn't take the idea of walking by her friend for the last time.

"I'm sorry about this," Ed said, taking the box from her at the door. He'd been kind enough to pull her rental car—a basic Toyota Corolla that smelled faintly of cigarette smoke—to the curb for her. "I hope you understand that this isn't what I wanted at all."

"I know," she said as she opened the trunk for Ed. He placed the cardboard box inside. "Thank you for all you did. And for trying to keep me."

He enveloped her in a hug, and Stacey fought hard against the tears that were clogging her throat. Not now. Not here. This was hard enough. With a heavy breath, she broke the embrace and smiled up at her now-former boss.

"Don't worry. I'm going to be fine."

Ed shook his head as he stepped back. "Put me down as a reference on your résumé. I'll tell anyone who calls what a damn fine employee you are."

"That means a lot. Thanks."

As Stacey rounded the car, she glanced upward. There, in the window of her old office, stood Hannah.

Shit.

With a quick wave, Stacey ducked into the car. The tears were coming now, and she couldn't stop them. She cranked the engine and glanced in the mirror. Of course, there wouldn't be a break in the traffic.

Trapped by a long line of cars, she sat there, her tears coming fast. Sobs racked her, and she closed her eyes for a minute, trying to get ahold of herself.

She'd lost her job. The one thing she'd been confident in, been good at, was gone. Everything was crashing down on her, and the one bright spot was Rob. Maybe there was still a chance that things could work out between them. She knew she'd hurt him by missing that flight, and she still regretted that bitterly. But with each time she looked in the mirror, she was reminded of the work he had done with her.

She hadn't lost any more weight that she could tell. But even though the change was slight, the mental change had been much greater. She didn't despise mirrors anymore. Looking at herself more objectively, she could tell that a lot of her earlier disgust didn't have as much basis in reality as she'd thought. Her body wasn't gross, or disgusting. Was she still out of shape? Yes. But Rob had seen beauty in her, had seen confidence that just needed the right environment to grow. He'd provided that, and now?

Now she needed to show him that she could be the kind of woman who was right for him. All she needed was a chance.

A break in the traffic came, and as Stacey's tears cooled on her cheeks, she nosed the rental toward Healthy Living.

He might not be texting her back. He might still be at his father's bedside. But she could still go and honor the commitment she'd made to him here. And when he returned? She'd be ready and waiting to be the kind of partner he needed.

If he'd let her. And she prayed that he would.

In the middle of the afternoon, parking at the deck across from the gym was a dicey proposition. She circled for what seemed like ages before finally grabbing a spot near the top of the deck.

The elevator smelled, and it was dirty. She opted for the stairs, her breath fogging out in front of her in the cold. Her heart beat hard against her ribs, more from nervousness than exertion.

Was he here? Would he be coming back soon? She'd asked him in a text, but he hadn't responded. She'd settled for sending him one last *I love you* and hoping for the best.

But now? Now she needed him. And she needed to be needed by him. To give and to take, to feel that same partnership they'd been nurturing before his father had fallen ill. She'd done without him as long as she could, had honored his need for space.

The DONT WALK sign was lit when she arrived at the corner, and she bounced on her heels as she waited. They made small *click*ing sounds against the pavement.

She didn't have any workout clothes. No gym bag, no water bottle. She didn't care. If Rob was here, she'd work out on every last damn machine they had to prove to him that she was committed. That she regretted letting him down. That she loved him.

Finally WALK lit, and she dashed across the street, the warm, bright lights of the gym's interior welcoming her. Yanking open the glass doors, she took in the delicious warmth of the heating system.

A quick scan of the counter didn't yield the one sight she'd been hoping for, but there was, at least, a familiar face. Brandi was at the smoothie bar, one hand on top of the blender as she chatted with a tall man in red track pants.

Stacey waited, her insides vibrating. Rehearsing what she'd say when she saw him, she almost didn't hear when Brandi finished up and spoke to her.

"What?"

"I said, hello," Brandi smiled, an expression that seemed a bit guarded to Stacey. She smiled back, trying to remember if she'd ever done anything to make Brandi dislike her.

Well, nothing other than falling in love with her boss, and then letting him down at the worst possible time.

"Sorry, I was kind of distracted. Is Rob here?"

Brandi shook her head. "No, he's still out of town."

Fighting hard to stay positive, Stacey bit her lip, took a deep breath, and tried again. "Do you know when he'll be back?"

Brandi busied herself rinsing out the blender's pitcher as she answered, "Not for sure, no. He did leave a message if you came in."

Kissing her would probably be a bad idea, so Stacey just leaned forward instead. "Really? What is it?"

Brandi set the pitcher down in the base with a decisive *click*. "I'll be training you from now on. He said that things got too complicated between you, and he needed to simplify."

Stacey stepped back, trying to discern the feeling that had just ripped through her chest. No, that was too much. Just his words. She'd figure out his words.

Complicated. He needed to *simplify*. She'd complicated his life, and he needed to simplify, so he was cutting her out.

"Oh. I see."

Brandi shrugged one shoulder. "If you're here for a workout, then I can get you started, but I've got another client coming in about twenty minutes. We can set up some individual times for you if—"

"No. That's—no thank you. I need to cancel my contract." Even though her tears were flowing again, Stacey's voice was calm and even.

"Really? That's too bad," Brandi said, and this time Stacey wasn't imagining the edge in the woman's voice.

"Yes. I'm leaving Atlanta. Moving away. So there's no need to keep my membership here."

Brandi's perfectly plucked brows knitted together in confusion. "Wow, that's out of nowhere. Where are you going?"

Stacey laughed. "I've got no idea. But anywhere but here looks good right about now."

His hands were locked at ten and two. His eyes never left the road. The radio was on, but not because he wanted it. The low buzz of noise was a safeguard to keep him awake, in case the chill coming in from the crack in his window wasn't enough.

Of course, even if he was in a position to sleep, he doubted his mind would let him.

His father, Richard Armstrong Liston, had died.

Rob and his mother had been in the room when it happened. It wasn't dramatic, or terrible. He was there one moment, and gone the next. Like a candle had been snuffed out. But the hole that his death had left was something Rob was afraid would never be filled.

The miles disappeared under the rotations of his tires. He'd had to come home. When he threw clothes into his duffel on the night he'd gotten that call from his mother, funeral clothes hadn't been on the packing list. And then his entire extended family had descended. Cousins, aunts, old neighbors, former patients, they'd all shown up to his parents' home with food, or drink, or just curiosity.

Seeing his need to escape, Greta had suggested he go home to pick up his clothes, and after some nagging from Mom, Rob had agreed. After the meeting with the funeral home to discuss the arrangements, Rob had hugged his sisters and his mother and had set off for home. He'd be back in three days for the service.

The afternoon had nearly disappeared by the time he reached the outskirts of Atlanta. As the surroundings grew more and more familiar, Rob fought against the thoughts that assailed him.

He couldn't fight them for long.

Not when he passed the restaurant he and Stacey had gone to just a few weeks ago. Not when he drove past the orthopedist's office he'd taken her to twice. Not when the Redbox she'd pointed out at the pharmacy caught his eye.

Damn it, he missed her.

At the last stoplight before he reached home, he pulled his cell from his pocket. Gripping it for a minute, he shook his head, then dropped it into the cup holder.

Calling her out of nowhere like that was a dick move. He was hurting. Lonely. Angry at the world and everything in it. He couldn't promise that he wouldn't lash out at her for not being there with him, and he'd already forgiven her for that.

Waiting was the best option. He had to wait until he could talk everything through with her and get things settled the way they needed to be.

As the seconds ticked by, Rob began to second-guess his decision to go directly home.

There were pictures of his family there. Mementos, gifts his parents had given him. Being there would be almost like being back at home, surrounded by family, having to speak to near strangers about the fact that one of the most important people in his life was now gone.

Making a split-second decision, he flipped his turn signal the other direction and waited for a break in traffic to turn left, back to the highway. He could get his things later, but for now? He wanted to be surrounded by what he had built. He wanted the energy, the positivity, and, if he was honest, the memories he and Stacey had made at his gym.

There was always the chance that she might be there. He couldn't go to her, but if he ran into her at the gym? Well, they could figure things out, couldn't they?

He drove a little faster as he made it onto the highway. Yes. This he could do. Checking on his business, ironing out any snafus that had cropped up in his absence. Besides, his friends were there. He could be surrounded by people who understood him, who wouldn't press him to talk about the painful, gaping wound in his heart.

Since it was getting late, it was easy to find a spot in the parking deck. He grabbed his bag and locked his vehicle, then headed across the street and into the gym.

Once inside, he paused for a moment, just taking it in. He had built this place, this warm, inviting, *good* place. And before his father had passed away, he had been proud. Proud that Rob had pursued his dream and achieved a bit of success. Was the gym at the place where Rob wanted it to be? No. But that was the thing about having goals. There was always something new to strive for.

He rounded the counter just as Brandi came forward to greet who she thought was a customer.

"Hi, welcome to— Rob! I wasn't expecting you this early, I thought you were coming home tomorrow." She dashed over to him and gave him a quick hug. "We've missed you around here. How are things?"

Rob let his bag descend to the floor behind the counter. "Not good. He passed away last night."

Brandi's expression changed instantly to one of sympathy. "God, I'm so sorry." She gave him another hug. "If you want to talk, I'm here. Otherwise, I'll just act normal, okay?"

He could always count on Brandi. "Thanks. We're doing okay. And no, I don't really want to talk about it."

Brandi nodded and pinned a bright smile on her face. "The gym is doing really well. We actually grabbed a couple of new members this week, so the ones we lost from the Krav Maga debacle are being made up for a little. We're still a few down, but I think we'll make it up next month. I found a new belly-dance teacher, and she's coming in to interview next week."

Rob groaned. "A new teacher? I don't know about that, Brandi."

Brandi began slicing up a banana at the other end of the counter. "Don't worry about it. It's someone my sister knows from her knitting group. She's totally legit. And I'll handle the interview, so all you have to do is sign off if you want to."

Rob rubbed at several days' worth of stubble on his chin. "Well, I trust you. Actually, I trust you a hell of a lot more than I trust myself right now."

"What do you mean?"

Rob sank down on the stool behind the computer terminal. "Just—it's not a big deal. I handled some things really poorly. I shouldn't have been as angry as I was, but I was hurting, and I didn't know what to do."

"Hey, you have to do what you have to do. Don't worry about it. Oh." She tossed the bananas into the blender with a dollop of almond butter and protein powder. "That client of yours came in a few days ago. Stacey Hough."

What was left of his heart flipped over. "How did that go?"

Brandi shook her head, bending down to the small fridge beneath the counter. "Not good. She canceled her contract."

"Canceled?"

"Yeah, she acted really weird. Well, it was kind of my fault. I was a little pissed at her. I was just worried about you, and if she had made things harder for you, I wasn't exactly about to roll out the welcome mat for her. But she said she was moving away, so she needed to cancel."

Rob shook his head to clear it. He couldn't have heard that right. "Moving. She said she was moving?"

"Yeah. And when I asked her where, she just said 'anywhere but here'. Weird." Brandi turned on the blender, and the blur and noise matched the maelstrom inside Rob's head.

Moving. Just when he had decided that he had been too hard on her, and that he needed her, and when his life was completely upside down, she left him too?

No. Too much had happened to him. Sitting back and taking this was not an option. He was going to make something happen now— for good or for ill.

Chapter 30

The pungent scent of permanent marker filled the living room once again as Stacey uncapped the writing implement. Gripping the lid in her teeth, she wrote BOOKS on the side of the storage box. Recapping the pen, she shoved it in her pocket, and then hefted the box. She stacked it with the others along the wall nearest the door.

Propping her hands on her hips, she looked around her living room.

The surfaces and walls were bare now. Her couch and coffee table would be going to Hannah's place as soon as Hannah could borrow her brother's pickup truck, probably tomorrow. She'd spoken to her landlord, and since she only had another month on her lease, he'd agreed to let her out of it early. Being a model tenant who always paid on time certainly had paid off.

Despite what she'd told Brandi, she did have an idea of where to go. Back home with her tail tucked between her legs. As much as she hated the idea, being close to Sabrina was worth the pain of having to see her parents more often. Bree was the buffer zone that had gotten her through high school until she could escape to college in Georgia. And honestly, Stacey was worried about her cousin. She wasn't acting as happy and in love as Stacey had presumed she would be. Maybe helping Bree through her relationship woes could help Stacey forget her own.

Straightening her ponytail, Stacey collapsed on the couch to catch her breath. Her cell phone, balanced on the arm of the couch beside her, caught her eye.

A million times since she'd signed that cancelation at the gym, she'd debated calling him. Texting him. Sending a damn carrier pigeon. Hoofing it to Charlotte. Anything to find out exactly how badly she'd hurt him and to see if there was any way possible of gaining his forgiveness.

She traced the dark screen with her fingernail. Not knowing what to do, she'd erred on the side of protecting herself. Silence. The only texts to come through her phone were from Sabrina:

> OMG you're moving back home! That's AWESOME! But so sad about your job. <3 you.

And then from Hannah:

> Jake will be back home tomorrow, and he said he'll be happy to move the furniture. Are you sure you don't want me to pay for it? My kids are going to wreck it, so I feel bad just taking it from you. Please change your mind and stay.
> I'll help you find another job. :'(

A few texts from other friends, and one from her mom, laced with just enough shame and backhanded compliments to make Stacey shudder. But none from the one man she wanted to hear from most in the world.

Her fingers curled around the phone and she closed her eyes, wishing for knowledge. Inspiration. The idea of what to do, the right thing to do. Without second-guessing this time, she opened the dark screen and sent him a text.

> Thinking of you. Miss you. I hope your dad is getting better, and that you are happy.

She paused in her typing, staring at the window to her left.

He'd stood there. Naked. Silhouetted by the streetlight the one time they'd been together in her apartment. She'd never gotten the chance to show him the change he'd made in her self-esteem. And that was one of her biggest regrets.

Shaking her head internally, she turned her attention back to the phone.

One day maybe I can see you again, and shed some light
on us. Until then, please remember that I do—and always
will—love you.

Before she could change her mind, she tapped the SEND button,
and watched the progress bar light up blue. There. Sent. Her words
were on their way to him, and nothing she could do would snatch
them back.

She didn't want to take them back.

As much as she'd love to scan through her texts and relive every
moment she'd had with Rob, she really needed to continue packing.
Placing her phone back on the arm of the couch, she stood, scruti-
nizing the rest of the apartment.

The kitchen was going to be a bitch to pack. She should probably
get started on it now. There weren't enough boxes to finish it, but
maybe in the morning she could go by the liquor store and see if
they had any more—

Her doorbell rang and derailed her train of thought. Frowning,
she stared at it.

Hannah wouldn't be off work yet. Maybe Tasha, her neighbor?
No, Tash was at class on Wednesday afternoons. Her landlord's
teenage daughter had mentioned stopping by to lend a hand with
packing, maybe . . .

Stacey swung the door open, and her heart stopped.

There, on the welcome mat she hadn't yet packed, with his phone
lit up in his hand, stood Rob.

"I'm here," he said simply, tapping the text on the screen. "I'd
love to see the light you mentioned."

Maybe it was the sadness. Or the desperation. Or the certainty
she'd had that she would never, ever see him again, never get the
chance to show him what he meant to her. But the hesitation was
gone. She could no more stop herself from flying into his arms than
she could stop herself from loving him. Both were an impossibility.

She clung to him, and her tears overflowed. His big, strong arms
wrapped around her, and when she could breathe again, she felt him
shudder slightly. Hugging him tightly, she willed every bit of love

and comfort she had into his strong body, which still lined up with hers more perfectly than she even remembered.

His heart *thump*ed against her cheek, his warmth bled into her, and with the beautiful scent of him filling her nostrils, Stacey finally felt what she'd been missing ever since that phone call that had made her doubt everything.

Home. When Rob was with her, she felt at home. And now, even though everything had gone wrong, somehow she knew that things would be all right. How could they not?

Her love was there and holding her once more.

Rob held Stacey tightly.

He couldn't stop the tears that sprang to his eyes as the delicious feeling of her in his arms registered. There was just too much emotion. The loss of his dad, the sight of her standing there, so beautiful, and yes, a little of the hurt that she hadn't been at his side for the entire ordeal. But it didn't matter. She was here now, and in his arms, and that was the way things would stay if he had anything to say about it.

She pulled back, and he wasn't surprised to see there were tears in her eyes, too.

"Why didn't you text me?"

He threaded his fingers through hers. "Let's go inside."

Stacey looked past him then, and finally seemed to notice that her neighbors were watching. She waved and backed into the apartment, and Rob followed, never letting go of her hand.

As the door shut behind them, he pulled her into his arms again. He didn't want to let her go, not now, not ever.

"I was so worried about you. When I went to the gym and Brandi told me you didn't want to train me anymore, I thought—"

"I know. That was my fault. I'd vented to Brandi a little, and, well—I'm sorry."

"I'm sorry too. I should've left and come with you anyway." She sniffed. "How are things?"

"My father died."

She looked up into his eyes then. "Oh God. I'm so sorry." She reached up and put her hand on his cheek. "And I wasn't there for you. You must hate me."

He reached up and caught her hand, bringing it down to his chest. "I could never hate you. That's in the past now, and all that matters is what we do going forward."

He leaned down and caught her lips in a kiss, pouring all of the feelings inside him into that one, sweet, simple gesture. She responded passionately, twining her arms around his neck and opening her mouth to him. He tasted her depths, tongue swirling over hers, tasting, touching, breathing in every part of her.

His hands moved down her back to cup her ass, bringing her high and hard against him. His blood was hot, surging through his veins as he sought to purge the bad memories with her.

She twined her fingers in his hair, tugging, the delicious pain fanning the flames of his passion. She was so soft, so perfect against him, and it was like they had never been apart.

He pushed her backward toward the couch, and as they fell in a tangle of limbs, her laugh wrapped delight around his heart. "I missed you," she whispered against his ear as his kisses trailed down her neck. "I missed this."

"You'll never have to miss me again, because I'm never going to let you out of my sight." His teeth grazed her collarbone, and she shivered. The reaction hardened him further, made him want to rip her clothes off and immediately sink into her delicious, wet warmth.

He reached underneath her shirt and his fingertips wandered their way up her belly, then her ribs, memorizing each centimeter of skin along the way. Threading his fingertips beneath her bra's band, he relished the feel of the softness of her skin. She moaned, arching her back a little as he moved his hands behind her. He brushed against the catch of her bra.

"Let me," she said, then sat upright and reached behind her.

He sat on the edge of the couch and watched as she unhooked her bra. Then she stopped.

His breath paused in his throat, and he waited. He knew what was coming next. What she would say, how she would look sheepish, a bit embarrassed, but the clear need would be written across her beautiful features. And he wouldn't deny her. He would go, and he would love her in the dark. If that was what she needed, if that was the only way he could have her, then he would love her with the lights off for the rest of their lives.

But she reached down and grasped the hem of her T-shirt. In one smooth motion, she pulled it over her head. Then he watched with disbelief as she slipped the bra straps from her shoulders and let the lacy white undergarment hit the floor.

Hands fisted at her sides, her face a study in concentration, passion, in the tiniest hint of fear, she stared at him as if daring him to comment.

He was stunned. Deliciously, wonderfully stunned.

"I—" She hesitated, then cleared her throat, color climbing up her cheeks. "I want you to see me."

"Stacey." He reached for her, gathering her into his arms, tucking her close to his chest. "You are so beautiful."

In the late afternoon light, her skin was incredible. Peaches and cream, softness all over, he watched his hands move over places they had only known in darkness before. The skin of her back, the sweet curve of her hips, all the way around to the softness of her belly, the fullness of her beautiful breasts that he had seen only once before.

He touched her everywhere, leaving no portion of her skin unseen, and through it all she kept her gaze glued on his face. He knew she was waiting for judgment, for disgust, for any kind of negative emotion. But she wouldn't find it from him. He found every square inch of her beautiful.

Once he had seen her, touched her, it wasn't enough. His lips followed where his fingers had quested, kissing from shoulders, chest, to the sweet tips of her puckered pink nipples. He loved looking up at her and seeing her lips part as he grazed the tip of her breasts with his teeth, so gently.

Her brilliant blue eyes were alive with passion, and finally, finally, he could see her react to him. Could worship the body he'd come to know through touch. Could truly connect with the woman whom he loved.

"Rob, I want you so much."

"I want you too," he said as his erection stretched the confines of his cotton briefs.

"Come on." She stood then, and held out her hand to him. "Let's go to my bedroom."

Chapter 31

Curiously bold, Stacey led Rob down the hall, wearing nothing but the jeans she'd been packing in. Never before had she felt this comfortable around anyone while wearing so little.

But Rob made her feel safe. Feel beautiful. Feel loved. The least she could do was to trust him enough for this.

She flipped the light switch on as she passed through the door, her skin prickling in anticipation.

This was it. This was the night. And nothing else mattered.

He pressed her down softly, the covers cool against her back. A brief brush of his lips on hers, and then he knelt between her legs, looking down at her like he couldn't get enough of the sight of her.

Feeling his gaze cover her, she reached down for the button on her jeans. Slowly, she worked it free, lowering the zipper. Lifting her hips, she began to work the material down her thighs. He took over for her, sliding them down past her knees, backing off the bed to pull them free of her bare feet.

Fear darted through her heart for a brief second, but she closed her eyes and took a deep breath. This was Rob. And he loved her. There was no need to be ashamed.

When she opened her eyes, he was looking down at her with the most beautiful expression on his handsome face.

Wordlessly, he hooked his fingers beneath the waistband of her panties and pulled them free, too.

She was naked. There was nothing to hide her body from sight. And the gorgeous man in front of her was totally transfixed by her nudity.

"Stacey, you are so beautiful."

She knew she wasn't. She wasn't perfect. But if this man—this bullheaded, bossy, strong, incredible man—wanted to believe it, who was she to correct him?

Smiling like a siren, she pushed up on her elbows and gave him her best come-hither look.

"I'd compliment you, too, but it's hard to see what I'm working with."

He didn't argue. Just shed his clothing and allowed her to look her fill. And look her fill she did.

God, why had it taken her this long to let him turn the lights on? Rob in the dark was incredible. But Rob in the light?

Heaven had a mascot, and he was right here in front of her.

He was beautiful, and he thought she was beautiful too. She held her arms up to him and he came to her willingly, holding her tight, kissing her with incredible fervency.

Somehow, being together in the light felt so much more intimate, more special, than anything they had done before. She watched his face as he kissed his way down her body, and though she tried, she couldn't find anything other than adoration and passion written on his chiseled features.

He kissed her everywhere, and then she returned the favor, kneeling alongside him, bending to press her lips to the center of his chest. She had pulled her ponytail free earlier, and her hair fell around her, making little tickling trails across his skin as she kissed her way down his taut torso, past his belly button, down to his jutting erection.

Cupping his cock with both hands, she looked up at him. His jaw was tight, hands fisted in the covers, and a drop of crystalline liquid appeared at the tip of his hard shaft.

"I want you to watch this," she said. And as she opened her mouth to enclose the head of his cock, he groaned. She felt more powerful than she ever had in her entire life. The salty-sweet drip coated her throat, and she smiled around him as she took him deeper. Velvety skin so soft, it made all the deep places within her weep. She wanted more of this, wanted all of it, forever.

She set up a rhythm, taking him deep into her throat, then pulling back. Her cheeks hollowed out as she sucked his cock harder. His hips lifted with her rhythm. But she wasn't satisfied. Her body begged for more. This was delicious, it was wonderful, but it couldn't satisfy her totally. She needed to have him inside her for that.

So good. He felt so good inside her mouth, her tongue swirling around his head and then gliding down the underside of his shaft. One hand cupped his sac, and her other splayed across his abs to feel his reactions to her every move.

"Stacey, I can't last much longer like this." His voice was a hoarse rasp.

She let go with a slight *pop*. Smiling, she licked her lips. "That's okay, if you want to. I can keep going."

"I would rather fuck you." His bald-faced statement earned approval from her, and as he rose up to pull her toward him, she let him have his way. Gripping her arms, he turned her and pressed her down into the softness of the pillows beneath her.

Before, he'd been slow, gentle. Exploring her, as if needing to get to know every part of her. This time? This was no sweet exploration. This was possession. With every kiss, every touch, every nip and lick and pinch, he was claiming her. Owning her. Her body knew its master, and obeyed as he commanded. When his head dived down between her legs, she curled her fingers into his hair and let out a long, low moan.

This. No one could ever make her feel like this, not like Rob did.

He sealed his lips around her clit, and his tongue flicked the sensitive nub. Over and over again he tortured her, and teased her, made her lower belly tense and release. His ministrations set up an aching throb of need within her.

It was good, God, it was so good, but it wasn't enough. She needed his cock.

"Please, Rob. I need you."

"What do you need, baby?" His breath blew against her sensitive labia.

"I need you to fuck me. Now." Before she had asked, now she demanded. She could not wait any longer.

He rose on his elbows then, over her, looking down at her as if she were the answer to every prayer he had ever uttered. She would never get used to feeling like this.

"Ready?" he asked, his voice rough.

She nodded.

The blunt head of him parted her, stretched her, and as he entered her they both let out a sigh together. Their breaths mingled, their bodies joined, and Stacey stared up into Rob's eyes as he moved within her and made her his.

She held him tightly as he rocked, plunging deeper into her warm depths. Her body stretched to accommodate him, her inner walls wet and welcoming, and she gripped him with all the strength she had.

She never wanted this to end, never wanted him to leave, but the fire burning within her could not be sustained forever. She was burning, burning up, and he was the one holding the torch.

Higher and higher her passion crested, and she dug her nails into his shoulders, then his hips, urging him deeper, faster. She needed more, needed him.

He grew harder inside her, his hips pistoning in and out in an unrelenting quest for their mutual pleasure. And just when Stacey thought she could not hold on any longer, he reached down between them and found her clit.

She screamed against his chest. Her mind and body shattered, and she had no choice but to ride the wave of pleasure to its completion.

He came not long after, one stroke, two, and then he collapsed atop her, his hot, wet pleasure filling her body in the most delicious way.

Stacey held on to him tightly, turning her head to the side so she could breathe. His heart *thump*ed against her cheek, and there in the light, she smiled.

Of all the men in the world, this one was hers. And she could not be more grateful.

He loved her all through the night, pouring his emotions into every encounter they had. And never once did they turn off the lights, though they did opt for the softer lamplight once the sun went down.

Staring down into the sunny blue of her eyes as he entered her was as close to heaven as he'd ever felt on earth. Seeing her smile, laugh, nuzzle against his skin as they held one another began to heal the wounds in his heart.

Around three in the morning, they began to talk. She told him about her project, the fire, how she had felt when she'd lost her job. And he told her about his father's decline, how hard it was to be strong for his mother and sisters, and how his mother had told him about his father's pride in his accomplishments.

When the emotions overcame him, she held him as he let tears fall. For what he'd lost, yes, but also for what he'd gained.

And then he kissed her, and she kissed him back, and slowly, gently, they made love into the morning.

When he opened his eyes, the sunlight streamed through what should have been a solid wall.

He blinked twice before he realized he wasn't back at home, and he wasn't in the hospital lobby. He was with Stacey. Well, he was in Stacey's bed. She wasn't beside him.

Sitting upright, he propped his elbow on his raised knee and yawned. He should get up. The clock on the table beside him declared the time to be 9:15. There was a lot to do today. He'd have to get up and head back to Charlotte tomorrow in order to arrive in time for his father's memorial service.

The memory still hurt, and he was pretty sure it always would. But now there was someone to hold his hand and stand beside him through it all.

Tossing the covers back, he swing his legs over the edge of the bed. The future. It wasn't something they'd discussed yet, but he knew what he wanted to do. The only question now was what her answer would be.

His clothes were piled on the floor, and he slipped into his pants before walking into the hall to look for her. Bare feet on her hardwood floors made no sound, so when he walked into her kitchen, he found her with her back toward him.

He blinked. And blinked again.

She was standing at the stove, humming as she stirred something in a pan. There were pink straps crisscrossing her back, a pert bow tied above her ass. Her naked ass. She was naked except for an apron, and if his nose was correct, she was cooking breakfast in the nude.

"Good morning," he said, smiling wolfishly as he leaned onto her bar.

She yelped and turned quickly, her spatula still in hand. "God, Rob, you scared me."

"Sorry. Was just admiring the view."

She blushed then, a beautiful pinkening that he was pleased to see ran straight down her breasts, which he could glimpse past the upper portion of the apron. "I thought you might like some breakfast in bed."

He slipped onto the bar stool. "I'd much rather watch you make the breakfast."

Her hand whipped behind her then, as if she was checking to make sure she was still naked. "Yeah. I thought, maybe, I should try being a little more confident."

"I definitely approve."

She turned back to the stove then, glancing at him over her shoulder, and resumed her stirring.

He waited an appropriate amount of time, but eventually the temptation was too great. Her squeal when he grabbed her generous ass was incredibly satisfying.

"Rob!"

"You're too delicious," he said, nuzzling the nape of her neck, where a few curls had escaped the messy topknot of her hair. "Forget breakfast, I want to eat you up."

"It's almost done. You can have me for dessert."

With her dismissal clear, he meekly retreated to the bar stool to wait.

Once turkey bacon and oatmeal had been consumed—pretty damn good, too, he had to admit—they showered together. The whole time he mentally rehearsed what he would say.

Would he come right out and just do it? Begin with saying how much she meant to him? Or how proud he was of her for embracing her flaws and becoming the woman she'd wanted to be?

He still hadn't decided while they were getting dressed and Stacey's phone chirped at her.

"Crap," she said with a grimace. "Hannah's brother is on his way with the truck. I'm giving Hannah my living room furniture."

"Right, the move," he said casually, as if it had just come to mind. He'd thought about almost nothing else all morning. His question wouldn't have an easy answer if she was still determined to hightail it out of the city. "Where were you planning to go?"

"Wilmington. My family is there," she said, shaking her head as she finished buttoning her top.

Easing down on the bed, he looked at his hands, which he'd folded between his knees. "Was that plan set in stone?"

She stopped, one button halfway in its hole. "It's not—well, no. I just didn't see any reason to stay here with my job up in smoke and us, well, whatever we were."

Pinning her with a direct gaze, he went for it. "You don't have to go anywhere if you don't want to. You could stay with me. I love you, Stacey. I don't want us to be apart again."

She didn't move for a long moment, and he wondered whether he had done things wrong. Said enough? Too much?

"I would love to stay with you." She smiled, and her eyes grew wet. Rubbing at them quickly, she laughed. "I never wanted to leave your house anyway, but I figured I'd never get back."

He stood and pulled her into his arms. "I love you, Stacey Hough. I want you to be my wife. Will you?"

"Yes." She laughed, tilting her chin to look into his eyes. "I'd love to marry you."

And he kissed her, thanking his lucky stars that the universe had brought to him the one woman who completed him. She'd come to him for help, but she was the one who had made him whole.

Epilogue

One year to the day after Richard Armstrong Liston's death, Stacey and Rob stood hand in hand, watching his ashes drift away on the tide.

They'd been married the evening before, in Stacey's hometown of Wilmington, in a small ceremony. Only Sabrina and Rob's childhood best friend, Scott, were in attendance, to act as witnesses. There would be a reception back home in Atlanta, and another for Stacey's family in Wilmington in a couple of days.

With the sea breeze at their backs, and their hands entwined, Stacey leaned her head against Rob's strong arm.

"Do you think he would be happy?"

Rob smiled. "Probably not outwardly. He'd make some gruff comment about how I shouldn't be wasting time on sentimental crap, and should go back to school and make something of myself. But inwardly? Yeah. I think he'd definitely be happy."

"Are *you* happy?"

He turned to Stacey, and she looked up into the stormy gray of his eyes. "How could I be anything less than happy when the most wonderful woman in the world is now mine?"

Stacey wound her arms around his neck, happier and more in love than she ever could have imagined. "Lucky for you, you're stuck with me forever."

"Lucky for me," he agreed, and he kissed her.

ONE TOUCH

Eliza's last relationship ended in ruins, and she's anything but
eager to jump back into something serious. A trip to Hawaii
for her best friend's wedding couldn't come at a better time.
Showing up without a date is the least of her worries.
In fact, it may even play into her wildest fantasies
when the perfect hunk of a man appears before her . . .

ONE LOOK

With Chandler's divorce behind him he's ready to move on,
so he heads to Hawaii for his cousin's wedding. The moment his
eyes encounter Eliza's sultry curves and sensual lips, he's more
than ready for a night of nonstop sex. But despite the heat of
their unbridled carnal pleasure, Eliza is still afraid to tell him
about her forbidden desires. And when their casual affair
follows them home, it threatens to alter their lives forever.

Keep reading for a special excerpt.

Chapter 1

The cart had a flat spot on one wheel, and the *thump* was driving Eliza insane. But there was no way she was going to take the time to go back to the front of the small grocery store and swap it out. She'd already seen three people she knew, and two of them had looked away almost instantly. After this much time it shouldn't hurt, but it still did. Being a pariah in her hometown wasn't exactly how she'd pictured living her life, but it was her reality now.

Setting her jaw, Eliza moved through the produce section and checked her list. Spinach, cucumbers, tomatoes . . . If she shopped smart, she wouldn't have to do this again for a month. Getting fresh veggies only once a month wasn't ideal, but neither was living in a town that was convinced she was some kind of sexual deviant.

Her ratty sneakers didn't make a sound on the polished floor of the grocery store. The cart was half full, and as she rounded the final corner toward the registers, her name smacked her in the back of the head like a mallet.

"Eliza Jackson! Oh my God, it is you."

She winced, then turned. "Oh, hey, Marshall." Eliza crossed her arms to cover the worst of the holes in her Green Day T-shirt. Part of the fun of being a chemist was ruined clothes when coworkers weren't as careful with chemicals as they should be. "How are you?"

Marshall looked her up and down, a somewhat leering smile on his face as he adjusted his grocery basket. "I'm doing great. You still at Quality Testing?"

"Yeah. I'm lead chemist in the pharmaceutical division." Eliza smiled politely, even though her insides were shaking. She wasn't stupid. This wasn't an old high school friend interested in catching up. This was something else entirely. "What about you?"

"Eh, I'm at Eubank Financial. Anyway, I heard you dated Tyler Hagans for a while. He's a buddy of mine."

Eliza's hands tightened into fists, and her smile froze.

Marshall continued, oblivious to her discomfort. "I have to say, I didn't know you were gay."

Her teeth hurt as she clamped them together hard. Her words were muffled as she spoke without releasing the clench of her jaw. "I'm not gay."

Marshall's laugh was mocking. "From what I heard, liking girls is the least weird thing about you. Anyway, you go do what you do. Have fun, but watch out. I've heard some of that kinky stuff you're into is illegal."

With a wink, Marshall turned and walked away, leaving Eliza to stare after him in shock and hurt.

When she could breathe without her chest feeling like it was cracking in half, Eliza turned and pushed her thumping grocery cart to the checkout line. But before she could start loading her items onto the conveyer belt, the cashier flipped off the lighted number 1 sign.

"Sorry," she said, giving Eliza a distrustful look. "This lane is closed."

Closing her eyes for a second, Eliza took a deep breath, then pulled her cart to the express lane, which was the only one left open. The red-shirted manager gave her a look, but started scanning her items anyway.

"Thanks," Eliza muttered as she accepted her change and receipt. The guy didn't say anything, just gave her a tight-lipped smile before cheerfully greeting the customer behind her.

Blasting her favorite band's latest album all the way home didn't help improve Eliza's mood. It hurt, damn it, and she was tired of pretending it didn't. By the time she made the left onto her street, her jaw ached and her eyes stung.

She hadn't done anything wrong. She'd just been honest about her fantasies, and when she and Tyler had broken up over it, he'd trumpeted her most secret desire to the world, complete with embellishments. It was the worst kind of betrayal, and even now, six months later, she wasn't sure how to deal with the hurt. Other than to hide in her house and vow to spend the rest of her life as a celibate hermit, that is.

Throwing the gearshift into Park, Eliza released her seat belt in the same motion. Silence fell over her like a blanket as she cut the engine. Her skull thumped back against the headrest and she blew out a breath. This was nothing new.

"It doesn't matter," Eliza grunted as she shoved open the car door. The cool breeze hit her skin, raising goose bumps in its wake. Trudging across her lawn with her grocery bags dangling from her forearms, Eliza fumbled through her keys to find the one for her front door. She was so distracted that she almost tripped over the box on her front steps.

"What the hell?"

Bending low, she examined the label. It had come from North Carolina. Maybe it was Bree? A shot of excitement tore through her, and she trotted up the stairs and pushed through the front door in a matter of seconds.

Dumping her bags and keys at the table by the door, Eliza turned and headed back to the stoop. Her blood pumped with anticipation as she carried the package through her messy house and straight to the kitchen table. Grabbing one of the knives from the butcher block on the counter, she grinned.

"What have you sent me, Sabrina?"

The sharp knife made quick, neat slices through the packing tape, then clattered to the table as Eliza abandoned it to pull open the cardboard flaps.

"What in the world is this?"

It was pink. Not just pink—pink was much too tame a name for this color. As Eliza withdrew the scraps of fabric from the box, dangling from their tiny strings, she decided that the only real name she could give that color was fuchsia. Or maybe magenta. Or maybe a color off the spectrum that hadn't been named yet. She had to blink three times to ease the pain from the brightness. And it wasn't just pink, it was a pink bikini.

Digging through the rest of the box, which contained the other half of the magenta monstrosity, a bottle of sunscreen, and a tank top with some sparkly letters on it, Eliza finally came up with an envelope from the bottom of the box. Her name was written in Bree's extra-swirly cursive.

The paper crinkled as Eliza ripped open the envelope and unfolded the letter. A plane ticket fell out. Eliza barely glanced at it; she was already reading.

> *Liza,*
>
> *I hope you like the little care package I sent you! If you've already read the tank top, you know that I'm asking you to be my bridesmaid. I know it's kind of presumptuous to buy your plane ticket without asking you first, but you're always complaining that you never get to go anywhere, so here it is! I'm flying you out to Hawaii for our wedding, which is November 9th. You can stay the whole week, our treat! You're such a good friend, Liza, please say you'll come and be my bridesmaid.*
>
> *Love you bunches! Call me after you're done reading so we can celebrate together!*
>
> *Bree*

When she realized that her tongue was actually drying out, Eliza closed her mouth and let the paper flutter to the tabletop.

She'd known Bree was dating a guy, but she hadn't known it was serious. And a wedding in Hawaii, only a month away? Eliza shook her head. Damn. Bree didn't waste any time.

After yanking open the refrigerator and taking a regenerating swig of apple juice, Eliza went down the hall to retrieve her cell phone. A mound of bags in front of the door jogged her memory. Oh yeah, the groceries. She should probably start putting those away.

Tucking the phone in the crook of her shoulder, she hauled the bags to the kitchen.

"Oh my God, Liza! Hey!"

"Hey Bree, I got your little box of goodies." Eliza winced at Bree's delighted squeal, which went straight through her eardrum.

"Ohmygod, isn't it the best news ever? You can come, though, right?"

"Well," Eliza drew out the word as she pulled open the door to her pantry. "I'm not sure."

"Why not?"

Eliza sighed, her arms full of canned goods. "It's a long way away, and I'm not sure if I can get off work—"

"Horseshit." Bree's tone was firm. "You haven't taken a vacation in three years, and I know it. They can do without you for a week."

"I'm just not sure if I feel comfortable. I don't really know any of your family other than your crazy mom, so I'll be kind of lonely, and—"

"If you can honestly tell me you're not lonely there at home, then I'll lay off you."

Bree had been the one friend Eliza had confided in after the shit with Tyler blew up. She knew how miserable Eliza had been, had even begged her to move down to North Carolina and work for her father's company. The offer had been tempting, but Eliza couldn't stand the thought of leaving her hometown. Even if that same hometown hated her.

"Fine," Eliza groaned. "I'll go. But I'm going to regret it. I've got to go shopping, find stuff to wear so I won't embarrass you."

"You won't. It's going to be awesome."

"And no fixing me up. Promise me, Bree."

The silence on the other end of the line was suspect, and Eliza raised her brow. "Bree . . ."

"Fine." Bree's exasperated tone made Eliza grin. "Deal. But promise me you'll keep an open mind, all right? There are a few guys there that I think would be perfect for you. You know that Tyler was a small-minded asshole, and there are tons of guys who'd kill for someone more adventurous in bed."

Eliza pretended not to hear that last part. "Okay, let me get going. I've got a lot to do if I'm going to be ready to go in, oh, twenty-four days."

Once the call was disconnected, Eliza took a deep breath. Okay. She could do this. And the more she thought about it, the better it felt. Get away from all the small-minded smalltown people? Maybe she could even pretend to be someone else, someone confident, who owned their slightly unorthodox sexuality.

She allowed herself a small, genuine smile. Maybe Eliza the hermit could become Eliza the bombshell for a few days.

24 days later . . .

Eliza's heels clicked against the tiled floor of the airport. Shifting the strap of her carry-on on her shoulder, she wobbled just a little, but pulled it back before it turned into a stumble.

Why the hell had she thought it'd be a good idea to wear high-heeled boots to fly? Waiting until she'd actually reached Hawaii to begin her bombshell routine seemed like a much better idea now. She'd held up the TSA security line for a good three minutes while she fumbled with the zipper on the left one. They were still new and kind of stiff, which didn't exactly make for easy removal. And then her gate had been all the way at the ass end of the airport. Of course. After that, though, the first leg of her trip had been fine. Now she just had to make it to her connecting flight without falling on her face. Hopefully she'd get used to walking in these monsters before she showed up at the resort. There, the last thing she wanted to look like was herself.

"Sneakers," she said beneath her breath as she glanced at the flight monitors mounted to the wall. "Sneakers for the return flight. That or flip-flops. I don't care if it's November."

A speaker crackled overhead, barely audible over the noise and chatter of the busy airport. Eliza pulled at her dove-gray pencil skirt, which was trying to ride up as she walked. She needed to hustle; the flight would be boarding sometime in the next ten minutes, and she was still five or six gates away. It was gate C-4, wasn't it? She should probably check.

Shoving her long brown hair back out of the way for about the twentieth time that day, she unzipped her bag and started to dig through it. Of course she'd had to pull everything out at the security desk because of the whole boot fiasco, and her other boarding pass had been shoved in there somewhere. But walking and digging through her bag at the same time wasn't the easiest thing to do in three-inch heels.

Glancing back to make sure nobody was close behind her, Eliza ducked to the side of the busy corridor and started digging in earnest. Was it maybe in her medicine bag? Nope, just her vitamins, Tylenol, various just-in-case cold and flu meds. Oh, maybe she'd stuck it in the little lingerie bag. No, not there, either. After another minute, her bag was in shambles and she still hadn't laid a finger on her boarding pass.

"Wait a minute," Eliza said, yanking open the side zipper. "Aha!"

The boarding pass wasn't the only thing in that pocket, though, and before she could snag the pass and pull it free, the weight of her tablet pulled the zippered flap out of her hand. A clatter rang through the corridor as her tablet landed face-first on the polished floor.

"Ohmygod," she moaned as she bent over to pick it up, praying that the protective case had taken the brunt of the fall.

"Here, let me get that for you." An incredibly deep voice from right behind her made her jump. The bag slipped from her shoulder and bounced free, pill bottles and panties scattering in a four-foot radius.

"Did I startle you? I'm so sorry."

She looked up then. The sexy voice belonged to an extremely well-muscled guy in dark-washed jeans and a sage-green sweater that almost matched his eyes. His light brown hair was tousled in that careless but gorgeous way, and as he knelt down beside her she had the strangest urge to run her fingers through it.

"I saw your tablet fall, thought I could lend a hand since you've got yours full. Looks like I just made it worse, though. Here, let me help you." He reached for the nearest object that had fallen out of her bag, which just happened to be one of her brand-new black lace thongs.

"No!" she squawked in alarm. "No, don't touch that."

"Hey, I didn't mean—"

"Please, just let me get it." Not trusting her ankles to support her with the damn heels, Eliza began the humiliating task of crawling on the airport floor to retrieve her belongings.

"I'd be happy to help you; after all, it's my fault." The guy reached for her bag.

She jerked it back, her nerves jangling. "No, no, please, really. It's fine." She shoved stuff into her bag as fast as she could, well aware that the burning in her cheeks meant they were a nuclear shade of pink. Hell, she might even be as pink as that bikini. That might be a good name for it—*mortification magenta.*

"All right, if you're sure." The guy looked a little disappointed, but Eliza couldn't form the words of an apology. It was like a giant wad of idiocy had wedged itself in her throat. She'd made an ass of herself in this huge airport, and now she was going to be late to catch her connection if she didn't hurry. What the hell would she do if she missed her flight? He watched her for a while, but then with an apologetic smile, turned and walked away. She couldn't help but mentally kick herself as she watched him leave.

Once everything was shoved back into her bag—including her thankfully undamaged tablet—she couldn't zip it anymore, but she struggled to her feet and hustled to the gate anyway. When she finally arrived at C-4, boarding had already begun, so she joined the last of the line.

"Have a nice flight," the gate attendant said as he scanned her pass.

"Thanks." Eliza caught a glimpse of her reflection in the window. At least that fall hadn't messed up her new outfit. And her hair, which she'd taken a helluva long time to flat-iron that morning before leaving, still looked shiny and bouncy. That little dose of relief lasted all the way down the Jetway and even as she stepped onto the plane.

But as she moved down the aisle, looking for seat 22B, her relief burned up and the smoke turned into a mixture of embarrassment and despair.

The hot guy who had caused her to spill her whole bag in the middle of the terminal was sitting in none other than seat 22A.

This was a five-hour flight. She was going to have to sit next to this guy for five freaking hours, all the while remembering how she'd acted like a total klutz.

Sometimes life really sucked.

Chapter 2

A sudden noise made Chandler Morse glance upward. There, in the aisle, stood the woman he'd tried to help earlier. Her cheeks were red, the corners of her full lips pulled down as she sank into the seat beside him.

Well, this is a nice surprise. The sight of her pert ass as she bent over to pick up her tablet had fired him like nothing had in a very long time. His divorce had strung out over a year, and while he couldn't deny that it was the best thing for him, he couldn't bring himself to break the vows he'd sworn to until the ink was dry. But for some reason this woman had drawn his eye. Maybe it was the blush. Or the way her full hips flared, framed so well by that form-fitting skirt. He couldn't deny things hadn't gone well earlier, but he'd done his best to apologize. Maybe being stuck beside him on a plane for a few hours would help her forget about that unfortunate accident.

"Hey, nice to see you again," Chandler said, but she didn't look over at him. Her cheeks reddened further as she shoved her open bag beneath the seat in front of her.

His lips curled into a smile as she fumbled in her bag, trying to rearrange the contents so it would zip again. Her black sweater was V-necked, the loose knit large enough that he could occasionally see flashes of skin. Her dark hair swung with her movements, catching the late morning light that shone through the small window beside him. And her ass, well, that was curved and tight and his palms fairly itched to touch it.

She sat up then, and he pretended to be very interested in the flight attendant giving the safety talk at the front of the plane.

"Mind shutting the window shade?"

He glanced over at her. She was squinting in the brightness that glared off the airplane wing.

"Sure," Chandler said with an easy smile. He slid the shade down.

"Thanks." She unfolded her boarding pass and smoothed it across her lap. It was easy to read her name.

Eliza Jackson. He tried it out silently. It suited her. *Eliza. Liza.* Nice name for a beautiful woman.

"So, where are you from?"

Chandler's question was met with silence as the plane rounded onto the runway.

Finally, Eliza glanced over at him, her dark lashes shuttering her eyes. "Um, the Midwest."

Undaunted by her non-answer, Chandler smiled. "Nice. I'm from North Carolina. Thus the slight drawl." He gave his trademark grin, the one that never failed to get a woman to smile back at him even if she didn't want to.

Nothing from Eliza. She seemed determined to focus on the floor, or the seat back in front of her. Basically anything to keep from looking at him. Of course, he couldn't really blame her, but he was disappointed anyway. Had his failed marriage screwed up his game that bad? The aircraft picked up speed as it moved down the runway.

He tried again. "I live near the coast, the Outer Banks. You ever been? They're some of the most beautiful beaches in the world."

"No. I haven't." She closed her eyes as the plane lifted off, her knuckles white as they gripped the armrests.

Chandler watched her as the plane trembled with the effort of its ascent. A little line appeared between her brows, as if she wasn't entirely comfortable with the process of flying. He wanted to reach over and grab her hand, reassure her, maybe even see if her lips were as soft as they looked.

Instead, he opted for conversation.

"Ever been to Hawaii before?"

She shook her head, not bothering to open her eyes.

Undaunted, he continued. "Me, either. It's kind of a forced vacation for me." He snorted a little. Working vacation, more like. His cousin was getting married, and Chandler had been roped into playing the role of best man. Fortunately, his job as private investigator could be flexible, when he needed it to be. "Are you vacationing?"

"Not really," she bit out as the plane hit a decent-sized bump. She tucked her chin into her chest. Like she was trying to make herself as small as possible until this was over.

A longing built in his chest, and he almost reached over to pull her tight against his side, protect her from the fear. He crossed his arms to keep from doing something stupid. So what if they had chemistry? Right now she obviously needed to get through the take-off. He'd wait until the plane had leveled off, and then he'd attempt conversation again. Draw her out. Get her phone number, if the fates were kind.

But when she finally opened her eyes, Eliza reached into the seat pocket and grabbed the first magazine she came to. Crossing her legs away from him, she turned on one hip, clearly marking their conversation as over.

Chandler blew out a breath. Oh well. He'd fucked that one royally when he scared her into dropping her panties all over LAX. The mental image caused him to smile again. She'd squawked like a chicken when he almost grabbed that thong. It was worth it to see her beautiful cheeks go pink.

Closing his eyes, he let his head fall back against the seat. Might as well get some rest. There was a dinner tonight at the resort so the wedding party could get to know one another. And if he knew Gregory, it would be wild, full of booze, and run really late. A nap was definitely in his best interest.

Too bad Eliza wouldn't be joining him. A little bedtime fun with her would definitely make his dreams sweeter.

The sudden jolt of the flight's touchdown woke him. Chandler blinked blearily, then stretched as much as the small area allowed him to. His arm brushed by Eliza's, and as he started to mumble an apology, he was struck by the sight of her face.

She was looking straight into his eyes. Her irises were such a deep, dark brown, like expensive chocolates. Caught in her gaze for a moment, he waited.

"Nice nap?"

"It was," Chandler said, stretching as the plane slowed its headlong roll up the landing strip. "Did you enjoy the flight?"

"Not really," she said, fumbling with her seat belt. "Flying's not really my thing."

"You should fly next to me more." He grinned. "I'll keep you safe."

The smarmy line was meant to prick her, and it did the job.

"By the way, you snore," she snapped and bent down to retrieve her bag.

"You're lying," he said calmly as he unfastened his belt. "I've never snored in my life."

She had the good grace to blush, and Chandler grinned at the sight. But the instant the plane stopped, she launched herself out of her seat to move into the aisle. Unfortunately for her, the rest of the passengers had the same idea, and she was forced to stand there, halfway in the aisle, with nowhere to go until the line started moving.

Well, it was unlucky for her, but it was damn incredible for Chandler. Her ass was now at eye level, and he definitely enjoyed the view.

Her toe tapped impatiently, and when the crowd of people finally began to thin, Chandler stood and moved behind her into the aisle.

"I'm Chandler, by the way."

"Nice to meet you, Chandler, but I've got to grab my bag and catch the shuttle. So, see ya. Have a good trip."

She turned left inside the terminal, taking short, choppy steps that echoed inside the crowded Hawaiian airport. Sensing that now wasn't the time to push her, Chandler waited a minute or two before following.

Hell, it wasn't his fault his shuttle was in the same direction. And besides, now he could continue to enjoy the view.

Eliza wanted to punch something. God, could that have gone any worse? While her sexy neighbor slept, she'd centered herself, intending to practice her bombshell routine on him when he woke. It had started out promising enough, but then he'd had to pick at her. She'd promised herself on this trip she'd be confident, happy, completely the opposite of Eliza from Appledale, Ohio. But that plan had imploded as soon as Chandler started teasing her.

A groan escaped her and she stopped right in front of a Coke machine. It was probably just self-defense. For the last few months, any time a guy had come up to her, she'd tried her best to keep them at arm's length. After her relationship with Tyler had gone down the crapper, she couldn't stand the thought of letting another man that close. But Chandler . . . He was nice. He seemed normal. He was hotter than hell, and sweet, and funny. Everything inside her had screamed he looked way too good for her, and she should stay far, far away.

Biting her lip, Eliza glanced over her shoulder. Maybe she should go find Chandler and apologize for snapping at him. It wasn't his fault she'd completely lost all interpersonal skills over the past six months.

The crowd shifted and moved, and she had to duck sideways to avoid being run over by one of those golf-cart security cars. No sign of Chandler. Oh well. Maybe it was for the best, so she didn't embarrass herself in front of him again. There was still time for her to salvage this trip, so she'd do it. New Eliza mask firmly in place, she turned down the corridor toward the baggage claim.

Bree had said that the resort shuttle would be there to pick up her and another wedding party member, and she didn't want to keep anyone waiting.

The baggage claim area was crowded, and Eliza scanned the moving carousel for her bag. It tumbled to the bottom of the wheel all the way on the other side. Eliza muttered, "Excuse me," about seventeen times before she was able to get to the edge of the conveyor belt.

Her bag was on top of another, and as she reached for it a kid climbed onto the edge, overbalancing and knocking into her. Her outstretched hand grabbed for the handle and missed as she righted herself.

"Are you okay?" Her question to the kid went unanswered as the child's mother grabbed his arm and dragged him back from the carousel, yelling the whole time. Poor boy. Eliza turned back to the conveyor belt and sighed. Now she'd have to wait for it to come around again.

"This is yours, right?"

"Chandler?"

It was him—big, incredible smile; broad shoulders; and all. He'd grabbed her bag and was now holding it out to her.

"I saw that kid bump into you. It's not your day, is it?"

"Um, it's not that bad." Eliza smiled as she took the bag from him. "Thanks a lot, I really appreciate it."

"No problem. It was the least I could do."

Together they moved through the crowd at the baggage claim toward the airport exit. Tucking her hair behind her ear, Eliza glanced up at Chandler. This was her chance. His eyes were bright as they looked forward, strong, defined jaw dusted with just a hint of five o'clock shadow. God, he was hot. He was way out of her league. But maybe . . .

"Listen, I should really . . ."

She was about to say "apologize" when she caught sight of the van at the curb. The driver was holding a sign that said "Jackson" and "Morse." The clear escape route definitely appealed to her inner coward. A few more minutes of prep would go a long way to helping her conquer her doubts. Not with Chandler, but maybe the next guy would be easier for her to communicate with.

"Sorry, that's me. But it was really nice to meet you. Thanks for everything," she said, and hustled over to the van. Yeah, so she'd meant to explain, but this was a neat way to get out of it. There'd been enough humiliation in her life over the past half a year without adding this particular slice of humble pie to it. She'd make it to the resort in plenty of time to change for the evening's dinner party, and never have to see the handsome Chandler again.

She wasn't sure if that was a good thing or a bad thing.

"Hi," she said to the driver as he took her bag. "I'm Eliza Jackson, for the Hough-Trailwick wedding?"

"Of course." He smiled. "Welcome to Hawaii. Please, take a seat inside."

With the aid of the handle by the door, she climbed into the van, choosing to take the bench nearer the back of the vehicle. Her hands trembled a little as she unzipped her bag and started digging for her cell phone. It was kind of a relief to know that the awkwardness with Chandler was over. He'd been way too nice, too attractive. It was damn intimidating. A shaky sigh escaped her as she pulled her phone free. She needed to start small, and Chandler had been anything but.

Hopefully Bree was right, and there would be single guys at the wedding she could try again with. This week was supposed to be about letting go of the past and being a completely new Eliza. And she could do that now, if she focused and tried really hard to forget about her awkward—

"Hey there." Chandler grinned at her as he climbed into the van. "I guess we're going to the same resort. My cousin Gregory is getting married there this weekend, to Sabrina Hough."

"Oh shit," Eliza said, then clapped a hand over her mouth.

Chandler barked a laugh as he settled into the bench in front of her. "That good, huh?"

The van door slammed as the driver moved around the vehicle, finally climbing into the front seat. "Next stop, Hau'oli Resort!"

Eliza tried to focus on regulating her breathing, but it was hard to do. Chandler started up a friendly conversation with the driver, and she couldn't be happier to be left out of the chat. God, this was a nightmare.

How was she supposed to be this different, confident person when he would be there all week long? He'd seen her clumsy, awkward, blushing like a fool. She wanted to melt into the seat cushions and disappear.

When the van finally pulled into the lot of the resort, she almost screamed with relief. All she wanted was to run to her room and hide for the rest of the day, possibly the rest of her life.

Chandler climbed out of the van first, and stood there waiting.

"Please move. Just walk to the back of the van, grab your bag, and go," Eliza begged in a tiny whisper as she yanked her bag onto her shoulder.

But he didn't respond to her pleas for mercy, just stood there and waited for her to emerge from the van door. And when he extended his hand to help her down, damn it, she couldn't help but be grateful for his assistance.

"Thanks," she said, not daring to look him in the eye.

"My pleasure." His accent was soft, not twangy at all, giving a pleasing, lengthy mellowness to his words. And as she passed by to retrieve her suitcase, the cologne that had been teasing her the entire flight tantalized her nostrils. It was light but musky, a delicious masculine scent that made her want to burrow her head against his chest and breathe him in.

"See you later," she said, then grabbed her suitcase, threw the driver a tip, and booked it into the resort.

She was a chickenshit, but that wasn't news. But now she had some extra work to do to get ready for tonight. Chandler would be at that party, and somehow she was going to have to come up with a way to make up for her complete lack of grace and manners during their first meeting.

Too bad he'd already seen her thongs.

ABOUT THE AUTHOR

REGINA COLE, lover of manly muscled arms, chest hair, and mini-marshmallows, has been reading romance since her early teens. While she loves a love story of any heat level, she's been drawn to the erotic side and is enjoying every minute of writing it. When she's not frantically pounding away at the keyboard, she can be found fishing with her family, playing with her dogs, trying out strange new recipes, or snuggling with her hubby. Readers can find out more about Regina (that she also writes historical romance as Gina Lamm, for example) at reginacole.net.

www.ingramcontent.com/pod-product-compliance
Lightning Source LLC
Chambersburg PA
CBHW020752250626
47155CB00003B/1037